EXTREME PROMISE

X-TREME LOVE SERIES

KAY MANIS

To my readers.
Here's one last Happily Ever After.

CHAPTER 1

HINDLEY

I BOLTED toward the exit of the dress shop, jaw clenched as I shoved the glass door so hard, the frame bounced back and nearly smashed me in the face. Their exasperating jeers echoed behind me.

The cool winter air hit my skin but didn't temper the heat coursing through my body. I jammed my hands deep into my coat pockets and scanned the city sidewalks right and left. Should I scream? Should I run? Maybe both.

Suddenly, my phone vibrated. Again. Shit.

I didn't need to see the phone to know who was calling. The man had been blowing up my phone for days. He'd left several messages, none of which I'd listened to for fear his words would send me spiraling out of control.

Run, definitely run.

My heels set a blistering pace as I raced down the street toward Dana's car.

"Hindley!" Rory shouted behind me.

I sprinted down the street and never looked back. I refused to acknowledge his presence. He'd humiliated me.

"Hindley, wait!" Dana's voice joined in.

Their cries didn't faze me. I was on a mission. Get home, vomit, crawl into bed and hide from the world. I'd developed the pattern years ago.

I searched up and down the street. Bustling cars jammed the busy thoroughfares of downtown Austin. In my periphery I spotted Rory and Dana gaining on me. I darted out into traffic, narrowly missing a car and two bicycles.

"Fucking cyclists," I mumbled.

"Hindley!" Rory's frantic cries drifted down the street.

Good. Be worried. Served him right.

I leaped onto the sidewalk across the street just as strong, beefy hands grabbed my shoulders.

I squirmed out of his hold and prepared for an all-out sprint to Dana's car. I positioned my feet like a runner on the starter block but one massive arm grabbed my waist and lifted me off the ground before I could dash away.

My body trembled. Oh, God, not again. *He's back. Back for you. Run!*

"Hindley, what the fuck?" Rory grumbled in my ear. His voice wavered with fear and annoyance.

I beat his hands that were clasped across my stomach and kicked my legs as they dangled in mid-air. "Put me down!" My voice resounded across the street and caught the attention of a few passersby.

"Not until you tell me what the fuck is going on with you." He gripped me tighter.

His deep voice brought me back to the present. It was Rory. My Skater Boy. But I was still pissed at him.

"What the fuck is going on with *me*?" I mocked. "What the fuck is wrong with *you*?"

Rory's hold loosened.

I slid down his chest and whipped around, my eyes darting between his.

"Hindley, what's wrong?" Dana scooted up beside Rory and

dropped her hands to her knees as she gasped for air. "You nearly got waxed by three cars crossing the road."

"Like you care." I rolled my eyes and folded my arms across my chest.

Dana straightened and her head jerked back as if I'd taken a swing at her. In reality, my words had. If anyone cared about me, my best friend, Dana Di Grazio did.

I scanned both their faces. Their expressions mirrored my own. Anger, resentment, but most of all fear.

"You both told the dress designer that her material looked like baby shit yellow," I huffed as my fists pounded my hips.

Rory and Dana glanced at each other but had the decency to stifle a laugh.

"I'm sorry, baby, but it did." Rory's smirk slid up one side of his face.

His mischievous expression normally warmed my heart, along with other parts of my anatomy, but not today.

The sting of unshed tears burned my eyes. I refused to cry. Not here. Not now. Not over such a lame excuse.

"It's three months before the wedding," I held up three fingers and shoved them in his face. "Three!" My eyes narrowed and my chest heaved with frustration. "I lost one dress designer already. The other has a wait list well into next year."

I gazed along Rory's lean body, at his legs encased in denim, showing off his muscular form. Not now. I shook my head to clear the sordid thoughts. Sometimes I hated how much he affected me.

"This woman was my last chance," I choked out, "my last chance." My words broke with my statement. But my emotions had nothing to do with a fucking dressmaker. The countless voicemails and phone calls barraging me had created the real fear and anxiety coursing through my mind. The anticipation of listening to the caller's voice scared the shit out of me. What could he possibly want?

"Baby, I'm sorry." Rory scooted closer.

I backed up.

"Hindley?" His brow furrowed.

Rory was scared and he understood my mood had nothing to do with a dressmaker. I both loved and hated the fact he could read me so well.

Dana darted between Rory and me. "Hey, why don't you and I stop at one more store? Regan told me about some awesome chick on the East Side."

Regan was a mutual friend who owned a sex shop in Dallas. I'd designed sexy stripper clothes and lingerie for her when I was in college and law school.

I stared at Dana, my brows furrowed. I didn't want to wear crotch-less panties with my nipples showcased through teaser holes in my wedding dress when I walked down the aisle.

"She doesn't specialize in wedding shit, but her designs are amazing." Dana shrugged her shoulders. "It's worth a try." Sensing I needed distance, Dana grabbed my hand and pulled me further away from Rory.

"Hindley?" Rory's usual husky voice broke in a whisper.

I wanted to reassure him everything was all right, that three months from now we'd be joined in wedded bliss. But the vibration of the phone in my pocket stole my confidence.

Could Rory endure the inevitable pain with me? For me? Could I even ask him to?

I gazed at him for answers to my silent questions as one lone tear rolled down my face.

Rory moved to wipe the moisture from my cheek.

I didn't stop him. I needed to feel his touch, even if the connection was fleeting.

"Can we go to dinner tonight? Just the two of us?" He slid closer.

His scent enveloped me like a warm blanket. I needed time and Rory understood. He was willing to give me the space I needed. But for how long? Long enough for me to sort out my shit and make things right?

"She'll call you." Dana jerked on my hand and pulled me away from my fiancé, the man who'd had my heart for almost a year.

I stumbled as Dana dragged me down the sidewalk with her not-so-unusual display of strength.

"Please call me, Hindley."

I glanced over my shoulder.

Rory's once bright blue eyes grew darker as he beseeched me.

He needed reassurance that I wouldn't run away for good. I nodded once. I would call him. I just didn't know if he'd ever want to see me again after I told him about the calls.

Was he strong enough to endure this battle with me, possibly for the rest of our lives?

Dana shoved me into the passenger seat and raced to her side then cranked the engine. As we drove away I glanced back at Rory.

One hand was shoved deep in his jeans pocket and the other gripped the nape of his neck. He released his hold and gave me a single wave.

"Mind telling me what the fuck is going on?" Dana asked as she maneuvered through the busy streets.

I twisted around in my seat and let out a sigh. I hated scaring Rory, but I needed time to think.

"This." I held up my phone. The screen illuminated the familiar name along with his title.

Dana stopped at a red light and glanced at my phone. Her gaze darted from the screen to mine, her eyes growing wide. "Oh, shit," she whispered.

"Yeah. Oh, shit." I repeated.

CHAPTER 2

RORY

"WHAT THE HELL is wrong with you?" Leif glanced over the back of his leather sofa.

The voices of some idiotic TV show blared throughout the living room. I pitched my bag in the entryway and scrubbed my hands over my face.

"What's up with the bag? You fuck up again, douche bag? Your old lady kicking you out?" Leif chuckled.

He wasn't far from the truth.

Something had spooked Hindley today while we were at the dressmaker's. I'd never wanted to go to the bridal shop in the first place, but between my schedule and hers, we didn't get a lot of time together any more.

Even before the smart-ass words had tumbled out of my mouth, I knew they'd been the wrong thing to say. But seriously, the dress looked like a baby had shit diarrhea all over the thing. And they were charging over six thousand dollars for the piece of crap. I chuckled.

"Since when is fighting with Hindley so funny?" Leif glared.

"It's not." I plopped down on the sofa.

"So why are you laughing?" Leif pushed the remote control, silencing the obnoxious voices on the television.

I shook my head. My racing thoughts refused to slow.

"Want a cold one?" Leif pushed off the couch.

Leif knew I didn't drink. His offer was for water. *My* water. Well, the water company who sponsored me—Sonora Water. I laughed under my breath as memories of Matt Davis floated through my mind. He was the company's marketing and promo director, and a complete douche bag when I'd first met him. Matt had tried to make a move on my girl, but Hindley shut him down fast. She'd already fallen hard for me and Matt knew it.

"You gonna share your joke with me now?" Leif nudged my shoulder with the water.

"I was just thinking of Matt Davis." I laughed out loud.

Leif's smug smile fell and his body stiffened.

"What?" I asked.

"Nothing, man." He shrugged. "What gives with the laughter?"

Leif had a way of turning the tables anytime he wanted to escape the scrutiny of his close friends and family. Most times I didn't let him get away with shit, but not today. Today I needed his help. "Something's going on with Hindley, man."

"What *kind* of something?"

"I don't know. She won't say."

"What makes you think that?" He twisted the top off his water and tossed the cap onto the coffee table.

I rolled my unopened bottle in my hands. The cool plastic did nothing to ease the fire burning in my gut. Something was wrong with Hindley. She'd shut me out. "I need to call her." I stood and dug my hand in my pocket.

"Whoa, Nelly." Leif grabbed my wrist. "Judging from the look on your face I'd say that's not a good idea."

"Why?" I glared at my best friend. He knew me better than

anyone. Well, anyone except the woman I was *supposed* to marry in a few months.

"Because you're a dumbass." He chuckled.

I flopped down on the couch and flung an arm over my eyes. I tended to fly off the handle and act rashly. Leif had been my voice of reason for years. Now the daunting task fell into the hands of Hindley Hagen. But she wasn't here.

My gut response was to corner Hindley and force her to talk to me but that wouldn't work with Hindley. I'd have to rely on Leif to help me sort this shit storm out.

"Where is she now?" Leif asked.

"She took off with Dana."

"Uh oh." Leif chuckled then guzzled his water.

"What's with the 'uh oh'?"

Leif and Dana had grown close over the last few months while we prepared for our wedding. Hindley and I had both hoped he and Dana might hook up, I mean how cliché would that be—my best friend and my soon-to-be wife's best friend falling for one another? *Wife.* The word rolled around in my head.

"Do you know something I don't?" I turned and glared at Leif.

"Hold up, cowboy." He held up his hand.

"Have you talked to Dana? Has she called you?"

He shook his head. "Just start from the beginning, dude. How bad did you fuck up?"

"No, not until you tell me what your 'uh oh' means."

"When chicks go off together in their posse it's not a good thing."

"What the fuck does that mean?"

"Hindley just needs a little girl time with her bestie. Don't sweat it."

"You sound like you have an inside track to the female psyche. Are you sure you're not gay?" I howled at the absurdity of my words.

Leif choked on his water.

I scooted closer and pounded his back.

His face burned bright red and he clutched his throat.

"Look dude, I am not putting my mouth on yours to resuscitate you so you better breathe, asshole," I said. "That's just gross, man." I laughed. The truth was, I'd do *anything* to save Leif. He was my brother. We may not be related by blood, but our souls were united.

He choked then sputtered, gulping for air as he wiped his mouth with the back of his hand.

"Dude, what was that about?" I asked. My brows furrowed as I scrutinized him.

"No more talking about me, asswipe." Leif nudged my shoulder, still coughing. "What gives with your fiancée? What the fuck did you do this time?"

This time? He wasn't far off. I was a natural at screwing up a good thing. I rubbed my hands up and down my jeans to dry the sweat. I'd fucked up. I knew it. I just didn't want to admit to anything.

"Your first mistake was going dress shopping with them." Leif chuckled as he shook his head. "I mean, talk about gay." He stared at the ceiling, and I couldn't help but feel like he was avoiding my gaze.

"Yeah, I know," I sighed, falling back on the couch. "But with our crazy schedules, it's just…"

"You must be desperate if your idea of spending quality time with your fiancée is going dress shopping."

"This was Dana's dress," I said.

"And…" Leif waved his hand as if presenting me with the winning door on Let's Make a Deal.

"And…" I swallowed. "I acted like an asshole."

"No surprise there." He laughed. "Could you be more specific about your assholeyness."

I drew in a deep breath and held the air in my lungs as if the action would redeem my "assholeyness". I'd come to rely on Leif's ability to help me understand Hindley. For whatever reason, Leif had a good hold on what made chicks tick—which was surprising since he rarely had a girlfriend.

I drew in a deep breath then exhaled. "I may have commented on the color selection of the dress."

Leif spewed water again as he burst into laughter. "Oh, shit. Let me guess, you gave your dumbass opinion to the sales lady? Or worse yet, the owner?"

I cut my eyes to the large picture window across the room and stared out over the hills of Austin, wishing they would swallow me whole. I was such a shit.

"Please tell me you did not make a smart ass comment about one of the dresses *Hindley* chose."

My silence answered him.

"Shit, Rory, what were you thinking? Don't you know when you're clothes shopping with a chick you have two answers, 'Yes, that looks amazing on you, sweetheart' and 'No, that doesn't make you look fat.' You say those things no matter *what* she asks you, no matter *what* she looks like."

"Where were you two hours ago, asshole?" I shook my head.

"So, what did you say that got you on your fiancée's shit list?"

"It wasn't just me, Dana thought it too."

"Dana's her best friend, she gets a pass. She's allowed to be brutally honest. You," he looked me up and down, "not so much."

"And just how do you know all of this?" I narrowed my gaze.

"Unlike you, I watch and observe people before I speak."

I tossed a throw pillow at his head.

He batted the cushion away with ease.

I missed the easy-going times Leif and I shared.

"Are you going to answer me or not, dill hole?" Leif raised a brow.

I wanted to punch the smirk off his face. Leif was right though. I hesitated, drawing in a deep breath. Obviously, he knew way more about girly shit than I did. He'd probably be just as appalled at my comment as Hindley was.

My eyes slammed shut to avoid his gaze. "I may or may not have compared the color of the dress to a dirty diaper worn by a baby with extreme intestinal problems." I exhaled and slumped against the couch, awaiting the wrath of my best friend.

The room fell silent. My fingers tapped on the water bottle. I cracked open one eye and turned to find Leif wearing a shit-eating grin and shaking his head.

"What?" I sat up.

"Seriously, you have to ask me 'what?'" He chuckled.

"Yeah, I know. Major douche maneuver."

"Major," he repeated. "So what did she say after your shit-for-brains comment?"

"She ran off."

"Literally?"

"Yeah, like she stormed out of the store and ran down the street. Dana and I had to do a full-on sprint to catch her."

"Oh, shit."

"Yeah, I know."

"There's more going on here, Rory." Leif's brow creased.

Shit. If Leif was worried then my situation was bad. "Tell *me*." I stared up at the ceiling and scrubbed my face. "This wasn't just about a dress, man. I mean, it was. But there's more going on she's not telling me and that's what scares me."

"What makes you say that?"

"She's been tight-lipped and jerky since I got in from California two days ago. I head out later this week for a competition in Brazil. Something in my gut says not to go though."

"Then maybe you shouldn't go."

"Dude, this is my profession."

"Dude, this is your *fiancée*!" He lurched forward.

Leif's accusatory tone annoyed me. His demeanor was in complete contrast to his usual happy-go-lucky personality. "What the hell does that mean?" I sat up.

"It means Hindley is now your priority."

His words rattled out as if the statement was so simple. But it was. "You're right, man. Something *is* going on and I need to find out what." I stumbled off the couch.

"Wait," Leif called out.

"What?"

"Give her some time. Let her hang out with Dana and sort this shit out first."

I stood in Leif's living room, paralyzed with the thought of losing Hindley. I had no clue about relationships. Hindley was the first woman I'd ever loved. Obviously, Leif had more insight into the female brain than I did. Maybe I should listen to him.

"Let me grab my shit and we can go down to the course." Leif nodded toward the double French doors leading to his back yard.

He was a skate park designer and had built a state-of-the art course on the property next to his.

"Let's run a few laps, get this punchy energy out of your system." He smiled. "Then you can call your girl."

I nodded in agreement. Leif was right, as usual.

"You got your gear?"

"It's in the bag." I nodded over my shoulder at the duffle I'd dropped inside his entryway.

"So you were just coming over to use me and my course, huh?"

"Among other things." I chuckled. "Thanks, man." I slapped Leif's back then grabbed my bag and headed toward his back door.

"For what?" He slid on his DC shoes and grabbed his own board.

"For always being there for me." I stared at my best friend, the man who'd always protected me and all my secrets. "I've fucked up a lot of shit in my life, but you've always stood by my side and pulled me out of everything."

His eyes snapped wide in surprise. I rarely shared my true feelings with anyone.

He nodded and chuckled. "All right, Mary Poppins, if you're done with the gay-ass girly talk, can we get going?" He signaled toward the door with his head.

I smiled. Leif's need to be outside and skate was his way of accepting my thanks without getting too deep. "Yeah, I'm ready to wipe your ass all over this course."

"Good luck, douche bag."

"I don't need luck, you prick." I swung the door open and walked out onto his deck. The late afternoon sun warmed me despite the chill in the air.

"Sounds like you're gonna need a lot of luck to get your fiancée back."

"Fuck you." I laughed.

"In your dreams." We both chuckled.

In my dreams, Hindley *was* the only person I wanted to fuck. No, fucking wasn't the right term, although the kinky shit Hindley and I shared was fun too. I loved Hindley. And besides my sister, Shelly and Leif's mom, Kara, I'd never loved a woman before.

I'd give Hindley some time, let her sort through her shit like she always did. But she was not running away from me no matter what demons chased her. I was faster and I would never let her go.

CHAPTER 3

HINDLEY

"HAVE you listened to any of his messages?" Dana asked as she pulled the car into an empty parking lot and shoved the gearshift into park.

I clutched the phone in my hand and shook my head.

"Are they letting that scumbag out?" Her eyes narrowed.

My erratic heartbeat silenced me. I feared the same question but had no answer. I had refused to return the phone calls because of my unease. "His parole hearing isn't for another two months," I whispered.

"You can't keep guessing like this, Hindley. Just listen to his message already. Let's yank the bandage off your wound and get on with it." Dana slid her hand over the console and wrapped her fingers around mine. "I'll be here, every step of the way."

I gazed up into her beautiful blue eyes, eyes that had seen more pain in her lifetime than I had. She was my best friend and I loved her more than life.

"Is that why you had a shit fit all over your boy earlier?" Dana looked behind us in the direction we'd fled.

I glanced over my shoulder as if Rory would still be standing in the middle of the street. We were miles away from the dress shop now.

"Kind of," I answered. "But seriously, Dana, baby shit yellow? Did y'all have to use such a horrible description, to her face?"

Dana laughed.

I narrowed my eyes and glared at her, my face tight with silent reprimand.

Her laughter ceased as she slapped her hand over her mouth. Her blue eyes cast downward.

At least she had the decency to look contrite.

A small chuckle escaped my lips.

She joined in and the car erupted with laughter.

"It did kind of look like baby poop, didn't it?" I snorted.

"Oh my God, you should have seen the sales lady's face, Hindley." Dana doubled over, her eyes tearing from laughing.

"I did!" I shrieked. "She looked like she'd just seen us *eat* baby poop, she was so offended."

"Fuck her." Dana wiped her cheeks with the back of her hand. "Someone needed to bring that bitch down a notch or two anyway. She was so pretentious, judging us from the moment we came into her high-priced store. She thought we'd wandered in off the street from some homeless shelter, like we didn't even have enough money to buy a free shopping bag from her."

"Right," I said.

Our laughter quieted, and I stared down at the phone clutched in my hand.

"Just listen to the messages, Hindley." She nudged my arm.

Dana was the bravest person I knew. And she'd always stood by me through good times and bad. I had no doubt that she would now.

"Okay." I released a heavy sigh and swiped the screen, bringing up the voicemail icon that glowed with the familiar name. Dragging in one last deep breath, I pressed the speaker button then played the first message.

"Hi Hindley, it's Jorge Montoya from the Dallas County District Attorney's Office."

The hairs on my neck stood on end.

Jorge Montoya was the assistant district attorney who had tried my original case against Donald Lee Westbank almost six years ago.

Jorge was a first generation Mexican immigrant. He and his two sisters fled their hometown of Saltillo after members of a notorious drug cartel shot and killed his mother, father and two older brothers then set them and their house on fire.

Jorge had fought his way not only across the border of the United States to enter legally, but through college and then law school, working and saving money from odd jobs to fund his own education. He claimed his motivation had always been to create a better future for his sisters and combat the gut-wrenching nightmares that haunted them. He approached every case as if he were fighting for his own family. Justice had been his passion and his motivation for years.

When Jorge had been unable to secure the maximum penalty for Donald Lee Westbank's crimes against me, he'd been devastated.

I clutched my purse and rocked in place as I listened to the deep, ominous tone of his voice. His message wouldn't be good.

"Your assailant, Mr. Westbank, is scheduled for another parole hearing in three months. New evidence was discovered a few weeks ago which may mean additional charges will be filed against him and brought before the grand jury. There may be another victim. I'd like to speak to you before the case goes public."

Another victim? Case goes public?

Oh, shit.

"Please call me as soon as possible, Hindley. My number is…"

Jorge rattled off a litany of phone numbers and contact information, but I didn't hear them. Four haunting words rang in my ears. *Donald. Lee. Westbank. Public.*

"Hindley, this is good news." Dana's voice cut through my thoughts. "If they convict him on new shit, then he won't be up for parole, maybe never again, depending on what he's done."

My stomach lurched. I threw open the car door and did what I always had when the conversation turned to Donald Lee Westbank. I puked.

"Oh, sweetie." Dana crawled over the console behind me. Before I could blink, she dragged my hair back and stuck a bottle of water in front of my face. "Drink this."

I grabbed the already opened bottle and sucked in a small mouthful, swishing the water around to wash out the taste of *him* from my mouth. I spat the contents on the ground with as much disgust as I had for *him*.

Dana pulled me back into the car and tugged the door closed. She brushed the damp hair from my face then slid across the car and fell into her seat, taking my hand in hers. "How many times has Jorge called, sweetie?"

I couldn't hide from Dana. She'd seen the anxiety and fear in my eyes for the past few days. So had Rory.

"Enough." I wiped my mouth with the napkin she gave me.

"Are you going to call him back?"

My eyes fluttered closed as my head fell against the seat. I drew in a ragged breath. *You are stronger now, Hindley. You're not a weak little college girl any more.*

"Hey." Dana's voice echoed in the interior as her hand squeezed mine.

I opened my eyes and stared at her.

"I'm here, you know that."

I tilted my head and my shoulders slumped.

"Rory's here too. We all are, Hindley. You're so much stronger now. Things will be different this time."

"You're right." I nodded.

"You can't let this motherfucker get out, Hindley. Especially if he's done this to another person."

"You're right," I repeated with more force.

"I'm not saying you owe anything to anyone, Hindley, because you don't. You *absolutely* don't. But you do owe this to yourself. You need closure with this scumbag. Maybe this is how you'll find it."

Enduring another trial? In public? Could I handle the stress again? *You can. With Rory, with Dana, with your family behind you, you can.*

"You're right," I sighed.

"You sound like a broken record." She smiled.

My mood lightened. Dana did that for me. She brightened even the darkest of my days.

"Hindley, during the first trial you never told us that fucker had raped you. You endured the pain of his assaults all by yourself, and…" She choked back a sob.

Dana was right. During my first trial I'd never told anyone Donald Lee Westbank repeatedly raped me while I was drugged out of my mind. Only after the tapes of his attacks went public did my family and friends find out about his sexual assaults.

I glanced up at her. Her face looked tortured as tears welled in her blue eyes and her chin quivered. The look was new for Dana. She never lost control.

"I can't imagine your pain, Hindley." She stuttered through her tears. "But I want to. I want to help you this time. Whatever you decide, you know I'll be here." She stretched her body across the console and grasped my shoulders.

I wrapped my long arms around her petite frame. She was small in stature but Dana was the epitome of strength for me. My *secret* was out. I had nothing to lose. And Dana was right. If another victim existed, I had to stand up and fight.

"Can you take me back to my place?" I asked.

Dana released me as she leaned back into her seat. "You're not going to call the DA back now?"

I shook my head. "Not yet. I need to talk to Mom and Dad. And Rory," I added.

"Will that make a difference? What they say, I mean?"

"No. I'll call Jorge and talk to him. I just don't want anyone to be surprised when the new trial breaks."

"I'm here, Hindley. Always and forever." Her gaze swept over me, her half-smile hiding her dimples.

My best friend was worried for me. But she was willing to walk through the fire to put this asshole behind bars for good.

"I'll be okay." I squeezed her hand in reassurance.

"And if you're not?"

"Then I have you. You'll kick ass and take names. No prisoners, right?"

"Damn straight." She laughed. "Don't fuck with us, the dynamic duo."

"Dynamic duo." I echoed.

"Just promise me one thing, Hindley."

I tipped my head and stared at her, my brows wrinkled.

"Please let us inside this time."

I knew what she meant. After my trial I'd shut everyone out. No one had known my deepest, darkest secrets. They assumed my assailant had been a voyeur, watching me dress and undress. I'd only shared the truth with Rory, but now the entire world knew I was a victim of sexual assault—multiple sexual assaults after videos of my attacks had been spread all over the internet.

If there was another victim though I couldn't let her suffer alone. Not like I had.

"I promise, Dana. I won't do this alone. I can't."

"You *can* do this, Hindley. You're strong and brave. The combination is both a blessing and a curse."

"What do you mean?"

"You were strong enough to keep a secret from all of us, but not strong enough to fight off your mind."

I stared at her. She was right. My mind had tortured me for years and almost won.

Dana swallowed. "I just need to know that when you're weak, when you're down, when that darker person inside you takes over your mind, you'll call me. Please, Hindley. I can't watch you suffer again." Dana hiccupped a sob as tears rolled down her face.

My stubbornness to reach out for help had caused her guilt. "I promise, girl. For real. I won't go back there. I can't."

She wiped her face. "Let's get you home then." Beautiful dimples drilled into her cheeks. Dana twisted the key then her car roared to life.

"I don't deserve you," I whispered.

"No. You really don't." She laughed. "Very few people do, actually."

I shook my head. Dana Di Grazio was as self-deprecating as me. We just handled our emotions differently—I self-mutilated, she slept with random men. In the end, neither coping skill had helped us. My biggest wish was one day she'd realize that too.

Dana was my rock. I would need her strength more than anyone's if I had to face this asshole again.

"Dynamic duo?" I stuck out my hand and raised my brow.

"Always." She grabbed my hand and squeezed hard. "Dynamic duo here to kick ass and take names."

"Yep." We shook hands.

"Let's go fry this motherfucker and make sure his sorry ass never sees the light of day again." She nodded.

I mimicked her movement of solidarity.

With Dana's declaration I released her hand and fell back into my seat. I had people to support me now, people who knew the truth and weren't afraid to fight for me. With my family and friends on my side, we could face Donald Lee Westbank. *I* could face him in court again. This time I'd stand strong and I'd win.

CHAPTER 4
HINDLEY

I TOSSED my keys on the side table and shut the door to my duplex. Well, *our* duplex soon. Just the thought of sharing my life and all my personal possessions with Rory sent my heart racing.

I loved him with every cell in my body, but I'd treated him like crap earlier on the street, running away from him, filling his mind with doubt. My foul mood wasn't his fault, and taking out my frustration on him wasn't fair.

I walked down the hall toward my bedroom. The sound of running water caught my attention. *Shower.* Yes, I needed my skin on Rory's, his mouth pressed against mine, kissing me, rubbing me, wiping away my pain like he always had.

Steam filled the bathroom and the faint sounds of his humming echoed in the air. I stripped off my clothes and swung open the glass door.

Rory stood in all his glory, naked and unashamed. His body was strong and solid, tanned like sweet cinnamon. His head tilted back and he ran his fingers through the thick hair laden with suds. His eyes were closed and his lips hummed a familiar tune. "I Won't Give Up" by Jason Mraz. Our song.

I stood in the doorway of the shower, feeding on the sight of him—his muscular legs, his taut stomach, his broad chest. He was the epitome of strength.

His shoulders flexed as he massaged his head. The rivulets of water cascaded down his golden body like a waterfall. My eyes fixated on his tattoo. The body art I'd discovered the first morning I'd woken up next to him. Skater Boy. *My* Skater Boy.

"Are you going to stand there and stare at me all day," he growled, "or are you going to get in here so I can rub my hands all over your naked body?"

My stomach tightened at the sound of his deep voice, his rich tenor sending blistering flames between my legs. I ached for him. I'd never be fully fulfilled without Rory Gregor's touch.

"Just admiring the view, Mr. Gregor." I slid the door shut but stood a few inches away. I wondered how anyone as perfect as Rory Gregor could want someone as damaged as me.

"So was I."

I gazed up and saw Rory's blue eyes liquid with lust and desire. All for me.

He stepped away from the downpour of water and slid his hands around my face.

His intense scrutiny paralyzed me.

"Do you have any idea how much I love you, Hindley? How much I'd do for you?"

My thoughts drifted back to the memories of when Rory had taken care of me, protected me, loved me unconditionally. I was indebted to him.

"I'm sorry," I whispered as my forehead fell against his broad chest.

"For what, baby?" His hands slid down to my shoulders and he turned my back toward the hot spray of the showerhead. The water beat down on my aching muscles.

"For earlier," I said, lifting my head.

His eyes pierced mine and his grip tightened. He looked bewildered, as if he had no idea what I was talking about.

"For being mean to you on the street and walking away," I said.

He shook his head and water streamed down his face. "No, I'm sorry." His hands moved up to my neck and slid up into my hair. "Now let's get you clean, my dirty little Drunk Girl." He tilted my head back and chuckled.

The water washed over my hair, but the spray was cold compared to the heat rolling off his body. Water slipped over my scalp and ran down my face. My eyes fluttered closed and I gasped.

His mouth slipped over my hardened nipple. He sucked the tip to a painful point, his tongue teasing me.

"Ah," I moaned, "oh, God, Rory." Yes, I needed his touch.

His hands slid down my ribs.

Goose bumps erupted over my sensitive skin despite the hot water pelting my backside.

His mouth trailed down to my stomach. One hand wrapped around my back and his fingers caressed my ass.

My legs wobbled and my insides melted.

"Perfect," he murmured against my skin. His other hand cupped my breast and his nimble finger tugged at my nipple. "You're perfect, Hindley."

I blinked, opening my eyes despite the dripping water. Before I could focus on his lips, his mouth covered mine, his tongue devouring me. I matched his primal need, searching inside him, clutching his body as if he were my savior.

He ground his hardened mid-section against me with a low growl as his mouth took me captive.

My muted moans echoed over the pounding of the water beating against my heated skin.

"So perfect." His lips skimmed over mine with familiar words as his hands moved lower, sinking between my legs.

So perfect. So perfect.

Oh, no. No, no. I fought to force down the images racing through my mind.

Someone pressed me face down against the mattress. The creaking springs deafened me and swallowed my voice. He ground me into the bed with his hips. His stubble-ridden face scratched my bare shoulders and the bed bounced with his thrusting. My stomach lurched with the constant rocking motion. His putrid smell suffocated me and burned my nostrils.

"So perfect."

The voice burned through my senses like acid.

Rough hands slipped underneath me. "So perfect, and all mine." His fingers tugged the zipper on my jeans.

I opened my mouth to scream but was choked by the smell of soured alcohol and cigarettes. I held my breath and pushed down the bile.

"So perfect." He whispered in my ear then his tongue licked across my cheek.

Oh, God, no. No, not again. Please, please wake up. Please let this be a nightmare.

Nightmare.

"Hindley!" A voice shouted.

I shook my head, willing away the memory.

"Hindley."

The voice grew louder, pleading for my attention.

Fingers closed around my upper arms.

I clutched at the hands to free myself. "Get off!" I screamed. "Let me go!" I yanked on my arms, but he gripped me tighter.

"Hindley! Open your eyes, it's me, it's Rory."

My body stiffened and blood roared in my ears. I could barely hear his voice.

"Hindley, baby." The man pulled me close to his body.

I shoved him away. The once warm water pounded cold against my body—like the man who'd attacked me.

"Hindley, please. It's Rory. Come back, baby. I won't hurt you. You're safe with me."

Rory? *Rory.* My Skater Boy.

The water stopped and a warm towel enveloped me. He had come for me. My eyes fluttered open.

Rory's blue eyes darted between mine, worry etched across his face. "Oh, baby." He lifted me then walked into the bedroom, lowering us onto the comforter. "Talk to me, Hindley. Tell me what happened. What did I do?"

"Rory," I whispered.

"Yeah, baby, it's me. Are you all right?"

I turned into his chest and burrowed in to him like a wounded animal.

He tightened his grip and held me close. He knew I needed his warmth and protection.

"You're shivering, baby. Let's get under the covers."

"No!" I clutched at his chest. "Just hold me. Okay?"

"Okay." He pressed a soft kiss against my head and moved us lower in the bed then dragged the comforter over our bodies. He rubbed his hand over my shoulders and down my arm, his fingers skimming my skin. He remained silent, never asking a single question.

He knew me. In time I would open up.

I nestled my face into his bare chest, savoring the familiar scent of the man I loved. I wondered how anyone could love me, love this shell of a woman Donald Lee Westbank had left behind.

You're not a shell. Not any more. You're strong, brave, fearless.

"The district attorney's office called me," I whispered.

Rory's body stiffened but he held me tight. "What? When?"

"Two days ago."

"You've known for two days and you haven't told me." Concern and aggravation resounded in the deep vibrato of his voice. "I knew it. I knew this motherfucker was in your head." He pushed up further in the bed. "What did the district attorney say?"

"I haven't talked to him."

Rory leaned over me and stared, his jaw clenched. "You still haven't talked to him?"

I shook my head. "He left messages. I listened to them today. But I haven't called him back."

"What did he say? What does he want? I thought fuck face wasn't due for parole for several more months."

I exhaled into Rory's chest. "He's not."

"Then what is it?"

Rory's thumb caressed my hairline. The light brown flakes in the center of his blue eyes darkened.

"What does the DA want, baby?"

The worry and concern in his voice broke my heart. I paused, mustering the strength to talk about the phone call. My breathing grew shallow. "He said they have new evidence against Donald and they may bring on new charges." I punched out the words.

"What kind of evidence?" Rory turned me to face him. "What has he done, Hindley?" His eyes darted between mine.

My gaze slipped to the towel still wrapped around me as I fiddled with the edge.

"Hindley?" Rory's finger slid under my chin and raised my head to meet his gaze.

He was beautiful, and worried, which worried me. "I don't know," I whispered.

"He didn't say?"

"I didn't call him back. He just said he wants to talk to me before the case goes *public*." I jerked from Rory's hold. If he couldn't deal with the public scrutiny that a new case may bring, I would be devastated.

"What the hell does that mean?"

Protector Rory reared his head, but I wasn't sure who he was defending.

"Hindley," he said, "please look at me."

His voice was softer now, pleading with me. My eyes rolled up to meet his.

"I'm here, for the long haul," he said. "I'm going to be your husband. Don't ever forget that." He smiled and caressed my lips with a chaste kiss. "I know you're strong and you've done this before, on your own. But you don't have to any more. Not this time. I'm here for you."

"I know." But did I? I reached out to rub his face.

He leaned into my embrace and cupped my hand with his own.

His eyes shimmered with love and adoration and he squeezed me tight, infusing me with his strength. I *did* know. Every ounce of my being filled with the assurance of Rory's presence. He was here *with* me, for me, for the long haul.

"Nothing will ever change how I feel about you, Hindley. Nothing."

His eyes pierced me. His love permeated every cell of my being. His affection was the sustenance for life I craved. And tonight I was starving. "I love you, Rory."

"I love you too, baby." He leaned in and kissed my forehead. "You need to call the DA though and find out what the fuck is going on."

"I will," I sighed. My hands skimmed up his chest, over his broad shoulders and into his hair. "But I need to do something else first." I leaned in closer, my towel dropping away as my lips connected with the skin on his neck. I dug my fingers into his hair, pulling his head back to reveal more of his throat for my partaking.

"Are you sure?" He pulled back, his forehead wrinkled.

He was uncertain because of my earlier freak out in the shower. With Rory, actions always spoke louder than words.

I sat up, straddling his massive thighs. I towered over him in my power position and stared at his beautiful face. My wet hair skirted across his cheeks. I lowered my mouth onto his and prepared for a feast. Passion and fire consumed our kiss.

Rory's hands slid over my shoulders and skated down the heated skin of my back. His fingers gripped my ass and he rolled me on top of his already thickened cock. He filled me, completely, body and soul.

I moaned into his mouth as his hips pushed deeper into me. I rose up on my knees and lowered onto him again, riding him fast and hard. "Rory," I sighed, his name like a reverent prayer with each downward motion.

Rory growled.

The vibrations from his deep tenor skimmed over every nerve ending. Our movements sparked a fire deep within and I pulsated with need.

Rory pulled his lips from mine and moved to my puckered nipples, sucking one taut in his mouth.

"Oh, Rory, God I need you."

His hands gripped my hips and he drew me into his body as his legs thrust him deeper inside me. "I need *you*, baby." His body accentuated every syllable.

I arched my back and pushed my chest further against his mouth, bracing myself on his thighs behind me. My legs burned as I rode on top of him, up then down, in then out. He grew thicker inside me, warning me of his release.

"Fuck, Hindley, you feel so goddamn good, I can't last."

"I want you, I want all of you," I mumbled. "Tell me what I do for you, Rory."

"You fuckin' undo me, Hindley." His mouth moved to the other nipple, sucking and biting down hard.

"Awwe!" I screamed. "More!" I needed Rory. I needed him to exorcise the demons inside me. "Fuck me, Rory."

"Oh, hell yeah, I will." Rory flipped us over, his body now on top of mine, hovering over me. Suddenly his movements stopped.

My eyes flew open and I stared at his beautiful face. Trepidation filled his expression and his forehead wrinkled with concern. I understood. He was afraid his new power-position would set me off.

"I need this, Rory. I need *you*. I need you to fuck him out of my mind."

His eyes darted between mine like a wild animal unsure of his next move.

"Now!" I slapped his ass hard.

His eyes popped wide then narrowed. "Oh, Miss Hagen, you naughty girl." He smirked, his sideways smile lighting all my girlie parts on fire. "So this is what you want, huh?"

"Yes, sir." I nodded.

He latched under my knee with one hand and lofted my leg onto his shoulder while he braced himself next to my head with his other.

"I'm going to thoroughly fuck you now, Miss Hagen." His hips pulled back as he slid out of me.

"Good." I tilted my head and smirked. "I wasn't sure you still had it in you, Mr. Gregor." Yes, I was poking the lion, but I needed to be devoured.

He slammed into me, balls deep.

"Awwe!" I screamed. Before I could breathe again, he crushed me, harder.

"Oh, God." I moaned.

With the next thrust, he sent us sliding up on the bed.

"Put your arms over your head," he growled. "Push your hands against the headboard." His eyes flashed with primal need and carnal lust. I didn't dare disobey him.

"Yes, sir." I grinned and slid my hands over my head like a good submissive. I pressed my palms against the slats in the bed.

He crooked his arm around my other knee and brought it over his shoulder. Both legs dangled against his back. The new angle drove him so far inside me I almost asked for mercy. But I wanted, no I needed to be completely filled with Rory Gregor.

"I'm going to fuck you, Hindley because that's what you asked for, right?"

I nodded.

"You know it's *me*, right?"

I nodded again and bit down on my lower lip.

"Say the words out loud, Hindley. I need to hear you."

"Yes," I whispered. "It's you." My eyes fluttered closed.

"Eyes, Hindley."

My lids popped open. Protector Rory stared down at me, master Rory, the man who wiped away all doubt.

"It's me with you," he repeated. "It will *only* be me with you from now own, got it?"

I nodded a third time.

"Say it."

"Only you," I whimpered.

He pounded into me again, his rhythm and angle sparking a fire deep within me. Beads of sweat glistened on his forehead as the tendons in his neck strained from supporting himself.

"Only you," I repeated. The burning need within my belly spiraled up my chest and through my heart as my orgasm built.

"Damn right," Rory proclaimed. "Only." He slammed harder. "Me." He pulled out, staring down with his dark blue eyes before hitting me hard in my core.

This angle catapulted me to a new world, a place where nothing or no one existed but the two of us. "Rory!" I screamed out his name as my climax shot me into another stratosphere.

He pounded against me several more times then stilled as he released deep inside me. His body shook in my arms, his orgasm thundering through him. He released my legs and collapsed on top of me, gasping for air, his chest rising and falling against me.

Being blanketed with Rory's body calmed me.

"I'm hurting you." He pushed up and balanced on his hands.

I wrapped my legs around his waist, drawing him back down. "Stay here. Stay here, inside me." I clung to his arms. "Please."

"Okay."

His hungry gaze drove me mad. I tightened my inner muscles.

"Hindley." He shook his head and laughed.

The vibrations of his voice sparked my need. "What?" I giggled, feigning innocence.

"There it is." He balanced on one hand, wiping away the damp hair from my face with his other.

"There's what?"

"The sound of your laughter." He paused. "It always leads me home."

"Ooo, how poetic, Mr. Gregor."

"I'll show you poetic, my soon-to-be Mrs. Gregor."

"I like the sound of that." I sighed into his neck as I peppered him with kisses.

"We can do this, Hindley. *You* can do this."

He didn't need to explain. I knew what he meant. I wasn't so sure I could face Donald Lee Westbank again, but Rory's confidence gave me strength.

He drew back from my embrace, his brow creased with a deep V. "You need to call the district attorney back, sweetie."

"I know." I dropped my hands from his shoulders and twisted to look at the bedside table.

"Hey." Rory's fingers caught my chin and tilted my head. "Forever." He stared at me. "That's how long I told you I would be here. And I meant it. Nothing or no one will *ever* change that, Hindley. Especially not this fuck face."

I nodded once as a tear rolled down the side of my face.

Rory leaned down and kissed my eyelids. "No tears, baby. You're strong. We're strong. We can do this."

"Okay," I sighed. "I'll call." My hands wound into his light brown hair. My thumbs skirted across the blond highlights created by hours in the sun. "But can I stay here like this a little longer." I squeezed my inner walls again. "Just you, inside me?"

"Baby, we can stay like this forever as far as I'm concerned."

"Forever." I smiled.

CHAPTER 5
RORY

"PLEASE HAVE A SEAT." The short Hispanic man waved to the two empty chairs in front of his desk.

A wooden nameplate sat on his desk. "Jorge Montoya." I smiled as I glanced at the woman who stood beside me. She was the reason I could read the man's name. Hindley was the strongest person I'd ever met. Today it was *my* turn to be brave for her.

Jorge's office was dull and dank, filled with mismatched furniture stacked high with papers and books. A small window in the corner provided the only natural light. Judging by the looks of his dying ivy plant, the rays weren't enough to sustain life. I hoped Jorge was a better attorney than interior decorator.

One large poster hung over his desk, framed in a plastic casing you'd find at the supermarket. The picture was simple but the words were profound—*Beyond a Reasonable Doubt*. On the facing wall was another poster attached to the wall with push-pins, no *fancy* frame. An American flag waved in the background with the words "And Justice for All" blazing across the front.

I liked him.

"Thank you so much for driving up to Dallas to meet with me

today." Jorge walked behind his desk and took a seat. "I know the drive from Austin isn't a short one."

Hindley slid into her chair. She chewed her thumbnail and bounced her knee.

I sat next to her, my hand on her thigh, giving it a small squeeze.

Her gaze met mine, her dark eyes wide. She looked like a deer caught in headlights. Large circles shadowed the tender skin underneath her lower lids. Last night had been fitful. She never rested easy when talk of Donald Lee Westbank permeated the air.

"I love you," I mouthed. "Forever."

She nodded once and smiled as the tension eased from her face. She turned toward Jorge, and like the strong woman she was, started our meeting on her own.

"You mentioned new charges. What's going on, Jorge?" Hindley fixated her gaze on him.

Meek, timid Hindley was gone, replaced by the power attorney I'd fallen in love with.

Jorge opened a large file on his desk and sifted through papers as if buying more time. He'd been the prosecutor at Hindley's original trial so he knew her case inside out.

"First, congratulations on your engagement. That's wonderful." He studied Hindley.

"Thank you." She smiled at Jorge then turned to me and gave my hand a squeeze. "I love you too," she mouthed silently.

My dick twitched and I cursed myself for being such a man, but I couldn't help it. Anytime I saw her lips curve into a delicious smile, all I could think about was—

Enough! Jesus man, you're at the courthouse.

"As you know," Jorge said, "Mr. Westbank isn't set for another parole hearing for a few more months."

Jorge's words doused my would-be hard on.

"I want to thank you for always volunteering to speak at his hearing," he said.

"Of course," Hindley replied. "Why wouldn't I?"

"Many victims won't. Speaking openly in front of your attacker is almost like being victimized all over again. But that's not why I called you here."

"You said there *might* be a new case."

Hindley scooted closer to the desk.

"Yes. The police discovered additional video tapes in an abandoned storage unit on the west side of Dallas."

Hindley gasped. "More," she whispered.

I squeezed her knee.

"Yes." Jorge thumbed through the papers. "Our video guys finagled with the tapes for quite a while but finally figured out what the images were. Knowing your case, there was no doubt as to the identity of the assailant."

Hindley stiffened underneath my hold and her hand slammed over her mouth. "Another girl?"

"Yes, a female, about your age."

"Oh, God." Hindley shook her head and her hand fell onto her lap. "Do you know who it is, the woman I mean?"

"Yes, she's been notified. That's part of why I've asked to meet with you."

Hindley's head cocked and her face wrinkled as she held Jorge's gaze. "Part of it? I don't understand."

"You weren't his first victim, Hindley. You were just the first one we discovered."

"Oh, shit," Hindley and I said in unison.

"This woman was also a college student like you when the attacks happened," Jorge continued.

"Did she know?" Hindley asked.

"No. Not until we told her and showed her the tapes."

"Holy fuck." I shook my head and rubbed my temples. "What kind of sick person does this shit?"

Jorge appeared unfazed by my outburst.

"Her case is a little more involved though," Jorge said. "I'm hoping the circumstances of the crime will play to our advantage."

"What do you mean, play to our advantage?" Hindley scooted to the edge of her chair.

"The victim is deaf."

Hindley and I gasped. The room heated as all the air evaporated. That motherfucker had taken advantage of a girl who couldn't even hear or speak.

I dug my hands into my scalp as my fingers yanked on my hair. My skin burned as if every square inch of me were on fire. I wanted to kick the desk over and smash anything in my way, namely Donald Lee Westbank.

Suddenly, a presence washed over me like a calming scent. The simple placement of her hand on my forearm brought me back. Hindley could tame my ravaged soul faster than any drug in the world. I stared down at her fingers wrapped around my arm then glanced up at her face.

"I'm supposed to be here for you," I whispered, giving her a half-hearted smile.

"You are." She squeezed my arm then turned her attention back to Jorge.

My eyes collided with his. I saw no judgment, only a man on a mission. We were comrades in a war to annihilate this sorry-assed excuse of a human being.

"She was twenty at the time of the assaults," Jorge said. "I can't give you much more information until we arraign him."

"What is that?" I asked.

"An arraignment is where they formally charge him with the crimes and he enters a plea." Hindley answered.

I often forgot my fiancée was an attorney. Of course she knew all the legal shit.

"He hasn't been arraigned yet?" she asked Jorge.

Jorge shook his head. "They're bringing him in from the state prison this week."

A shiver ran through me. "Did he drug the victim and videotape her as well?"

"We believe so, although we have no proof of the drugging, just as we didn't with you." Jorge remained focused on Hindley.

Does he think she'll crumble if he looks away?

I slid closer to Jorge's desk. "You said there was some sort of advantage to this case. What does that mean?"

Jorge's gaze drifted to me. "In the state of Texas we could only try Donald Lee Westbank with sexual assault against Hindley, which meant the maximum he could be charged with was a second degree felony, punishable by up to twenty years. Donald received fifteen. Texas penitentiaries are overpopulated though. They have to make room for more hardened criminals. As a result, men charged with crimes like Donald's have been granted parole earlier. Thankfully through your testimony though, he hasn't been released early." Jorge smiled at Hindley.

Her back stiffened.

"Because the victim is disabled, according to the federal government, he can now be charged with *aggravated* sexual assault. And that's what I'm charging him with," Jorge said.

"That's worse?" I asked.

"Yes," Hindley and Jorge answered in unison.

My brow furrowed as I scanned both of them.

"If we can get a conviction of *aggravated* sexual assault, the maximum prison time is ninety-nine years in the state of Texas." Jorge leaned back in his chair. "That means he wouldn't even be *eligible* for parole for thirty-five years, probably more with his prior conviction."

"So, wait," I shook my head at the lunacy of the penal system, "a man can be convicted and sentenced to ninety-nine years for repeatedly raping a woman, but only serve a third of his time." My internal temperature rose with every word I uttered. Suddenly, I wasn't worried about Hindley having to endure another trial, I feared I may not be able to withstand the ordeal. Would *I* be able to sit in the same room with this fucker and not kill him with my bare hands?

"Sometimes even less I'm afraid," Jorge said.

"This is so fucked up." I shook my head and bowed it in defeat.

"It can be," Jorge said, "but I think with Hannah, we'll be able to see justice served."

"Her name is Hannah?" Hindley leaned closer, hopefulness resounding in her voice.

"Oh, no," Jorge said.

I snapped my gaze to Jorge.

He stared at Hindley as he slammed the file shut. "I shouldn't have told you her name. Releasing any information could compromise the case since he hasn't been formally charged."

"You know I won't say a word, Jorge." Hindley reached across the desk and patted Jorge's hand. They were partners in the war against Donald Lee Westbank. And their team just increased by one.

"I want you to meet her, Hindley," Jorge said.

"I'd like that." Hindley smiled. "Is she still a college student?"

"She was at the time of the attack. She's a graduate now, almost twenty-seven."

"I'm so glad," Hindley said.

Hindley had been slammed with the news of Donald's attack while she was still in college. The assaults had almost ruined her and nearly kept her from finishing her degree. But she persevered. Hindley was strong. She was a warrior, and had even gone on to finish law school in record time.

"When is the arraignment?" Hindley asked.

"He should be here on Thursday. I've asked the judge to expedite the hearing. I'm hoping to have him in and out of the courtroom in less than an hour."

"Why?" I asked.

"Well," Jorge leaned closer, "I was hoping maybe you would be here. For Hannah."

"Of course I will." Hindley answered without hesitation.

My stomach twisted. Seeing this fucker in person could set her back. "Hindley?"

She turned and placed her hand on my knee. "I'm stronger now, Rory. I want him to see my strength. I want to be there for Hannah, to give her encouragement. I know what facing him is like, and I don't want her to go through that alone."

I loved Hindley fiercely. She protected the people she loved. Even though she'd never met Hannah, in Hindley's heart they were bound through tragedy.

"I'll be there too." I squeezed her hand.

"But you have a competition in Brazil this weekend."

My eye twitched with irritation and I fought to lower my voice. "You think I give a fuck about skating, Hindley? There's no *way* you're going into the courtroom to face this shitbag without me glued to your side." The relief in her expression surprised me. I shook my head and stiffened in my seat. "Seriously Hindley, did you think I *wouldn't* be there?"

She shrugged.

I leaned in closer. "You're going to be my wife. There is no one more important to me than you, Hindley. There *never* will be. I protect what's mine." I growled.

Her pupils dilated and her eyes widened then a small smirk lit up her face. She'd taken my words sexually though I hadn't meant them to be.

I raised a single brow in warning, or was it anticipation?

Hindley gave me a wink and turned to face Jorge. "What time is his arraignment on Thursday?"

"Probably in the afternoon. The bus will leave the prison Thursday morning."

"I'll be here," she said.

"*We'll* be here," I corrected.

Hindley glanced down at her lap where I'd intertwined our fingers. The diamond on her engagement ring sparkled in the dim light. She gave me a small squeeze then turned back to Jorge. "We'll be here, Jorge. Together."

CHAPTER 6

RORY

I GAZED AROUND THE COURTROOM, just beyond the railing. Jorge sat at the table to the right, papers spread across the desk. He turned and spoke to Hannah's family.

We'd met Hannah and her family yesterday. Thankfully, she read lips and communicated well with all of us. She and Hindley bonded instantly.

I studied Hannah. A slick-backed ponytail held her blonde hair high and called attention to her wide blue eyes. She studied Jorge's mouth.

The similarities between Hindley and Hannah astounded me. Other than the color of their eyes, the women could have been sisters. Donald Lee Fuck Face had a *type*. The thought nauseated me.

Today, Hannah's parents were present along with two brothers who flanked her. She seemed strong and determined, something I feared Hindley had not been at her own trial.

Jorge had assured Hannah, her family and Hindley the video-tapes wouldn't be shown in the courtroom at the arraignment. The judge would view them privately in his chambers. Hindley was grateful.

I glanced down.

Hindley rolled the hem of her sweater between her fingers.

I covered her hands with mine. "It's okay, baby," I whispered in her ear

Hindley's mother leaned in close from Hindley's other side. "Are you sure you want to be here?"

Hindley sat up and stiffened her back, her eyes wide with an unnamed emotion. "I have to be here."

"No, you don't." My lips pressed in a tight line.

She jerked around and stared at me. "Yes," she threw back her shoulders, "yes I do."

Hindley's declaration assured me she was not going to run from this asshole.

I nodded once in understanding and smiled. I was so proud of my Drunk Girl.

A man dressed in a brown suit adorned with a badge walked toward Jorge. I assumed he was a sheriff's deputy or court officer. The man bent down and spoke in his ear.

Jorge leaned in closer.

After a few moments of a one-sided conversation, the man pulled away.

Jorge's chair slid back and he stumbled to his feet. He stalked behind the deputy as they moved toward a side door and disappeared. The door slammed closed with an ominous thud.

"What's happening?" I asked Hindley.

"I'm not sure."

We sat in silence for what seemed like an eternity. My eyes roamed the courtroom, wondering how long the eerie space would be my home as we endured Donald's trial. I'd promised Hindley I wouldn't leave her while she was here for Hannah.

A scuffle broke out at the side door where the men had exited earlier.

I held my breath.

Jorge emerged, buttoning his suit jacket. His eyes darted from Hannah to Hindley then his gaze cut to the floor.

What the fuck?

Hindley gripped my hand so tight I thought she might cut off my circulation.

"Fucker," Dana whispered behind us.

I glanced back at Hindley's best friend.

She scowled as if to say, "Hindley's mine, asshole, I'll say what I want." Dana had been protecting Hindley her entire life.

"Fucker," I mouthed back to her with a nod.

Dana's blue eyes darted past me, growing wide.

Hindley and her mother gasped.

I jerked my head toward the door.

And saw *him*.

The man who had robbed my beautiful fiancée of the peace she deserved.

The man who'd stolen so much from Hindley.

I saw Fuck Face.

He was dressed in your typical black and white striped shirt and pants. The once dark material was now faded into shades of muted green probably from decades of wear. He shuffled, the shackles of his chains around his ankles clanking through the now silent room. His cuffed hands rattled against the chain around his waist as two guards escorted him.

His dark, greasy hair hung in his pudgy face and grayish-black stubble littered his jaw. He was the epitome of every news show's serial rapist and axe murderer I'd ever seen. Fuck Face whipped his head to the side to clear the dingy mess from his eyes. When he did, his gaze connected with Hannah. He didn't seem surprised to see her. He appeared pleased. A small smirk spread across smug mouth as if he were being introduced to an old friend he hadn't seen in years.

His eyes swept over her body.

Fuck! My stomach rolled and I swallowed down bile. It took every ounce of strength inside me not to leap from my chair, jump over the railing and rip this motherfucker's dick off then shove it down his throat.

Hindley's hands tightened around mine.

I turned to stare at her.

Her eyes were glued to Donald Lee Westbank, her body stoic and still, her chest void of movement as she held her breath. Her jaw clenched and her hands clamped tight around mine. I could count the beats of her heart through the vein in her neck as her blood pulsed and pounded with fear and fury.

Hindley's eyes narrowed.

I turned toward Fuck Face again. He stared directly at Hindley, his gaze piercing her. If looks could kill, Donald would be on trial for murder. Hindley's appearance obviously rattled him.

I cut my gaze to Hindley. She sat ramrod straight, her shoulders squared and her eyes hard and unyielding. I'd never seen this look on her before. She was a woman you did *not* want to cross. I changed my mind. If looks could kill, Hindley would be on trial, not Donald Lee Westbank. The man would not break her. Not today, not ever.

The sheriff's deputies finally turned the asshole to face the front of the courtroom and pushed him into a chair. A stout man dressed in a frumpy brown suit sat beside Fuck Face. He leaned over and whispered into the fucker's ear, pointing to papers laid out in front of them. Fuck Face ignored the man, instead leaning behind him to leer at Hannah.

Ah, shit.

Hindley had years of practice facing this asshat during his parole hearings. Hannah didn't.

Hannah seemed strong-willed and stoic when we'd met her yesterday, but I knew what Hindley had been through during her trial. I could only imagine what was happening inside of Hannah's fragile mind.

Without warning, Hindley withdrew her hands from mine and rested them on Hannah's shoulder in front of us.

Hannah turned and gazed at Hindley.

Hindley raised three fingers, making the sign for "w" in sign language and swung them across her chest from shoulder to shoulder.

I was so proud of Hindley. She'd wanted to communicate with Hannah in sign language and had spent last night in our hotel room, studying videos and learning certain words.

Hindley made a fist and pulled her hand down in front of her like a fighter warning his opponent, signing the word "strong."

We are strong.

Hindley gave Hannah a voice.

Hannah smiled and nodded her head then raised her fist and shook her hand. She made the same "w" sign with her fingers and waved her hand across her chest. She crossed her pointer and middle finger, bringing it to her chin and pulling it down, punctuating the action.

Yes, we are.

Hannah grabbed Hindley's hand and squeezed then smiled and released her grasp before turning in her seat to face the front.

We are strong. We *are* strong. *We* are strong.

In a world obsessed with superheroes, no two people were stronger or braver than Hindley and Hannah. We all had so much to learn from them.

"All rise," a deep voice rang through the courtroom. "The forty-second district court now in session. The honorable Tate Whitaker presiding."

Everyone in the courtroom stood. Sensing she needed my strength, I snaked my arm around Hindley. In reality, I needed hers. I really couldn't say for certain I wouldn't go ballistic on this motherfucker. But I needed to stay calm, for Hannah and Hindley.

A balding man with gray hair on the sides entered from behind the judge's podium. He stepped onto the platform and waved his hand. "Thank you, everyone. Please be seated."

We all sat and Hindley settled in next to me. She was strong, strong enough to admit she needed me. I loved being her rock.

The judge stared down at various papers strewn about his desk before removing his glasses and speaking into the microphone in front of him.

"All right, gentlemen, am I ready to call the matter of the People versus Donald Lee Westbank?"

His question and his doubt surprised me.

Jorge stood. "For the record, your honor, Jorge Montoya appearing on behalf of the people." He reached for his chair and sat again.

The man perched beside Donald stood. "Good afternoon, your honor, Jason Decca appearing on behalf of Mr. Donald Lee Westbank."

Donald remained seated.

"Mr. Westbank," the judge said, staring at Donald, "would you please stand next to your attorney and give us your full name and address for the record."

Donald leaned in to the microphone on his table.

"Donald Lee Westbank—"

"I believe I asked you to stand, Mr. Westbank." The judge's lip twitched and he raised a single brow.

Slowly the fucker stood.

That's right motherfucker, you're not in control any more.

Fuck Face rattled off the information. His voice sounded as dirty and grimy as he looked. The vibrations of his words grated over me like sand paper scraping against an open, festering wound. I had to silence the rest of his answer to block the bile rising up my throat.

Hindley shuddered.

I squeezed her tight.

"Mr. Westbank," the judge spoke again, "you've been charged with multiple aggravated sexual assaults of Hannah Noel Knowles starting on or about February 27, 2007 in Dallas County, Dallas, Texas."

I surveyed the courtroom and noticed a sign language interpreter stood next to the witness stand, repeating everything spoken in the courtroom through sign.

I peered at Hannah. She sat firm, unwavering. She couldn't hear a thing. Maybe the silence for her was a blessing. Fuck Face's voice was enough to make me want to vomit.

"That is a *first* degree felony punishable by five to ninety-nine years in the state penitentiary."

The judge's emphasis on *first* degree was hard to ignore. I hoped Fuck Face understood the case would give him the punishment he deserved.

"Do you understand the nature of the charge, Mr. Westbank?" the judge asked.

"Yes," Fuck Face grunted.

"You have a right to be represented by an attorney. Mr. Decca's presence is indication you are aware of that?" The judge raised his brows.

Westbank looked at his attorney and the guy nodded.

"Yes," the fucker said.

"Mr. Decca is your court appointed attorney. Should you feel you are not being fairly represented, you have the right to ask for a new attorney," the judge continued. "Do you understand this, Mr. Westbank?"

"Yes."

Fuck Face already annoyed the shit out of me with his single monotone answers. But given his disgusting presence and his voice, I was glad he wasn't saying more. I could only imagine him on top of Hindley, assaulting her, talking to her, using her body for his sick, twisted pleasure. My back stiffened and my head pounded like a native drum. Every muscle in my body contracted. I willed myself to stay in my seat and not beat the fuck out of something, or someone.

"Stop," Hindley whispered in my ear.

I didn't look at her, I couldn't. If I saw her, I'd be reminded of what Fuck Face had taken from her. She needed my support today. I didn't need to worry her. I drew in a ragged breath, slowly exhaling, willing my body to relax.

The judge continued. "You have the right to a trial before the court or a jury."

He had a *right*? What *right*? This fucker shouldn't have *any* rights. As if sensing my anger, Hindley squeezed my hand. I gazed down at her face.

Her eyes were riveted on the scene before us.

Be. Strong. Dude.

The judge read off Donald's rights—he could remain silent, anything he said could be used against him—all the other bullshit benefits that the constitution afforded him. Rights he didn't deserve. I was floored such a scumbag would have so many privileges.

The food from earlier lurched in my stomach, burning my throat. I should escape, take Hindley far away from this fucker. He deserved *nothing*. He should have no rights. He'd taken away Hindley's and Hannah's right to choose. The only choice he deserved was to select the weapon I'd use to chop off his dick—rusty razor blade or dull machete.

"Mr. Decca, how is your client pleading on these counts today?" the judge asked.

The courtroom vibrated with silence as everyone held their breath. I wondered if Hannah's life was like this all the time—void of sound.

They'd talked about a plea deal. Fuck Face and his lawyer were aware of all the videotapes, and this time, Jorge said he was certain the judge would allow all sixteen to be admitted into evidence, something the judge in Hindley's trial hadn't allowed.

I squeezed Hindley tighter, willing her strength to infuse me. I was a chicken shit. I was the *man* for God's sake. I should be strong for my woman.

"Guilty." His attorney's single word fired through the room like a shotgun.

Guilty. Guilty. *Guilty*? This fucker was admitting to his crimes?

A collective gasp buzzed through the room like an electric charge. I wasn't sure whether to be elated or pissed as hell. A guilty plea meant there would be a deal, and he'd serve a lesser sentence. But Hannah and Hindley wouldn't have to endure another trial, thank fuck for that.

The judge didn't seem shocked by the attorney's answer, nor did Jorge. Had they known Fuck Face would plead out all along and just hadn't shared the information? The thought pissed me off. Had we worried and stressed about a pending trial for nothing?

"The court will accept your plea of guilty, Mr. Westbank. We will assign a new date for sentencing not to exceed seven days from now. Court is adjourned."

The gavel hit hard. My heartbeat skidded to a stop. Adjourned? What the fuck? The hearing was over? Just like that?

Hindley slumped in my arms and I watched Hannah fall into her mother's embrace.

"All rise," the deep voice from earlier said.

With my arm around Hindley's shoulders, I lifted her with me as I stood. We both stared in confusion as the judged stepped down and disappeared.

The deputies led Donald Lee Westbank from the courtroom. His head hung against his chest and he never looked back at the women he'd attacked. When the door slammed shut, we all rushed Jorge.

"What the fuck?" I yelled before I could catch myself. I wanted to apologize, but the confused looks on everyone else's face assured me they wanted answers too.

Jorge turned to face us, shoulders slumped as he gripped his neck. "I'm sorry, I didn't get a chance to tell you. They entered the plea just minutes before he came into the courtroom."

I wanted to be angry with him, but it was obvious Jorge was already upset with himself.

"It guarantees he'll serve time without putting you all through another trial." Jorge's gaze shifted to Hindley's.

Jorge had been unable to secure the maximum prison sentence in Hindley's case. He didn't want Fuck Face to escape without the maximum punishment this time. For Hannah and for Hindley.

"It's fine, Jorge." Hindley reached across the railing and squeezed his arm.

Hannah stared from Jorge to Hindley, then to her mother for more interpretation. Whatever her mother signed must have appeased Hannah. She turned back to Hindley and signed, *We are strong.*

CHAPTER 7

RORY

HANNAH STUDIED Hindley's mouth as they spoke outside the courtroom. I watched the two interact as if they'd been friends for a lifetime. Today Hannah would give her victim impact statement, something Hindley hadn't done. Not because she wasn't afforded the opportunity, but because she hadn't had the strength to face Donald Lee Westbank during her trial.

When Hannah had asked Hindley to read her statement out loud while she signed, Hindley had choked on tears. She'd only been able to nod yes and grasp Hannah in her arms.

"I'd be honored," Hindley had said to Hannah minutes later.

A huge sigh had escaped Hannah's mouth as relief flooded over her face. "You'll be my voice," Hannah had signed.

You'll be my voice.

I'd had to fight back tears when I'd saw Hannah's words.

"They're ready for you," someone said from the doorway of the courtroom.

Hannah looked every bit the professional school teacher, dressed in a pink silk blouse and dark gray wrap-around skirt with matching boots. Her hair was pulled back in a high ponytail again.

Hindley wore a powder blue linen dress she'd purchased the day before. The cream colored cardigan covered her top and the pearl earrings and necklace her father had bought her when she graduated law school made her appear regal and royal with a sense of grace and elegance.

Hannah and Hindley stared at each other, nodded once, then joined hands and entered the courtroom, never looking back. Today, they didn't need anyone for strength. They had each other.

As the two women walked toward the front of the courtroom, Jorge held open the gate in the railing. They passed through and stopped at the podium near the witness stand. The staff had faced the lectern toward Fuck Face and his attorney rather than the judge, something Hannah had asked for. Hannah had said if he couldn't hear her, she wanted him to see her. She was fearless and fast becoming one of my all-time favorite heroes.

The judge nodded toward the front of the courtroom and the two women stood behind the podium, hand in hand.

The judge cleared his throat. "Please let the record show Ms. Hannah Noel Knowles is hearing impaired and the legal proceedings today will be interpreted by Ms. Gloria Steele, a certified interpreter with the National Association of Judiciary Interpreters and Translators."

The judge turned to the interpreter. "Ms. Steele, do you solemnly swear you are in fact a sworn sign language interpreter for the NAJIT and the proceedings you are about to interpret for this court will be true and accurate to the best of your ability?"

Gloria signed the judge's question then spoke and signed her answer. "Yes, your honor."

"Very well." The judge turned toward Hannah. "Ms. Knowles, as you know Mr. Westbank has pled guilty to the first degree felony charge of sexual assault against you."

"Yes," Hannah said, shaking her fist, the sign for "yes" I'd learned yesterday.

"While the plea agreement does not necessarily require the

approval of the victim," the judge continued, "I want you to understand the sentence and accept his agreement. Mr. Westbank and his attorney, as well as Mr. Montoya, the representative for the people of the state of Texas, have all agreed to a fifty-four year prison sentence for the crimes committed by Mr. Donald Lee Westbank against you. Do you understand the punishment?"

"Yes." Hannah said and shook her fist.

"Mr. Westbank admitted guilt earlier in this court and has waived his right to a trial. The law states that with the original plea deal, Mr. Westbank would be eligible for parole in twenty-four years, but as part of the agreement I have signed, I have added he not be allowed his first parole hearing until at least thirty-five years of his sentence has been served."

What the fuck? This jerk off could get out in thirty-five years. My stomach rolled. Someone squeezed my arm. I turned and found Hindley's mother staring at me as if to say, *This is the best we can hope for.*

I understood. Her daughter had suffered tremendously during the first trial. If we could spare Hannah the same heartache then we would take the deal. Fifty-four years with the possibility of parole in thirty-five though? The whole thing was totally fucked up.

"As Mr. Westbank has attested to earlier," the judge continued, "his age as of the present day is thirty-seven. This assures the court and the victim he will not be eligible for parole until the age of seventy-two."

Hannah's eyes darted from the interpreter to the judge then over to Donald Lee Westbank.

At least the smug bastard had the decency to stare down at his cuff-linked hands.

"I hope the sentence gives you some sense of peace and justice, Ms. Knowles," the judge said.

"Yes, sir," Hannah said and signed. "It does."

"It is my understanding you would like to give your victim impact statement, Ms. Knowles."

"Yes," Hannah nodded.

"Let the record show Ms. Hannah Knowles has elected Ms. Hindley Hagen to read her victim impact statement." The judge extended his hand. "When you're ready, ladies."

Hannah smiled and released Hindley's hand.

The blood roaring from my pounding heart deafened me. I feared I might not be able to hear Hindley's voice. Was this what life was like for Hannah?

Hannah and Hindley stood stoic, their similarities uncanny.

Hindley spread out the paper on the podium before glancing at Hannah. They turned and glared at Fuck Face, unwavering in their strength.

This man, this animal, this fucker would never intimidate these girls again. Yes, Hindley would have setbacks, but this opportunity to speak directly to her attacker would strengthen her in a way no one else could.

As the room fell silent, all eyes were riveted to the two women standing at the front of the courtroom. They'd endured so much at the hands of the monster sitting in front of them. Hannah and Hindley were formidable foes though. Nothing could break them. I was in awe of these courageous women.

Hindley read aloud, "My name is Hannah Noel Knowles."

Hannah signed the words.

"I am a daughter. I am a sister. I am a teacher. I am a friend. I am a survivor. And I am deaf. My voice may be difficult for people to understand so today I've selected another victim to speak for me. Someone whose voice was never heard." Hindley paused and drew in a deep breath. "Today our words will resound loud and clear through the courtroom.

"The court has afforded me the opportunity to speak in what they call a victim impact statement. But I am *not* a victim. A victim is defined as a person who suffers from a destructive or injurious action or agency. I have suffered, but I am not suffering. I was shamed by a vicious attack, but I am no longer ashamed."

Hindley glanced beside her.

Hannah nodded.

Hindley closed her eyes, drew in a deep breath and held the air for several heartbeats.

"Come on, baby, dig deep," I said silently, willing her the strength I knew she already had deep inside.

Hindley exhaled and opened her eyes, her gaze fixated on one man. Her attacker.

"Donald Lee Westbank raped me," Hindley's monotone voice rang through the room.

A thundering wave of nausea crept up my throat.

Everyone sat silent as Hindley and Hannah held Fuck Face's gaze. He would not run away from them today.

"Donald Lee Westbank raped me repeatedly."

Hindley's voice grew stronger.

"Donald Lee Westbank raped me repeatedly and videotaped the acts and stock piled the evidence."

My jaw clenched and my body burned as adrenaline spiked in my veins. Sweat beaded between my shoulder blades and my hands twisted in my lap. I didn't know how many more times I could hear Hindley talk about her rape.

There was no doubt this asshole was a sick motherfucker, but at the moment I was glad he'd videotaped his attacks. The tapes were irrefutable. The evidence meant my girl could finally get justice, accountability and reassurance Fuck Face wouldn't be released for thirty-five years at the earliest.

Hindley studied the paper then stared directly at Fuck Face as she continued. "There is no shame in talking out loud about the heinous acts committed against me. When we hide for fear of being judged and rejected we truly suffer. But when we stand together and call ourselves survivors, survivors of rape and sexual abuse, not just victims, we experience the healing power from speaking the truth. We are no longer shamed by the acts committed against us. We are empowered by the mere fact we survived, and thrived.

"I live with the scars from Donald's attacks every day, but the point is, I *live*. Donald Lee Westbank's attacks do not define me. I choose to survive, not to be victimized. In my strength I will help others be brave and courageous and confront their attackers. I hope to draft legislation to keep criminals like Donald Lee Westbank behind bars for life. I will not be paralyzed by fear."

Hindley glared directly at Fuck Face, her back straight and shoulders pulled back. "You will not break me. I will live my life. I. Will. Live."

Yes! My girl would not be broken. I'd wished Hannah had added "fucker" at the end of her statement, but that wasn't her style.

Hindley read from the paper again. "My name is Hannah Noel Knowles I am a daughter. I am a sister. I am a teacher. I am a friend. I am deaf. But most of all, I am a survivor. And so is my friend, Hindley Hagen. Today my words find their voice through hers. We give each other the power to survive through the gift of retelling our story. Standing strong and confident beside each other, knowing we are not broken."

Hindley glanced at Hannah. "We are brave. We are strong. We are survivors."

The two women spoke in unison as they signed, "We are brave. We are strong. We are survivors."

No truer words had ever been spoken, both silently and aloud.

CHAPTER 8

RORY

THE DOORBELL to our hotel suite chimed.

"Who's that?" Hindley called from the bathroom.

The courtroom scene from earlier had completely drained her. I was proud of how stoic and brave she and Hannah had been in front of Fuck Face, but as soon as the car door slammed shut after we left the courthouse, Hindley had fallen over the center console into my lap and sobbed. My heart broke. She was my hero, but even Superman wasn't immune to Kryptonite.

"It's room service, baby. I ordered dinner."

Everyone at the trial had wanted to go out for dinner to celebrate, but I sensed Hindley needed time alone to process the day's events. She'd relived her first trial. Even though Hannah had written the victim impact statement, the words and experiences were every bit Hindley's too. She'd given a piece of herself in the courtroom, and tonight she needed to find the missing parts of her soul.

"Oh, good, I'm starving," she shouted.

As soon as we'd arrived at our suite, I'd drawn her a bath and poured in scented oils provided by the hotel. I stripped her of her clothes as she stood, oblivious to my actions. She was lost in a world I couldn't bring her back from, and instincts told me not to.

Instead, I lowered her in the tub to let her process the thoughts in her head.

Her hunger encouraged me. I pushed open the bathroom door and peered down at her lounging in the clear water. My dick twitched at the sight of her naked body.

Eyes closed, her body lay still underneath the rippling water as her arms rested against the tub. She was perfect. Her lashes fluttered open and she gazed up at me.

"Chicken fried steak?" she asked, her eyes bright with anticipation.

Who knew something as simple as a southern meal would bring my girl back? "With mashed potatoes and corn," I said.

"Oh, yes," she moaned.

Fuck. Now my dick was rock hard. I slid the door closed. All I wanted was to strip down myself and join her in the tub, but she needed time to herself.

Making my way to the door, I breathed in deeply and exhaled slowly to tame my body before swinging open the hotel room door.

A young man in a burgundy suit stood beside a cart adorned with drinks, silverware and covered plates. "Should I bring it in, sir?"

"Yes, thank you." I stepped aside.

He wheeled the cart into the room. "Should I set the dinner up on the table, sir?"

Sir? God, I wasn't a sir. I was a dickhead, a dumbass, a—

"God, it smells so good," Hindley said as she emerged from the bathroom. She drew in a deep breath and tightened her robe as she walked toward the cart.

Tiny rivulets of water clung to her face and I wanted to lick her dry. *Shit man, pull yourself together. She needs you to be strong, not a horny asshole.*

"Thanks, man. I've got it from here." I waved off the room

service guy and I fished a twenty-dollar bill from my pocket, holding the money out to him.

He grabbed the bill and stared as if the money was a bug. His eyes went wide as he noted the denomination. "Thank you, sir."

Sir. Again.

"If you two need anything else, please don't hesitate to call. Push nine on your phone and ask for Thomas. I'm at your disposal all evening."

My disposal? "Um, okay," I said.

"Thank you." Hindley smiled at the cart, not even glancing at 'Thomas.'

The guy stared at Hindley, his eyes widened as he flashed her a bright smile.

"We *got* it, Thomas." I trapped the boy in a menacing gaze.

He cleared his throat. "Um, yes, sir. Thank you." He ducked his head and made a bee line to the door.

Just in time. I thought I was going to have to throat punch the kid.

"You hungry, baby?" I slipped behind Hindley and wrapped my arms around her waist.

"For more than just food."

Her raspy voice shot a bolt of electricity straight to my dick.

She leaned into me, her head resting against my chest as she tilted her head.

Oh, shit. What was she asking for? "Hindley?" I wanted her, but I wasn't sure tonight was the time or the place.

"Rory," she called back in a mocking tone. She turned in my arms, her deep brown eyes filled with desire I recognized.

Fuck it. I wanted her too. And if she was giving me the green light with those "Come Fuck Me" eyes, I was gonna give her what she wanted.

In one fluid motion I tugged on the belt of her robe and slid the terry cloth cover-up off her body then lifted her. Her legs wrapped around my waist and I made my way over to the bed.

"No," she whispered in my ear. "There." She nodded toward the chest of drawers against the wall.

I stared at her in confusion.

"I want you there." Her breathy voice had me hard as stone.

I wanted to argue, to carry her across the room to the plush bed, but who was I to deny my girl what she wanted. My dick throbbed so hard I was afraid I wouldn't even get my pants down before I popped a load.

I placed her naked body on the dresser as she spread her legs wide. She leaned back onto her hands, her head resting against the mirror.

Like a nervous teen, I fumbled with the zipper on my pants. Shit. Finally able to master the art of getting naked, I dropped my jeans and boxer briefs to the floor in one fluid motion. I gazed into her lust-filled eyes, her lids heavy with desire, and leaned into her, aligning my body with hers.

"I need you, Rory." She gripped her legs around my waist and her heels dug into my ass as I slid inside her. "Please, hard, Rory, harder."

Wait, *hard*? What?

I peered over Hindley's shoulder at my reflection in the mirror. My own eyes were wild with need. Wild. Need. Hunger. This wasn't right.

"No," I said, stepping back.

Hindley snapped out of her lust-filled state, bolting up. "What?" She panted. "What are you saying?"

"You're not going to use me as an escape, Hindley."

"What the hell are you talking about?" She clutched her body, trying to cover herself.

I stepped out of my clothes then moved closer. I slid her off the dresser and turned her to face the mirror.

Her head fell to her chest, her eyes downcast.

I pulled her arms down to her sides. "Look at yourself, Hindley," I whispered in her ear.

"No," she said.

"Look at yourself," I repeated.

Her head lifted, her eyes swimming with unshed tears.

I lifted her arms out to the side. "Do you see what I see?" I smiled at her reflection. I wasn't asking about her physical body.

"No," she choked out.

"I see strength. I see love. I see honor. There is no shame here. Remember what Hannah said. You are whole."

Tears spilled down her face, but I continued. I wouldn't let feelings of shame make her hide behind rough sex.

"You've been broken, I know," I said. "Someone stole your right to choose. But I promise you, Hindley, you are whole. And no man will ever hurt you again. I swear." I drew in a deep breath.

Her eyes darted between mine.

"You deserve love, real love, Hindley. You're worthy. You. Are. Perfect." I kissed her shoulder.

Her eyes brimmed with tears, but I held her gaze. "I am going to make love to you, Hindley, because you deserve to be adored, not fucked on top of a dresser in a hotel room."

Her chin sunk to her chest.

I let go of her arms and they dropped to her side. I tilted her chin until she was staring at me in the mirror. "There is no shame here any more." I perused her body before returning her gaze. "Anywhere," I punctuated. "Do you understand that?"

She remained impassive, tears spilling down her cheeks. My heart splintered as I stood helpless and watched her break down. I refused to let her hide any more though. Not from the fucker who had robbed her of so much.

"He's gone, Hindley. For a long, long time." I turned her in my arms and stared down at her distressed face. Her eyes narrowed as if trying to focus. "You are free, Hindley. You're safe. You're a survivor, remember?"

Her head fell against my chest and her body trembled in my arms as hers wrapped around my waist. I kissed her shoulder and neck, moving up to her hairline, smattering kisses over every inch of her I could reach.

"I'm free?" she whispered.

"Yes, you're free." I answered.

"Thank you."

"For what?" I leaned back to gaze down at her.

"For loving me when I didn't know how to love myself."

"Always, Drunk Girl." I smiled. "I'll always love you."

"Will you make love to me, Rory?"

Did she have to ask?

Her blank stare answered me. Yeah, she did have to ask. She was working her way back. She needed reassurance with every step.

I nodded once as I scooped her up in my arms and walked toward the bed.

She grabbed the comforter with one hand and tugged the cover back as I gently lowered her. She scooted over and lifted the sheets, nodding for me to join her.

I gazed down at my fiancée, the woman who, by some miracle, had agreed to be my wife. Hindley Hagen was the most beautiful person I'd ever seen, inside and out.

"Thank you," she said.

"Thank *you*." I slid in next to her.

"For what?" She dropped the comforter over us as I scooted closer to her.

"For loving me when I didn't know how to love myself."

"We're a pair, aren't we?" She bit her bottom lip.

"Peas?" I asked.

"Peas," she giggled. "Peas of a pod."

CHAPTER 9

HINDLEY

"I'LL GET IT!" Dana shouted over the hum of the stereo system as I danced around Rory's kitchen.

Only Dana could throw me a bachelorette party and have *me* doing all the cooking. For the safety of everyone attending, the fact I was preparing the food was actually a good thing. The woman would burn water if left alone.

"Oh my God!" Dana screamed.

I dropped the lid I was holding and jumped as the metal clattered on the tile floor at my feet.

"Dana!" I yelled. "What is it?" I chucked the dishtowel onto the counter and rounded the corner to the entryway of Rory's house but stopped in my tracks when a familiar face peeked through the doorway.

Regan Jackson, owner of 'Sex World,' a small sex shop in Dallas, and one of my dearest friends, stood in the entryway.

Tears burned my eyes as a wave of nostalgia hit me hard. I hadn't seen Regan in years. She'd never even met Rory.

"There's my sexy siren," Regan purred, her deep smile spreading wide. Her caramel colored skin glowed. I wasn't sure the alluring shimmer wasn't from some type of lubricant or naughty body lotion she sold at her store. The woman oozed sensuality.

"Oh, Regan." I flew into her open arms. "I can't believe you're here." I muffled my sobs in her embrace, confused by my sentimental reaction.

Her scent was familiar, cinnamon spice mixed with a bite of sexy—a potent mix proven to bring your blood pulsating to the surface. Regan had always empowered me, given me the tools to fortify myself, believe in myself.

"I just can't believe you're here," I repeated, shaking my head and wiping my tears. I pulled away from her embrace and scanned her petite stature. "You look amazing."

"She looks fucking hot!" Dana said.

Regan was fifteen years older than Dana and I but you'd never know it from looking at her. She stood just a few inches taller than Dana in bare feet, but today she was clad in her dominatrix, sex toy hostess attire. She wore a black leather bustier with a matching, form-fitted black leather skirt. Her raven-colored hair was slicked back into a high ponytail. Charcoal gray eyeliner and shadow rimmed her light brown eyes.

"What do I always say, girls?" she asked. Her ruby red lips curled up in a deviant smile.

"No one wants to fuck ugly on the inside," Dana and I said in unison.

Regan's motto had been engrained since we'd met her. She wasn't talking about a woman's physical beauty though. Regan trained women, helping them reach their inner diva. She always said, "When *that* girl shows up in the bedroom, the one who *knows* she's sexy from the innermost part of her being, it doesn't matter what she looks like on the outside, no man will ever be able to resist her."

Regan had been right. When I'd finally been able to harness my inner diva, Rory couldn't resist. He said he'd always been attracted to my inner strength.

"No one likes to fuck ugly on the inside?" Geneva repeated behind us.

"Umm, hmm," Regan buzzed as she pushed past us, rolling in a huge suitcase.

"What does that mean?" Geneva asked.

"You'll learn, sweetie." Regan chuckled.

"Are you staying the weekend with us?" I asked.

Rory had flown me and my closest girlfriends out to his beach house in California for my bachelorette weekend. He hadn't been happy about the idea of us going out to strip clubs, but when Dana had threatened him with his balls, he'd finally relented, only if we promised to stay inside the house. Dana had conceded, but the sparkle in her eyes when she'd agreed told me she had something up her sleeve.

"Uh, no," Regan answered as she gave Dana a wink.

Shit.

"Then what's in the case?" Geneva asked as she stood in the middle of the living room.

"Party favors." Regan waggled her perfectly manicured brows.

"Oh, hell no, Regan, not *the case*," I said. Her worst, or best some would say, sex toys lived inside her Trunk-O-Naughty Toys.

"Please, Hindley." Regan laughed as she scooted around Geneva and lifted the large suitcase onto the coffee table. "The invitation said Bachelorette Party not St. Mary's Nunnery Grand Opening, didn't it?"

All the girls encircled her case.

"You know, the nunnery, where you get none-ery." Regan threw her head back with laughter as her ponytail swayed over her shoulders.

My friends burst into laughter.

"Now, now." Regan clapped her hands and rubbed them

together as if starting a fire. Her fingers popped the three silver clasps on the case and she lifted the lid as everyone leaned in closer.

"Oh my god," Geneva said, covering her mouth.

"What the fuck is that?" Tamara, a girl from my old law firm asked as she pointed to the suitcase.

Knowing Regan as well as I did, I could only imagine what she was carrying inside.

"Did that thing go through security clearance at the airport?" Brianna laughed as she poked Jessica in the ribs.

Bri and Jess were two of my stripper friends I'd designed clothes for while I was in law school. They were dear friends, but we didn't get together often any more. I was so glad they'd agreed to come to California to share my special weekend.

"Not only did it go through clearance," Regan stepped back, crossing her arms across her ample chest, "two officers ordered one of each. Purple and black."

"Female officers?" Dana asked.

"Nope." Regan popped the "p" with her cherry red lips. She shook her head and chuckled.

"Holy shit," Jessica whispered. "I've never seen a dildo with so many attachments before."

"And you won't either," Regan answered. "This one was specially designed. I call it the Sexy Siren."

"You designed that?" Geneva pointed, her mouth gaping.

"Mmm, hmm." Regan withdrew the piece of machinery from the case. "I don't just sell dildos, vibrators and crotchless panties, ladies. I design them too. I have my own line." Regan's eyes sparkled with pride.

I was so proud of her. She'd turned her own small shop into a very lucrative business of naughtiness, evolving herself from a sex shop owner to a reputable sex toy designer. I'd helped draft her legal documents of incorporation and given her a list of patent attorneys to help secure her royalties for her "devices."

"This one is all for you, beautiful." Regan turned and walked toward me with the biggest dildo I'd ever seen.

"That thing is huge," Geneva squealed.

"But wait." Regan held up one finger. The room fell silent as she reached for a remote control in the case. Pushing a button, we all watched the monstrous, veiny plaything began to deflate.

"What the fuck?" Dana asked.

"You deflate the dildo to the size you need for insertion," Regan said as if she were explaining elementary math. The sex toy shrunk to a more reasonable girth. "We all know Dana's tight little pussy would need this thing uber small." Regan laughed.

Dana nodded. "Yep, shrink that bitch down to virgin size."

We all laughed knowing how promiscuous Dana was.

"Once it fits comfortably inside, then you depress this button." Regan pushed the control and we watched the dildo inflate and increase in size again. "Then fill the toy until you're *satisfied*." She winked at me.

"What does this button do?" Jessica pointed to the controller.

"That starts the vibration." Regan pushed the button and the plastic wiener jumped to life.

We all squealed and giggled.

"You can adjust the setting for the level of vibration." Regan held the dildo out to Geneva.

"Oh my God." Geneva's eyes rolled back as she gripped the toy. "It's like a wave of pleasure." She moaned.

"Or you can do pulsating vibrations." Regan moved the dildo over to Brianna and Jessica.

"Holy fuck," Bri sighed.

"And this one puts off heat." Regan smiled as she hit yet another button on the small control panel. She held out the rubber cock to Tamara.

Tamara stood stock still, obviously in shock. I knew Tamara wasn't a prude, but I wasn't sure if she'd ever been to a sex shop.

"Feel it," Regan coaxed.

Tamara's eyes went wide as they darted from the dildo back to Regan.

"Have you ever touched a sex toy?" Regan asked. Her words were soft and motherly, not judgmental.

Tamara twisted her lips and shook her head.

"Oh, honey, you're in for a *treat*." Dana smirked.

Tamara slowly stretched out her shaking hand.

"It won't bite, sugar." Regan spoke with her Texas drawl. "Well, not unless you hit this button."

Tamara jerked her hand back.

"I'm just kidding, sweetie. Feel it?" Regan stepped closer.

Tamara's eyes scanned the room as if asking permission.

We all nodded our heads.

Her hand ran the length of the impressive plastic tube. "Oh my God," she sighed. "It feels so...real."

"Right?" Jessica nodded her head.

Tamara's hand gripped the dildo. "Oh my God, this thing is growing." Her eyes flashed wide as she stared at Regan.

"Imagine that big, slick dildo growing thick inside of you right now." Regan waggled her brows. "Long, vibrating and heating up."

"Fuck yeah," Dana shouted.

Tamara's eyes rolled back in her head.

"Regan, this may be your best toy yet." Dana's blue eyes sparkled. "I want to order one. Purple for me."

"Yeah, me too," Jessica said.

"Me, three," Bri chimed in.

Everyone looked at Tamara, whose closed eyes and lax mouth were indicators of her satisfaction.

I feared we might be interrupting an orgasm.

Her eyes popped open. "It just heated up?" She shrieked.

"Mmm, hmm," Regan nodded. "Another added feature. This

one is top of the line. Nothing less for my girl." Regan's gaze found mine and she smiled.

Regan had been a rock for me during my original trial. We hadn't spoken of my attacks much, but I knew she understood. I was pretty sure her past included secrets just as dark and painful as mine.

"Do you want this one, Tamara?" I asked.

"But, it's yours," she stumbled with her words, lost in a euphoric dildo high.

"Actually, I made one for each of you." Regan smiled.

"No, shit?" Bri clapped her hands.

"Yes, shit." Regan laughed. "They'll be mailed to your homes in a few weeks. This one is the prototype."

"It's fucking awesome," Geneva said as she looked over Tamara's shoulder.

"I don't think I'm going to get this one back, am I?" I asked, looking at Tamara's orgasmic smile.

"Uh uh." Tamara shook her head as she adjusted her grip on the dildo.

"It's yours, Sexy Siren." Regan stared at me. "You can let her keep it and I'll mail you a new one."

"Have you ever used a dildo?" Bri asked Tamara.

Tamara's face flushed.

"You're in good hands with Regan." I patted her arm and smiled. "She loves helping women discover their kinky side."

The oven dinged.

"The pizza is ready you guys," I announced.

"Fun time's over." Regan grabbed the sex toy from Tamara's hand.

Tamara groaned.

"I have more goodies." Regan smiled, squeezing Tamara's empty hand.

Tamara's eyes shined with the same type of merriment I'd had when I first walked into Regan's sex toy shop years before. My visit to Regan's Sex World was the start of one of the most amazing friendships I'd ever had. I was sad I hadn't seen Regan in so long.

Regan stashed the toy in the accompanying case and secured the lock as the girls made their way into the kitchen.

"Thank you so much for coming, Regan." I pulled the pans from the oven.

"Are you kidding, sweetheart?" She turned and brushed my hair over my shoulder. "I knew this day would come and I wouldn't miss it for the world."

"What day?"

"The day you finally met the man worthy of you."

"Worthy of *me*?"

"Yes, Hindley, worthy of *you. You're* the big catch in all of this." She waved her hand around Rory's monstrous house. "Not this skater boy you've fallen madly in love with." She laughed.

"Thank you." My voice quivered.

"For what?"

"You taught me so much about myself, about my own sexuality. Even in the midst of my pain, you taught me not to be afraid."

"And yet, you still were. Until you met this boy, right?"

I shrugged my shoulders. "Somewhat, I guess."

"But Dana says you're happy now?" She raised her brow.

I smiled and nodded.

"And you're strong, Hindley. So strong. Even before you met Rory, you were strong. I'm so proud of you. What you did in this case, standing tall for another victim."

"I learned everything from you." I grabbed her around her tiny waist and pulled her toward me. "My two dynamo vixens." I nodded toward Dana who was now stuffing her face with pepperoni pizza. "You both have taught me the meaning of strength and courage."

"I think you have that backward, my dear," Regan said.

"What?"

"It's *you* who have shown *us* the meaning of strength and courage. I'm honored just to know you, Hindley." Regan's eyes glistened with tears.

"Are you going to cry?" I teased, poking her ribs with my finger.

"Tears of joy for you, Hindley. Only tears of joy." Regan cupped my face and kissed me on each cheek. "I knew you were special the minute you came into my shop, my little sexy siren. I would have loved to seen you on the stage, but I'm just glad you found someone who is worthy of you."

"You're too kind to me, Regan."

"And you're too modest." She squeezed me. "But that's okay. That's why you have me."

"Thanks for making me brave," I whispered as I embraced her.

"You've always been brave, Hindley." She pushed me away, staring into my eyes. "And I've always considered myself the lucky one for having known you."

I stared at Regan for several seconds as her words of adoration washed over me. Appreciating such compliments was uncomfortable for me, but I was learning. I *was* brave. I *was* strong. People like Regan and Dana and Rory were slowly making me believe in myself again.

CHAPTER 10

HINDLEY

"Okay, ladies, let's take your seats and get ready for the *show*." Dana smirked as she ushered everyone out of the kitchen and into Rory's humongous living room.

My stomach tightened with fear. The way Dana winked at Regan assured me I wouldn't enjoy this surprise. "Dana," I nudged, "Rory specifically said *no* strippers." I remembered how adamant Rory had been when Dana teased him, suggesting she'd booked three dancers for my bachelorette party. He and I had come to blows over the entire ordeal.

"Well, One Nighter ain't here now, is he?" Dana cocked her head. "What he doesn't know won't hurt him. Mum's the word, right ladies?" She gazed over the room full of girls.

They all nodded.

"Dana," I whispered, pulling on her elbow.

"Settle down, princess. It will all be okay, I promise." Without another word, she lifted a remote control over my shoulder and pressed a button.

The room sprang to life with the familiar beat of one of Rory's favorite '80's classic rock songs. "Walk this Way" by Aerosmith.

Shit. Shit. Shit. Rory will kill *you. Then he'll demolish my best friend, little Miss Liar Liar Pants on Fire over there.*

My stomach twisted and knotted in fear. Fuck. I glared at Dana. She was in *so* much trouble.

Loud whistles and catcalls captured my attention. I followed the girls' gazes and saw a man standing at the top of the staircase—fully clothed, thank God.

He wore a loose fitting T-shirt and unflattering work out pants. A flat back cap covered his face.

"Dana," I fumed.

"Have a seat." She nodded toward the empty chair next to her and pressed a wad of one dollar bills in my hand.

The other girls whistled and hollered as the stripper walked, no *strutted* down the stairs. His face remained hidden by the brim of his cap. My hands broke into a sweat and the dollar bills almost slipped from my hand.

The man slid his shoe past the final carpeted step onto the tile with a thud.

"Oh, hell yeah," Regan called.

Wait, those shoes. I knew those shoes.

He raised his head, revealing a familiar face. His luscious lips spread wide, his smile lighting my panties on fire. Small creases danced around the edges of his bright blue eyes.

My Skater Boy.

Rory sauntered toward me with the grace of a puma on the prowl, his smile slipping to a predatory smirk.

"Did someone ask for a stripper?" He grinned.

His low sultry voice sent goose bumps skittering across my skin.

"Um, yes we did, One Nighter." Dana winked at me. "How nice of you to show up."

Rory strutted toward me then straddled my knees with his legs. He bent at the waist, his lips brushing against my ear. "You didn't *really* think I would let some cockless motherfucker strip for you, did you Miss Hagen? Because trust me, if any man would have tried to take off his clothes for you, I would have ripped his cock off."

Oh, hell. The warmth from his breath shot sparks of pleasure across my skin.

Rory gazed over the room. "Ladies," his voice hummed, "are you ready for the show?"

"Fuck yeah we are!" Jessica yelled.

Wait? Show? What the hell?

"No way," I said, pushing up on the arms of my chair. "You can't strip in front of them." The thought of Rory baring his body in front of my friends set a tidal wave of green jealousy crashing through my veins.

"Watch me." He winked and tossed his hat off his head then pushed me down into the chair.

"Oh, hell yeah," Bri squealed as she caught the cap.

"Rory," I growled.

"Hindley." He chuckled.

His rich laughter reminded me of the Big Bad Wolf about to blow my house down.

Before I could protest more, he stepped up on the coffee table, his mid-section directly in front of me. All thoughts of why he should *stop* suddenly faded away as I anxiously awaited the show.

His hand slipped behind his shoulders and he grabbed a wad of his shirt as his hips gyrated to the beat of the song.

I'd never seen Rory dance before and I had to admit he had rhythm. *You didn't already know that from all the sexcapades?*

He lifted his shirt over his head, revealing his washboard abs and chiseled upper body. Visions of being wrapped in Rory's strong arms with my head resting on his muscular chest flashed in my mind. His body had become my safe haven from the storms raging inside me.

He twirled the shirt high above his head as his hips thrust and swiveled in rhythm to the music. He flung the T-shirt toward Dana and she caught the clothing mid-air.

Rory and Dana shared a knowing glance. These little shits had planned the entertainment.

Rory's empty hands slid up and down his shiny work out pants.

I wondered how he'd remove his clothes over his DC sneakers. Before I could conjure any ideas, he grasped either side of the waistband and literally ripped the pants off.

The room erupted in high-pitched cheers. My green-eyed monster roared to life but died down when my eyes roamed up his toned legs to the brightly colored underwear. Hello Kitty.

Rory thrust his hips forward and shoved Hello Kitty's face in mine.

I prayed he had on another pair of underwear beneath to keep his dick from springing out of the hole in the middle.

He jumped down from the table and straddled me, sitting up on his knees until his dick stood inches from my face.

"Oh, yes!" Regan shouted.

"Work it, boy!" Bri screamed.

Rory gazed down at me with the biggest shit-eating grin. His hands raked over my shoulders and down my arms until they rested on my wrists. He lifted my arms and wrapped them around his waist then pushed my palms into his meaty cheeks, forcing me to grab a handful of his ass as he thrust forward.

"Rory!" I screamed.

He leaned down. His lips brushed my ear as his hands kept mine planted squarely on his ass. "Unlike you, I let you touch the dancer." His hands dragged mine around to the front.

"No!" I shouted, fighting to pull my hands away.

Instead of putting them on his crotch, Rory opened my hands, palms down, and planted them on his abs just above the waistband of his boxers. His torso rolled forward and back like a slithering snake.

My Skater Boy had skills. What the hell? Did Rory used to dance?

His hands slid mine up his taut stomach.

I reveled in the divots of his muscular torso. His sculpted body reminded me of the first day I'd awoken to find his body in my bed. I licked my lips and rolled my eyes up to meet his. They were darker now and full of mischief…and promise. Oh, crap.

"Give him some dollar bills," Dana said.

"Yeah, yeah!" Jessica encouraged.

Rory released my hands and tilted his head as his hungry gaze swept over me.

Was he daring me? I chuckled and wiggled my eyebrows. Two could play this game. Slutty Hindley had just arrived to the party.

I pulled my hands away from his body and dug around the chair until I found the wad of bills. I gazed at his mid-section and licked my lips. "What can I get for this?" I flicked my hair back as I held up one dollar.

"Oh, shit." Dana giggled. "Girls, this may get *real* ugly. *Real* quick."

Dana knew the propensity Rory and I had of revving the sex speedometer from zero to sixty in a nanosecond.

Rory's salacious grin ignited a flame. The fire burned through every cell in my body quickly turning into an untamed inferno.

He slid his hands halfway into his boxer shorts and pulled open the waistband. "Put it in and find out." He nodded toward his pants.

"That's what she said." Dana cackled.

I rolled my eyes as I slid the dollar bill into his shorts.

Rory's eyes lit up as if I'd given him the best gift of his life. He lowered his face to mine and kissed my nose then pulled back.

"That's it?" I asked.

"It was only a dollar, sweetheart." Rory laughed and slid his fingers down my jaw.

I held up five one dollar bills. "What does this get me?"

Regan whistled and the other girls cheered me on.

Rory gazed down at his shorts as he lifted the waistband again.

His predatory gaze set my heart beating wild. He wielded a power over me. My body buzzed with need, and I swallowed with an audible gulp.

His gaze lowered to my throat and his eyes darkened as a film of lust washed over them.

I slipped the handful of dollar bills into his waistband. With a *snap*, his elastic band sealed tight around the dollars.

He slid in closer to me, his crotch lined up perfectly with mine. His fingers spread on the arms of the chair. As the rhythm of the music increased and the drums beat louder, his hips thrust into mine. His erection rubbed against the burning bundle of nerves between my legs.

I gasped and my eyes fluttered closed.

"Oh, yeah, baby!" Bri shouted.

All the chants and jeering faded away as my mind flooded with desire. My lids flickered open and I stared up at the man who'd captured my body, my heart, my soul, months ago. Instead of the usual lust in his eyes, tonight I saw love, I saw adoration. I saw forever.

"Open it." Regan nodded toward the box sitting on the counter. The present was wrapped in silver paper and tied with a purple bow.

The other girls had already left the party. Unbeknownst to me, Rory had booked them suites at a luxury hotel in Laguna Beach. My girlfriends were obviously *not* part of his evening plans.

"I wanted to be alone with you tonight," he'd said when I questioned why everyone was leaving the house so early.

Rory gazed over my shoulder as I pulled the wrapping paper away with great care and concern. I knew whatever lay inside had to be some type of sex toy if the gift was from Regan. My fiancé would be very appreciative. Rory said Regan was fast becoming one of his favorite people in the world.

I gazed at the elegant black box with the embossed silver edging. In the middle was a matching silver framed square with the words "Flying High" written in beautiful black script lettering. *Maybe not so much sexual after all.*

"What is it?" I asked. "An Ozzy Osbourne CD collection?"

Rory laughed.

He did like 80's rock and roll.

"Not even close." Regan smirked.

Oh, no.

Rory and I exchanged bewildered looks. I read underneath the script writing. In small lettering were the words, "Indulgent Fantasy Toys by Regan Jackson." A shiver of excitement—and fear—rolled up my spine.

"Open it." Regan nudged me.

I glanced at Rory one more time then lifted the top of the elegant box. Inside was a mass of nylon straps and ropes neatly folded in a die-cut container. *What the hell?* I glanced up at Regan in question.

Her deviant smile warned me.

"What is it?" Rory pulled the apparatus out of the box. The cording unraveled from his hands and fell in a twist of ropes and metal.

"It's a sex swing." Regan waved her hand in front of the box like a magician.

"Oh, fuck yeah." Rory chuckled.

"Oh, fuck *no*," I said.

"What?" Rory sagged against the counter and stared at me as if I'd cancelled Christmas.

"It's a portable swing that attaches to the door." Regan removed the contraption from Rory's hand and laid the *gift* on the counter.

"Did you design this?" Rory asked

"Nah, sex swings have been around forever. Portable ones like this are new though." She laughed. "I just reinvented the packaging. I want to make kinky sex toys appealing to everyone, not just the FetLife community."

"The *what* life?" Rory asked.

"Never mind." I pushed Rory aside. We didn't need to discuss fetishes right now. I stood between him and Regan. Unraveled on the counter, the *swing* looked like a torture device.

"Come on." Regan grabbed the band of straps and knobs and walked toward the stairs. "Let's hook it up." She waggled her brows.

"Now?" My voice shot up an octave.

"Hell yeah!" Rory pushed off the counter and bolted for the stairs.

"Wait!" I grabbed his arm. "This was *my* bachelorette party you invaded."

"And?" He flinched.

"And," I said, "you're not even supposed to *be* here, let alone use the sex toys I got from everyone."

"Oh, sweetheart," Rory purred as he slid his arm around my waist and tucked me under his arm. "That's *exactly* why I'm here."

I shook my head. Reprimanding Rory Gregor was a waste of time. All my friends were gone already. And staring at the toys littering the coffee table, I had to admit, trying them with my oh-so-sexy fiancé would be a dream come true.

"There's my Drunk Girl." Rory clasped my hand, and tugged me toward the stairs.

We ascended the steps and walked into his massive master bedroom.

Regan placed two metal bars over the top of the door. "This will secure it," she explained as she shut the bedroom door.

The swing fell in a mass of straps and she straightened the tangled mess. "Your arms go here." She held up two loops. "You can sit here." Her hand ran across the padded seat straps. "And these." Her eyes sparkled. "These are for *whatever*."

"What does that mean?" I cocked my head in skepticism.

"You can put your legs in them, your calves, or your feet....whatever floats your boat."

"Feet." Rory's lips curved and he waggled his brows. "Oh, yeah."

"The possibilities are endless," Regan continued. "There's a manual in the box if you get stuck though." She dropped the swing and stood back, staring at the apparatus now secured to Rory's door.

I stared at the swing, mouth agape in shock.

"Well, I'm off," she quipped with a flick of her hand then opened the door. "Love to you both. I'll see you at the wedding. Kiss, kiss." She pecked us both on the cheek then slinked through the small opening. "Have fun, my dearies. But not *too* much." She winked then pulled the door closed with a soft click.

Rory and I stood and stared at the *thing* hanging on the back of the door.

"Best wedding present. *Ever*." Rory smirked.

He glanced at me, his eyes drinking me in from head to toe.

I backed away from the door, and his gaze. "Oh, no you don't." I waved a finger.

"What?" He stepped closer.

"You crashed my *bachelorette* party, Rory Gregor." I crossed my arms over my chest in an effort to protect myself from his sultry gaze.

"So?" He inched closer.

"So…" My brain thumbed through the file folder of other offenses he'd committed during the night—undressing in front of my friends, serving as a make-shift bartender in his boxers. "It's called *bachelorette* for a reason, Rory. There aren't supposed to be any bachelors."

"Aren't strippers bachelors?" He cocked his head and leered.

My body snapped taut, caught in the web of his desire. The deep rumble of his voice stole the air in my lungs and paralyzed my body. Shit.

"And girls invite strippers to their bachelorette parties, don't they?" he asked.

Double shit. "That's different."

"How so?" He slid his hands up my arms and gripped the back of my neck.

Yeah, how so? Dammit, he was winning the debate.

His fingers massaged my scalp and his thumbs did wicked things to the erogenous zone just under my earlobe.

"Um…" My lids flickered closed.

"I just wanted to dance for you."

His childlike tone was in direct opposition to the hot breathy caress that wafted over my face.

My lids fluttered open.

He was inches from me, his eyes trained on my lips as he uttered a low growl.

"You call what you did tonight *dancing*?" I laughed. His moves earlier lit a fire between my legs, but he didn't need to know that. Not yet.

"You didn't like my dance, Hindley?" He pouted.

My name rolled off his tongue like rich, dark chocolate. His luscious lips begged to be bitten. All thoughts of why he should leave vanished.

He walked me toward the door and pushed my back flush

against the wood. The straps of the swing pressed against my clothing.

"Perhaps I should keep dancing then."

His provocative tone had every muscle south of my navel contracted in desire. The thought of Rory Gregor grinding into me again seemed like the best bachelorette party gift a girl could ever receive.

He slid his hands under my shirt and his fingers skimmed across my heated flesh.

I gasped. My head fell back against the door with a thud. I was a goner for Rory Gregor.

He lifted my arms and tugged the top over my head. When he pulled my shirt free, he gripped my wrists tight and held them against the door with one hand. With tantalizing ease, his other hand traced a line down the curve of my body. He stopped at the waist-band of my jeans and feathered his hand across my contracted abdomen. His thumb circled my belly button with slow strokes.

My chest heaved and trembled against his touch as I gasped for air.

Oh, holy hell.

Rory pressed his body into me, leaning his face down to caress his cheek against mine. The evening stubble littering his face grated against my skin.

Goose bumps rippled along my smooth flesh. A spark detonated in my belly and spread to my extremities like a wild fire. His erection rubbed against the thick material of my jeans. My hips gained a life of their own as they bucked and gyrated into his.

"Do you want to fly, Hindley?" he whispered into my ear.

Did I? Hell yeah, I did. I moaned, my eyes rolling back into my head. Hell, I was halfway to an orgasm already and he hadn't even touched me down there.

His hands worked the top button and zipper of my jeans and in seconds he had them off and discarded along with my shoes.

My eyes fluttered open.

Rory stepped back and surveyed my body from head to toe, eating me alive with his heated gaze.

And I loved it.

"You said something about dancing, right?" he asked.

I nodded my head, unable to speak.

He reached behind me.

The clattering of the belts echoed through the room and reminded me of the first time he'd restrained me.

"Put your hand in here." He held the handles in front of me.

As if in a trance, I obeyed, sliding my left hand into the soft material.

"Hold on to it."

I clung to the strap as if the handle was my only chance at survival. With Rory in command, I knew the harness just might be.

He secured my right hand with the loop on the other side.

My chest rose and fell as my breathing increased, every inhalation falling in sync with the rapid beat of my heart. With my hands now secure in the loops, my physical body was half way at his mercy—my mind was already his, I'd relinquished control months ago. His dark, penetrating gaze assured me he knew I was his.

"Here." He held up the stirrup. "Slide your leg through."

My brows furrowed. "I thought you were going to dance for me."

"Oh, I am." His tongue darted out to lick his succulent lips.

Oh, holy hell.

He chuckled low.

The vibrations skittered over my nerve endings, leaving me a wanting heap.

His hand slid under my knee and lifted my leg off the floor. "But first I have to make sure you can't touch the dancer." He slipped my foot through the soft, padded loop. "Isn't that what you said when you danced for me in the pole dancing studio? No touching the dancers, right?" He nudged my other leg.

In seconds, I was trussed in the swing, hands clutching the handles and my back pressed against the door. Old instincts and memories would normally have had me teetering on the brink of a full-blown panic attack, but I was used to Rory's physical restraints now. I enjoyed his domination. Giving away my control to such a powerful man had proven to be more intoxicating and erotic than I'd ever expected.

Rory turned and strutted toward the dresser, picking up his phone and pressing a few buttons. Suddenly, the sounds of "Walk this Way" by Aerosmith crooned through the room.

I smiled and bit my lip to hold in a chuckle, but failed.

He glanced over his shoulder. "Oh, are you laughing at me, Miss Hagen?"

His eyes shined bright blue, his expression expectant like the first time I'd seen his beautiful face in my bed.

"Tsk, tsk tsk." He clicked his tongue.

Oh, shit. His tongue. It did wicked, wicked things to me. My hello kitty was on fire with need and anticipation.

"I think I could make an exception for you though." His hips swayed to the music, but he made no move toward me.

I knitted my brows. "What kind of exception?"

He stalked toward me, every step synchronized with the drum-beat of the song.

Walk this way.

I wanted him to do more than *walk*. I licked my lips in expectation, praying he'd move faster.

His pupils dilated.

Oh, yeah, I could affect him too.

He stopped between my legs, his body mere inches from mine. "I think it's okay if I touch this lady tonight." He slid his hands along the outside of my bare thighs.

I trembled, thankful to have the straps to grip.

"But I don't like you this way," he said.

My eyes darted between his. He didn't like me?

His thumb traced my bottom lip. "Don't pout, sweetheart."

Was I pouting?

"I want you like this." His hands reached behind my knees and yanked me toward him.

My hands clutched the loops tighter as he lifted me completely off the floor. My legs splayed wide, held in place by the straps. I was bared to him.

"Oh, yes." His eyes widened. "But not *quite* perfect."

This time I *did* pout. My whole body sagged in disappointment.

"Oh, you're perfect." Rory stroked my inner thigh and moved closer to the juncture begging for his touch. He skirted the throbbing area. "But I don't want to be inside you just yet." He ground his crotch into mine, his erection hitting the bundle of nerves between my legs.

"Ahh." I wiggled, trying to rub myself against him. Hanging from the straps made movement impossible. "Rory," I pleaded.

His hips pulsed against me to the words of the song. I had no idea Aerosmith's lyrics talked about seesaws swinging and feet flying up in the air—which I was literally doing.

Rory grabbed another strap above me and yanked down hard.

My body slid up the door until my pelvis aligned with middle of his face. *Oh, shit!*

"Now *that's* perfect," he said.

His breath washed over my mid-section like a warm afternoon breeze. A salacious smile spread wide across his face.

"See saw swinging," he sang along with the song and chuckled, bobbing his head with the beat.

Oh, God. My panties were soaked.

He pressed his nose into the wet material of my underwear and dragged in a deep breath.

My face flushed from embarrassment.

He moaned with a guttural sound deep within him. "Now that is my absolute favorite scent." His eyes rolled up to meet mine.

He was wicked. Wicked, wicked, wicked. And I loved him.

Before I could draw in another breath, his tongue slid out from his plump lips and stroked me over my underwear. "Oh, God!" I struggled to push against him. Instead, my arms and body flailed against the door.

"Relax, baby," he whispered. "We have all night." His tongue danced with the music. "It started with a little kiss, like this." He hummed against the material as his long finger slid into my underwear and pulled the panties aside.

The moment his tongue connected with my sensitive skin, I thrashed my head against the door and moaned, anticipating the ride of my life. All too soon, he pulled away.

"Still mad that I crashed your party?" He mocked me.

I gazed down at the man I loved.

His face settled mere inches from my center.

I shook my head, unable to speak, my own tongue twice the normal size and adhered to the roof of my mouth.

He chuckled.

My nerves hummed at the huskiness of his laugh.

"Watch me eat you, baby," he growled.

Oh, God. I swallowed hard.

His tongue resumed its torture between my legs.

Heat blasted through my body and my head fell to the side as my eyes fluttered closed and rolled back in my head.

"Eyes, Hindley."

His deep voice demanded my attention.

I gazed down.

Rory's mouth worked me over until I came, hard, screaming out his name through muffled sobs.

My body trembled from the aftershocks as Rory lowered me

down the door. His hands slid under my thighs and lifted my legs, holding the weight of my body. When my hips aligned with his, he slowly slid inside. When had he stripped of his clothes, I wondered, but not for long.

His massive body pressed into mine, filling every inch of me. He adjusted his arms around my legs and angled my body until he hit my magical spot.

A heated tingle rolled up my spine and my eyelids fluttered closed but I forced myself to focus on him. A dark shadow of lust and need rolled over his blue orbs. His eyes burned liquid with desire.

The song on the stereo faded away and a new one rang out— Nora Jones, "The Nearness of You."

"A very eclectic mix, Mr. Gregor." I laughed.

He pushed deeper inside me.

I gasped and heaved a gulp of air.

"What can I say, Miss Hagen, I'm a complex man." His lips brushed against mine as he pushed my hips away, then pulled me toward him, swinging me against his body.

"Oh." His depth took my breath away and suddenly I understood the design of the swing. I moaned and lifted up silent thanks to Regan for her thoughtful gift.

Rory's tongue took full advantage of my open mouth as his lips pressed against mine.

I was lost to him. I always had been.

Rory circled his hips to the light rhythm of the song as he swung me back and forth, rocking me against him.

My hands itched to touch him, to rub my fingers across his chiseled back, but I couldn't. The loops around my arms held me firmly in place.

His mouth moved across my jaw and down my neck.

I succumbed to him, my head tipped to the side as his tongue danced across my skin, teasing me, working me into a fevered frenzy.

"Oh, Rory," I moaned, my hands numb from their death grip on the handles. My body tightened as my climax loomed.

Rory's hands slid up my stomach to my breasts which were still covered by my bra. His thumbs pressed down on my nipples, sending a rippling effect to my sweet spot.

He bucked against me. "Look at me, beautiful," he whispered.

My lids opened wide.

He stared at me, his eyes half-hooded and hungry. "You are so beautiful, Hindley."

I smiled at his declaration. Making me believe I was beautiful had become Rory's mission in life. In that moment, I did feel beautiful. I felt treasured despite my trussed-up position.

"Every day of my life I want to make you feel the way you do right now." His hips thrust against me, propelling him further inside me.

Oh, fuck.

"Every day of my life I want you to know how much I love you." His eyes trailed to my lips.

A tight band clenched my chest.

"Every day I want you to know that I can't exist without you. Wherever you are, I want you to feel me inside you." He tightened his hold on my hips as he swung me against him. "All of me. Near you. Holding you."

A tingle sparked at our connection and trailed up my body, paralyzing me.

"You are my dream come true, Hindley."

His breath skimmed across my neck.

"You're so beautiful, inside and out. And every day I will treasure you." He pushed me back and withdrew then swung me forward until he seated deep inside me.

With one last thrust, I exploded, clamping internally as my body surrendered to his movements.

"I love you, Hindley."

His words echoed in my heart.

Rory rocked against me, growing thicker as he pushed my thighs further apart. Suddenly, his body spasmed and shattered, spilling his love inside me. His head dropped and his lips met mine. With one blistering kiss, he seared us together for all time, his body washing away all my fears and doubts.

As Nora's song faded to a close, I realized Rory would forever be a part of me, body and soul. With him, I would always feel beautiful.

CHAPTER 11

HINDLEY

"IT LOOKS GORGEOUS, HINDLEY." My mother kneeled in front of Dana, straight pins clenched in her teeth.

I stood beside her, staring as she secured the last pin in the hem of Dana's dress. "It is, isn't it?" I said.

"It's amazing." Dana perused her body from head to toe. "I told you you could design something more beautiful than that piece of shit dress at the bridal shop."

My mother scowled at Dana.

"What?" Dana glared back. "It was a piece of shit, ask Hindley. The thing looked like a baby had crapped all over it." She winked at me. "But this," she waved her hand along the dress like she was on the Home Shopping Network, "this is sheer perfection, my dear." She flashed a mega-watt smile, displaying her famous Di Grazio dimples.

"You really like it?" Even though I'd been making clothes for ten years now, I was still apprehensive about showing my designs to others for fear of rejection.

"Like it?" Dana batted her hand at me and huffed. "It's *incredible*, Hindley."

"It really is, sweetheart." My mother stood and slipped her arm around my waist.

I surveyed Dana from head to toe. The lilac colored satin dress glimmered in the afternoon sun and clung to her like a second skin. Purple was Rory's favorite color and the lavender shade accented Dana's olive skin tone and blue eyes.

"I didn't think we'd *ever* find a dress to fit these massive things." Dana jiggled her breasts. "But somehow you found a way to actually design a dress that could tame my girls." She laughed. "You should do this shit for a living, Hindley."

"You really should," my mother agreed.

I'd struggled with which career path to take since I'd left my law firm. A profession in clothing design had entered my mind, but self-doubt always had me burying the idea.

"I really want to travel with Rory." I held out my hand to Dana to help her step off the coffee table.

"Well, I'm telling you, when everyone sees the pictures of your wedding dress, I don't think you're gonna have an option." Dana smoothed the satiny material across her stomach.

I smiled at her comment. We'd searched everywhere for "the one"—that perfect wedding dress brides talk about, the one that screams your name when you see the perfect design and glows like the gown was dropped from heaven. I had awoken one night after a failed shopping trip to Dallas, unable to sleep. In a fit of frustration and irritation, I'd designed a dress, *my* dress, "the one."

Rory had issued two edicts for the wedding. He wanted my hair down and my shoulders bare. I had teased and asked him if his instructions were for the dress or our honeymoon.

"Not the wedding night," he'd answered, "I want your hair tousled in a sexy mess and your body *completely* naked the entire time we're on our honeymoon."

I giggled out loud.

"What's so funny?" My mom picked up the extra pins and material littering the table.

She'd never been an expert seamstress, but she knew enough to help me when I needed her.

"Just thinking about Rory and my dress."

My mother's hands flew up in the air. "Oh my God, speaking of *your* dress," she waggled her finger in my face, "we need to get your shoes so we can finish the hem." Her words raced like a wound up toy car. "And then there's—"

"Calm down, Mom." I stroked her arm. "I've still got almost two weeks."

"Two weeks?" she squeaked out as if she'd seen a cockroach. "Oh my God, Hindley, what are you thinking? We've still got—"

"Take a chill pill, Caroline." Dana brushed up against my mother and rubbed her back. "That's what maids-of-honor were invented for. I promise we'll get everything done. Your daughter is as hopelessly OCD as you are. I have five to-do lists sitting in my car and two more on my phone."

I scowled at Dana. How could she leave her to-do lists in the car? And why did she still have five?

"Shopping for shoes is top priority, right Hindley." She winked at me outside of my mother's sight.

Honestly, I couldn't care less. I'd walk down the aisle barefoot and naked if I needed to. Marrying Rory Gregor was all that mattered.

"I'm coming in." Rory's deep voice boomed through the door. Speak of the devil. "If you're naked cover up. If you're naked *and* my fiancée, then everyone else get the hell out of here."

Dana chuckled.

My mother frowned.

"Rory," I scolded, even though a charged tingle ran up and down my body. The thought of being naked with him right now sounded amazing. Vivid memories of our sex swing flashed through my mind. We were back in Austin now at my duplex, but somehow Rory had snuck the portable sex swing through security in his carry-on bag.

My mother tossed a blanket over Dana.

"You're safe, One Nighter," Dana said. "It's only me."

Rory's fingers spread wide as he peeked through, his blue eyes dancing with mischief. "Dang it." He snapped his fingers in disappointment.

"What? You were expecting a little nip action?" Dana teased.

"Dana!" my mother and I barked in unison.

"Oh, please. You're the biggest horn dog on the planet now, thanks to lover boy over there." Dana nodded toward Rory then glared at me. "And you," she jutted her chin toward my mother, "you and your hubby eye-fuck each other to death every time you're in the same room together."

"Dana," my mother seethed through gritted teeth as her face flushed beet red.

My stomach rolled.

"Well, all right, Caroline, way to go." Rory butted up next to my mother and held up a hand, waiting for her returning high five.

My mother had the decency to look offended, but I could see the hint of amusement in her eyes.

Gag.

Dana swatted Rory's arm and winked.

Oh my God, she winked at my fiancé. My eyes narrowed as I chucked daggers at my best friend.

"What?" Dana shrugged with her hands in the air. "Don't get mad at me. It's you two fuck monkeys that are doing the horizontal mambo on a daily basis, not me."

"Get! Out!" I pointed toward the hallway. "Go get out of that dress now before I sew your lips together."

"Oh, girl, don't do that," she hollered from the doorway. "Men all around Texas will be crying their eyes out if they found out they can't get their dicks in my mouth."

Rory and Dana roared with laughter.

My mother rolled her eyes.

I shook my head but smirked. That was Dana. And I loved her.

I stared at Rory in the mirror as he brushed his teeth. My tiny bathroom barely contained both of us. I should remodel my side of the duplex. But Rory and I had talked about one day building a house here in Texas. We still weren't one hundred percent sure where we would live after the wedding. He traveled so much, a home-base seemed impossible.

"You look tired," I rubbed his back.

He glanced up at me in the mirror and our gazes locked. Even with the dark circles under his eyes, he was still the most beautiful man I'd ever seen.

"Is everything okay?" I asked.

He nodded once then rinsed and dried his mouth.

"You're not having second thoughts about marrying me, are you?" I raised a brow.

He stood silent, staring at me in the mirror.

Oh, shit, what if he was? I chewed my lip.

He turned then slid a hand around my waist and drew me to his bare chest. His thumb tugged my lip from between my teeth.

My body melted into his and my forehead fell to his shoulder.

"I'll miss you, that's all," he answered.

He was leaving for Colorado tomorrow for a competition. He'd asked me to go, but I had so much going on with the wedding, I just couldn't. Plus, something inside told me maybe a break from one another right before our big day would be good for us.

"I'll miss you too. Especially snuggling with you." I burrowed deeper into him.

He tightened his hold.

Nervous energy radiated from his body. I couldn't pry though. Being pestered wasn't Rory's style. When he was ready to talk, he would.

"Let's go to bed." I twined our fingers, and pulled him out of the bathroom.

"Great idea, Miss Hagen."

I glanced over my shoulder

He waggled his brow and his lips lifted in a half grin.

"To sleep."

He groaned.

"You're exhausted," I said. "And that's no way to start a competition."

He shook his head as he turned down the covers then nodded for me to crawl in.

I scooted over to the edge, making room for him to slide in next to me.

"Sleep now, baby, cuz when the honeymoon rolls around, that sex swing is getting a work out," he said.

I giggled and snuggled in under his arm.

"It's nothing to laugh at." He gently kissed my head. "I plan on thoroughly fucking you, Mrs. Soon-to-Be Gregor."

"I like the sound of that."

"What? Of me thoroughly fucking you?"

"No." I slapped his chest but laughed. I had to admit, him fucking me sounded like fun too. "Of being Mrs. Gregor soon."

He drew away from me and gazed down at my face. "I like it too. I never thought I would, but I do."

I scrunched my face. "What do you mean, you never thought you would?"

"I never thought I would get married. Never thought I wanted to."

I pushed up on my elbow to stare down at him. "But you want to, right? Now, I mean?"

He slid a hand into my hair and grabbed the back of my neck then fused his lips to mine in a scorching kiss.

A sharp tingle ignited at the base of my skull and zipped along my spine, shooting sparks of passion to my toes.

His lips pulled away from mine too soon. "You couldn't get away from me even if you tried, Drunk Girl." He studied my face and his lips curled into a smirk.

Images of the little boy we would create some day flashed in my mind. Our child's bright blue eyes would light up with mischief as his shaggy blond hair fell in his face anytime he got into trouble. Which, being Rory's son, would be a lot.

"I can't wait to start a family with you." I smiled.

His body stiffened and his hand fell from my face as he rolled over onto his back. He stared at the ceiling.

"Rory," I whispered.

He closed his lids.

"Talk to me, baby." I pushed up on an elbow and peered down.

"I don't know, Hindley."

"Don't know what?"

"If I can do that."

"Do *what*?"

He tilted his head toward me, but remained silent. His blue eyes flashed darker and his gaze held such pain and agony.

Be a family. Be a father. That's what he meant.

"But you said you'd love anything that was a part of me." I hadn't meant to sound so desperate, but being a mom had always been a life-long dream for me. "I mean, I don't want kids right away, but eventually…"

"I know." He reached to stroke my face.

I jerked away and sat straight up.

"Please don't pull away from me, Hindley."

"So what are you saying, Rory, now you *don't* want kids?"

He inhaled and closed his eyes.

I held my breath, unable to move, fearing I may pass out.

"I never said that. I never said I *don't* want kids." He heaved a sigh and his lids fluttered open. "But I never said I did either."

Shit. Shit. Shit.

My heart stopped. I loved Rory with my entire being. Loving him had never been a choice, falling in love with him had happened by accident. For better or for worse, he was part of me now. I couldn't exist without him. But would I have to sacrifice having children to be with him?

He sat up and crossed his legs, his hands resting on my knees. "Can we not talk about this right now. I'm so—"

"Not talk about this right now?" I laughed. "Not talk about it?" I scooted off the bed and stood. "When do you think we *should* talk about this, Rory? On our first anniversary? Our fifth, hell maybe even our tenth after a decade of a childless marriage?"

His eyes went wide and he sat up straight.

"We damn sure will talk about this. Now!" I folded my hands over my chest and pursed my lips. Everything in me told me to fight.

Rory slumped back and his head fell against the headboard. He stared at his hand as his thumb rubbed circles on his palm. It was a nervous tic he'd developed as a child.

"Why, Rory?" I whispered.

"You know why, Hindley." His hushed voice faded into nothingness as he dropped his chin to his chest.

I crawled onto the mattress and kneeled in front of him. I placed my finger under his chin and lifted his head, not surprised to find his eyes closed.

"I know it's because of your family, Rory." I spoke softly as if coaxing an injured animal. "You're not like them though. You're not like your mother and stepfather."

His eyes opened and shimmered with unshed tears. "How can you be so sure? How do you know I won't be a horrible father once we have babies?"

"Oh, Rory." I lurched forward and wrapped my arms around his massive shoulders, squeezing him tight in reassurance. "I know because your heart and my heart beat as one."

His body shuddered under my hold.

"I know you'll be an amazing father because you saved me, Rory Gregor. When no one else could, you came into my life and saved me."

I pushed him back, my need to see his face overwhelming me. I wiped away the tears staining his cheeks. "When I was unconscious in my hospital bed after my accident…" I peered down at the scar on my arm. The puckered skin was a daily reminder of how far I'd gone to escape the ghosts of my past. Rory had brought me back. "I was dreaming, dreaming of sinking into a dark underworld where my most terrifying nightmares haunted me."

I slid my hands down his muscular arms and wrapped my fingers around his wrists. I brought his hands to my chest and pressed his palms against me as I stared into his eyes.

"It was *you*, Rory Gregor." I squeezed his hands. "It was *you* whose words brought me back from the nightmares pulling me under. It was *you* who saved me. *Your* words, *your* voice, they brought me comfort and peace. You're the reason I came back. I knew I would always be safe with you."

I caressed his cheek. "You have protected me. That's how I met you, on our very first night together, remember? You've protected everyone you've ever loved your whole life." My fingers slipped down his throat and rested on his broad chest.

His heart raced.

"And when *we* decide to have children," I said, "I know beyond the shadow of a doubt *you* will protect them with your life. Just like you've guarded everyone you've ever loved."

His eyes darted between mine. Fear marred his beautiful face.

I pressed his hand against my chest as I palmed my other hand against his. "Our hearts beat as one, Rory. The night we first met, when we first kissed, I felt our connection down to the tips of my toes. Since then, our lives and our hearts have been intertwined. Making babies with you is just the natural next step."

A small smile tugged his lips.

"There isn't a man alive who I'd choose to be the father of my children except you. There's not a man more qualified than you." I leaned in and placed a gentle kiss against his lips.

"But—"

I pressed my finger against his mouth. "You have issues, Rory. I have issues. We all do." I tilted my head and shrugged. "But you're better than your past." I sat and crossed my legs. "Maybe this trip to Colorado would be a good time for you to get some closure."

"How?" His brow creased and he cocked his head.

"I don't know. Maybe go see your mom, talk to her."

He shook his head.

"Rory, I don't know the specific answer to relieve your anxiety about being a good father, but I do know you can't wait around and let your past dictate your future. To make a better life for the two of us, you'll eventually have to talk about it all, to someone."

He held his breath and sat still.

My stomach clenched with worry.

"Would you come with me?" he asked.

"To Colorado?"

"No," he answered. "Go with me to talk to someone I mean. Maybe *your* therapist."

I'd never heard Rory ask for help with anything—even learning to read. Teaching him had been my idea.

I crawled over his legs and curled up in his lap. Wrapping my hand around his neck, I slid my fingers into his hair. "Haven't you figured it out by now?" I smiled up at him.

"Figured out what?"

"I'd do *anything* for you, Skater Boy."

His eyes shined and a breathtaking smile spread across his face.

"I'd do anything for you, Drunk Girl."

"I know. And one day, when we're both ready, you'll do anything for our children too."

He dipped his head and brushed his lips over mine. "Okay," he murmured against my skin.

An invisible band snapped tight against my chest.

"Just…" He paused.

I leaned back but clung to his neck.

"Just, not right away, okay?"

"Okay." I kissed his lips. "But we can practice. Right?" My mouth skimmed across his neck and over to his ear then I clamped down on his lobe.

He flipped us over.

"Oh," I yipped.

His large body loomed over me. His warm smile took my breath away. I couldn't believe such a beautiful man like Rory Gregor was all mine, and would be for the rest of my life.

"It's like I always say about skateboarding." His lips curled into a devilish grin.

"What?" I asked.

"Practice makes perfect."

And with that, I was lost in Rory Gregor once more.

CHAPTER 12

RORY

THE COLD COLORADO air slapped my face like a scorned lover as I stepped through the sliding glass doors of the airport and out into the bone-chilling wind. I hadn't been away from Denver *that* long, but already I'd forgotten how brutal some late winter days could be.

I maneuvered my way around the wandering passengers and quickened my stride as I raced to the rental car lot.

"Sign here," the rental car agent said, pointing to the screen of his hand-held device.

"What am I signing?" As a lawyer, Hindley had taught me never to sign anything unless I had full disclosure.

"It's your standard rental car agreement, sir." He assured me with a nod. "Don't worry, Mr. Gregor, I would never try to screw you over. You're a legend here in Denver. Folks wouldn't take too kindly to me taking advantage of you. You're the greatest X Games athlete of all time."

I smiled at his accolades. I wasn't sure I was the *greatest*, but I was learning to take a compliment. "Thanks…" I searched his shirt for a nametag.

He pointed to the badge on his chest. "Name's Randy."

"Thanks, Randy."

He scrolled through the tiny computer screen. This rental car agreement was so different than any other I'd ever signed before—mainly because I could actually read this contract. Thanks to the love of my life. *Hindley.* I was in Colorado for her.

"And this here clause says that—"

"It's okay, Randy, I'm sure the document is a standard agreement."

"Yes, sir, it is."

I grabbed the stylus and signed my name in the box on the illuminated screen.

"Could I bother you for one more autograph, Mr. Gregor?"

"On one condition," I said.

His brow furrowed. Worry swept across his face as if I'd threatened to take away his Oreos.

"Please," I smiled, "call me Rory. I don't even know who Mr. Gregor is."

Randy's head tilted.

Obviously, he was intrigued by my statement. My admission was as foreign to him as the words were to me. But I was here in Denver to get answers.

Randy raced inside the small office.

Before I could blink, he'd returned with a magazine. *Vanity Fair.* I'd hated the photo shoot.

After Hindley's story broke last year, the world fell in love with my drunk girl. By default, they fell in love with me too. Magazines and film producers had flocked to us for our story. Even my agent had to get an agent.

In the end, we'd decided to do photo shoots, three of them, some of the biggest magazines on the market. They offered us a lot of money to put our faces on their covers. Why people wanted to read our story still boggled my mind. But the money was insane, and Hindley convinced me the payout would go a long way in funding Shelly's learning center, so I'd agreed.

I grabbed the magazine from Randy, about to ask for a pen, when he produced one.

"You've done this before?" I chuckled.

"Never," he said.

My eyes caught his. A hollowness cast a shadow on his already dark brown eyes. They reminded me of Hindley's, more than just in color. I waited, wondering if he would disclose his story, the reason why he'd really asked for my signature.

"It's for my daughter, Mr.—" He glanced to the magazine cover.

I followed his gaze and noted Hindley posed in the photo. She straddled my lap as I sat on a skateboard. My forehead was on her chest, my eyes closed. Her cheek rested on the top of my head, her face turned toward the camera. She looked vulnerable but strong as she gripped my arms and squeezed her legs around my waist. The camera had captured her spirit perfectly. She was my protector.

"It's for my daughter, Rory." Again he paused.

I glanced up and saw the familiar pain etched across his face.

"She's a cutter," he whispered.

In that moment, I fell in love with Hindley Hagen all over again. Her strength, her willingness to be vulnerable and share her story of sacrifice with the world, inspired me every day. She'd made a difference. I hoped to be as brave in my own life.

"And my daughter thinks you're 'to die for', as she says." Randy used air quotes and laughed, rolling his eyes.

The mood lightened with his mock disgust. "What's her name?"

"Miranda."

"Miranda," I repeated. "It's a beautiful name."

"She's a beautiful girl."

Randy's eyes beamed with familial love any father would have for his daughter—*should* have for his daughter.

Hindley was right. If I ever wanted to experience unconditional love, I had to settle my shit with Marion Gregor once and for all.

I took the pen from Randy with a new determination. Signing

my name for fans was so different now that I could personalize my words. I didn't hesitate for a minute on my inscription to Miranda.

Be brave. Be strong. Be free.
    Love, Rory and Hindley Gregor

No, we weren't married yet, and officially Hindley's name hadn't changed. But I wanted Miranda to keep our picture forever, the same way I would keep Hindley. Before long she would be mine and I wanted those words etched on the cover for everyone to see.

I handed the pen and magazine to Randy.

He scanned my words. "Thanks, Rory," he choked out. "My daughter really is so brave."

I dug in my pocket and dragged out a packet of gum. I pulled a piece out and tore off the wrapper. "May I?" I reached for the pen.

Randy handed the marker to me.

"This is my agent's phone number." I jotted down Luis's contact information. "I'll be in California next month for a competition. Hindley and I would love to meet Miranda. If you want, we'll fly you out to the competition, put you up in our hotel and hang out a bit while you're there."

Randy's mouth hung lax and his eyes popped wide. He looked like he'd seen an alien.

Shit, had I offended him?

"Hello?" I held the pen and the gum wrapper toward him.

His hands fumbled with both as he clutched them against his chest.

"I…I…don't know what to say, Mr.…" He smiled. "Rory."

"Say yes." I smiled.

"My wife and I would be honored. Miranda will be so excited. Yes. Yes, we'd love to come."

"Great, then it's done. Just call Luis. He'll schedule everything. I know Hindley will be excited to meet Miranda."

Randy stared at me as if I had three heads. "She's a lucky woman."

"Who?" I fumbled with my bag.

"Hindley, your fiancée. She's lucky to have you."

"I think most people would argue it's the other way around." I chuckled. The urge to phone Hindley flooded me. I needed to tell her she was right—as usual. I patted my front and back pockets, searching for my phone. "Shit!"

"What's wrong?" Randy ripped a long strip of paper from the hand-held machine.

"I can't find my phone."

"Do you want to use mine?"

I laughed. "I don't even know her number."

"Whose number?"

"My fiancée's. Isn't that horrible. Her number is programmed into my phone." Hindley and I had both been forced to get new cell phone numbers a few months ago when a crazed fan stalked us day and night.

"You don't have her phone number memorized?" Randy asked.

"I did, but her old number was leaked to the press and we had to get a new one."

"Want me to call your agent and get the number from him?" He held out a strip of paper. "This is the rental contract."

I grabbed the document and stuffed the paper in my pocket. "No, no. I'll call him when I get to where I'm going." Dread filled me like cement in a cinder block mold thinking about where I was headed. "But thanks."

"Here's the fob. The car's in space fourteen. Black Camaro." Randy pointed down the line of cars next to the shed.

"Camaro?" I chuckled, taking the fob and map he offered. "Are you trying to get me arrested?" I loved fast cars. And I loved driving cars…fast.

"This one is souped *down*." He grinned. "But the car's still got some punch. Be safe."

I nodded. "Thanks, Randy."

"No, thank you, Mr.—Thank you, Rory."

"I'll see you next month?" I looked over my shoulder, awaiting his response as I inched closer to spot fourteen.

"Absolutely!"

His smile grew.

I chuckled to myself.

Randy the Rental Car Guy was the proud father of a daughter who had obviously been through hell and back. He was the type of father a kid needed. The kind of father I wanted to *be* one day.

As I climbed into the Camaro and slung my bag in the back seat, I studied the map, surprised I could finally read one. Amid the mass of streets and avenues on the paper, I located the region I wanted with ease—Five Points. The map had the area labeled incorrectly. The neighborhood should have been called "My Childhood Hell."

CHAPTER 13

RORY

I SQUIRMED in the leather seat of the idling Camaro and thumped the steering wheel with my finger. The heater blasted warm air as I stared out of the driver's side window.

The house looked the same, but different. The rotted wood around the front door and chipped paint on the siding spoke of the inhabitants' lack of self-respect. The porch stairs still sagged and tilted to the right. The tattered red and white striped awnings covering the front windows whipped in the wind. If my past was any indicator, I feared the occupants would look much the same as the dilapidated shack of a house staring back at me.

I surveyed the cracked driveway and noticed only one car. My recon, aka Luis Marquez, had disclosed my num-nuts stepfather was still in the county jail for a battery charge after a bar fight—typical asshole behavior. Vic's one felony ensured his safety—from me. I didn't want trouble, but I wouldn't sit back any more and take his shit either. I only wanted one thing. Marion Gregor. My mother.

I clicked off the engine and nudged the car door open with my booted heel. Scanning the street, I crossed the road but stood paralyzed at the curb, unable to step onto the uneven sidewalk leading to the front door of my childhood home. Well "home" was using the term loosely. The structure had held me captive like a jail cell for many years, until the state decided to place me in a real reformatory.

I trudged toward the front door, side stepping the stairs for fear of my own safety. I hefted myself onto the porch from the ground with ease and recalled the hundreds of times I'd jumped over those stairs on my board, trying to perfect my skateboarding moves. For the first time since I'd landed in Denver, the dread that had hollowed the pit of my stomach finally lifted.

I tugged on the screen door, surprised to find the structure held fast. I laughed as I surveyed the torn mesh covering—as if locking such a simple wooden door would stop anyone in the ghetto neighborhood from breaking in. Most of the homes in the area bore bars across every window.

I drew in a deep breath, my throat burning from the sub-freezing temperature. I knew the reception I would receive from my mother would be colder than the frigid Colorado air whipping around me. I fisted my hand tight and my stomach cramped. I drew in a deep breath, but no matter how hard I tried, I knew I'd never be able to prepare myself to see the woman who'd banished me to hell when I was only a teenager.

With a shaky hand, I banged on the rickety door. The frame rattled, and I wondered if I had broken the thing off its hinges.

A dog inside barked, his high-pitched yapping splitting my already pounding head in two. Why the fuck had she gotten a dog when she didn't even give two shits about her own kids?

"Coming!"

The rasp in my mother's response confirmed her addiction to Marlboro Reds.

"Shut up, you little shit!"

The dog yelped in pain.

I envisioned Marion Gregor kicking the innocent thing.

Multiple locks clicked and the knob twisted, along with my

intestines. The door creaked open and a gnarled face stared back at me. I almost didn't recognize her.

Her once vibrant blonde hair was shorter and an ashen mess dulled with gray streaks at the roots. Lines creased the corners of her eyes and the edges of her mouth. She'd always been a head shorter than me, petite like Shelly, but age and lifestyle had robbed her of another inch.

She puckered her lips and stared.

My mother was weathered, worn and weak. A pang of guilt hit my chest, but only lasted a second as her words ripped through me like the shrapnel from a tainted bullet.

"Oh, *now* you grace me with your presence. Come to gloat, did ya?"

I stood still, more from annoyance than shock. Why had I expected my visit to be anything different? A normal mother would be proud of her son's accomplishments, welcome him with open arms, offer him a home cooked fucking meal for God's sake. Not Marion Gregor. She served guilt in four-courses at her dining room table.

"What? Ain't ya got a smartass comeback for your momma?" she asked, raising one thin brow.

I shook my head and swallowed. The bile in my throat threatened to choke me. I gritted my teeth. "May I come in?"

My mother stared me up and down.

I glanced down at the small dog who hunkered low to the ground as he slinked forward.

He was so small and seemingly insignificant. I would have expected my stepfather to own a menacing pit bull or some equally intimidating animal, not something barely bigger than a rat.

The pitiful animal lifted his head and yapped several times.

Without even looking down, Marion kicked at the tiny thing, sending him sliding across the floor.

The defenseless creature scampered under the coffee table, tail tucked between his legs, and trembled.

Not even animals were immune to the *motherly* affections of Marion Gregor.

My mother pushed open the tattered screen door and stepped aside to let me in.

Inside, the place reeked of stale smoke and cheap wine. The interior hadn't changed much, but the house felt smaller. A hot wave of apprehension smothered me. I'd never been claustrophobic, but inside my childhood home, the walls caved in on me.

My mother darted around me to the sofa, picking up the newspaper and clothes strewn across the cushions. "Sit." She motioned toward the end she'd just cleared.

I stared at the cracked and worn coffee table. A lit cigarette balanced against a plastic green ashtray, the smoke filtering up in one long stream, floating away into oblivion.

"Uh, do you want something to drink?" she asked. Her voice wavered, awkward and unsure.

I glanced at my mother.

She sat on the other end of the couch, her hands knotted together as her eyes scanned the room.

She was nervous, as if she feared her husband was close by and would beat the fuck out of her for allowing me inside their festering shit hole of a house.

I knew the feeling well. My stomach knotted with unwarranted anxiety. My stepfather was in jail, I reminded myself.

"I'm sure my house is nothing compared to yours." Her lip snarled as she hissed her venomous comment.

I stood in silence, unwilling to engage her. A first for me.

She waved her hand in the air. "Our house does me and Vic just fine. You can sit on my furniture, *Rory*."

My stomach rolled with the sarcasm in her voice. She couldn't even say my fucking name without getting spiteful.

I lowered myself onto the dingy cushion, surprised when the small dog jumped on the sofa and stared at me, wiggling his butt.

"Get off the goddamn couch, Candy."

Candy? Was he a *she*?

My mother swung at the dog, but *Candy* skirted her hand as if used to the abuse, and jumped into my lap.

We'd never had animals growing up so I wasn't sure how to respond to the dog. *Candy* circled twice then curled into a tight ball in my lap. Her brown eyes begged me for something familiar. Something I could offer her. Protection.

My mother moved to grab the dog, but I held up my hand. "She's fine. She can stay." I looked down at the dog.

Her small frame, huge ears and beady eyes marked her as a Chihuahua. Her fur was sand-colored and solid except for a lone diamond-shaped white spot on her forehead. She tucked her ears and trembled against me.

"All small dogs shake like that," my mother said.

I reached down and stroked Candy's head, not surprised when she flinched. After several loving caresses, her trembling subsided. She drew in a heavy breath and nestled in further to my touch.

"Yeah, I'm sure any living creature shakes when you beat the shit out of them." I glared at my mother.

She inhaled a long drag of her cigarette. "You looking to hash up old times are you?" She exhaled the smoke. The hazy mist streamed through her wrinkled lips and polluted the already toxic environment.

"Sort of," I said. Candy was nearly asleep in my lap as I petted her belly.

"Well, I don't care what you say," she puffed out her chest and lifted her chin, "you ain't gonna make me feel one damn bit guilty."

"Guilty for what?"

She sat silent. We both knew for what. I just wanted to hear her say it. Hear her say she was sorry for all the shit she'd allowed her husband to do to me and my sister.

"Why didn't you ever take his name?" I asked as I stared down at the dog.

"Whose name?"

My eyes cut to hers. She was sincere in her ignorance.

"Victor's last name." God, just saying his name out loud churned my stomach and had my free hand balled in a tight fist. "McKinney. You always kept my last name, Gregor. Why?"

Her head fell back against the couch cushion as she pondered the question.

The ticking of the clock hanging on the opposite wall thundered through the awkward silence.

She released a heavy sigh. "What do you want, Rory?"

"I just want to know his name," I said.

Her head snapped up and her eyes went wide as she stared at me. "Whose name?"

"My father. I just want to know his name."

Her face puckered as if she'd bitten into a pickle. "Why?" she asked.

I sunk into the couch and exhaled a breath I didn't even know I'd been holding. "I want to talk to him, meet him, let him know I exist. You owe me that."

"I don't owe you a goddamn thing you selfish little prick!" She jumped to her feet. "You run off and make a big life for yourself, become some star athlete, hoity-toity little rich boy who thinks his shit don't stink. And you never gave your momma nothin'!"

I sat still as Candy trembled in my lap. She may be afraid of my mother, but I wasn't.

Marion jutted her chest and squared her shoulders, glaring down her nose. "And now you're marrying America's sweetheart. You didn't even send me an invitation to your wedding. You think you're too good for me now, Mr. Hot Shot Athlete? *You're* the reason Victor's in jail. You're not worth shit."

I squared my shoulders and sat up, my back ramrod straight. "First of all, I don't owe you shit. Let's get one thing straight right now, *Mom*." I laughed at the irony. "Why would I help the woman who allowed her husband to beat the fuck out of me every day then call the cops and let them arrest me when I decided to stand up and fight back?"

She opened her mouth to speak.

"No," I held up my hand, "don't say a fucking word. Not only did he beat the shit out of me *and* you, he molested your own daughter. What kind of mother lets that happen?"

"I did the best I—"

"The best you could?" I shook my head and roared. "God, to say your best isn't good enough is a complete understatement."

My mother had the decency to avoid my gaze, staring off through the dingy window she stood by.

I gazed down at Candy curled up in my lap. She trembled and her ears pressed back against her head. I hadn't meant to scare her. I stroked her back and scratched the top of her head. Hindley had taught me how to care, how to love, unconditionally. I was here because of her. To get closure. Fighting with my mom wouldn't help.

"Why?" I stared down at the dog. "Why did you stay with him?"

After a long silence, I gazed up at my mother.

She'd lit another cigarette. The glowing stick dangled between her fingers. Her hand trembled and she bit on her thumb.

"Mom?" I uttered the word despite the sour taste in my mouth.

Her shoulders slumped and she picked her fingernails. Her eyes cut to mine as smoke from the burning cigarette curled around her head.

"Why?" I asked.

She straightened and smashed the barely smoked cigarette into the plastic ashtray. Her lips pursed and her eyes narrowed as she glared at me. "So now you're trying to *blame* me for all your fuck ups?" she hissed. "Like outing me and Victor in your stupid interview with Paloma Monroe wasn't enough."

I remembered my interview with Paloma. She'd asked specific questions about my past, but I'd remained vague, only hinting to the abuse I'd endured under my mother's roof. I wasn't surprised to learn Paloma's investigative team researched and reported on the allegations of abuse and neglect at the hands of Victor and my mother.

"That bitch is the reason Vic is in jail. And you." She pointed her finger at me.

"What are you talking about?"

"Those nosey assholes came snooping around here. I opened the door, thinking Paloma wanted to get my side. They took one look at me and called the cops."

I stood, tucking Candy to my chest. "Why did they call the cops?"

She bowed her head and kicked at the coffee table. She didn't need to explain why. Her face had probably been black and blue.

"Look, I don't really give two shits where Vic is or what happens to him. If anything bad comes his way, it's a direct result of his own fucked up actions. I came to get answers for myself, to reconcile my past." I stared my mother up and down with a bone-chilling glare.

Her shabby clothes couldn't hide the bones poking through the thin material of her dress. She was battle-torn and weary, all of her own doing. She was pathetic and weak, and there wasn't an inch of empathy inside me for the broken woman standing before me.

"I don't know why I thought I'd get any answers from you. I'm done." I shook my head in frustration. This was a mistake from the start. Hindley said I needed closure. She didn't understand that for some childhood wounds, complete healing wasn't possible.

Victor McKinney was a sick, demented son of a bitch and my mom was a weak and pathetic human being. They were a perfect match. The realization was the only closure I would get.

I gazed down at Candy. She trembled in my hands. I tucked her into the crook of my arm and stalked toward the door.

"Royce Hamilton."

I barely heard my mother's words over the thrumming beat of my heart.

"What?" I turned toward her voice.

"Royce Hamilton. His name is Royce Hamilton," she repeated.

"My father?" I choked on the words, staring at my mother in stunned silence. I had a name.

She clasped her hands and twined her fingers. She stared down at the gnarled mass, unable to meet my gaze.

"Is Royce Hamilton my father?"

Her head lifted and her eyes cut to mine. They were sky blue like mine, and for the first time in my life, a glimmer of true regret shimmered inside Marion Gregor's gaze. Had she loved him?

"Yes. He's your father."

"Does he live here, in Denver?"

She shrugged her shoulders. "I don't know. He used to."

"And he walked away from us, from Shelly and me?"

"He's not Shelly's father."

Her answer was flippant, as if the words wouldn't shatter the foundation of my world.

I stumbled back, staring down at the tattered and stained shag carpet. Shelly and I didn't have the same father? My gut wrenched as if I'd been hit with a sledgehammer. The room closed in on me, its stifling heat unrelenting. I had to escape this God-forsaken toilet.

"It was a one night stand," she whispered.

I rushed toward the door and gripped the knob, shaking my head.

"He didn't mean anything to me," she continued. "And neither do you."

Her words held no power over me any more. I'd heard worse from her in my life. Like all kids who grow up in a dysfunctional home, I'd hoped one day my mother would embrace me, tell me she loved me and she was sorry for all the wrongs she'd done. That would never happen. Just because Marion Gregor lacked the ability to love me didn't mean I suffered from the same fate. I had other people in my life to fill the void of my mother's love, and I had plenty of my own love to dole out.

I opened the door and stepped outside.

"Where are you going with Candy?" she yelled at me.

Typical Marion Gregor—more worried about a dog than me. Her concern wasn't for the animal. She'd been abusive to the defenseless pup since I'd knocked on the door. No, she was pissed because I was taking something away from her, something she considered her own. Something she could abuse.

"The dog's coming with me."

Candy shivered in my arms, more from the shrill of my mother's voice than the freezing wind battering us.

I lifted her small body, stuck her inside my leather jacket and zipped up the coat until only her head was poking out. The prominent white diamond on her forehead reminded me of the diamond on Hindley's finger. *My fiancée.*

I glanced over my shoulder, not surprised to see the scowl on Marion's face. "I'm taking the dog with me where she'll be safe," I said. "Something I should have done with my sister a long time ago."

Without another word or glance back, I closed the door of my childhood home, on my past, on my dreams of having a real mother. I was more determined than ever to give *my* children a better life, a better home, a better mother and father than I'd had.

The dog pulled her head inside and nestled deeper inside my jacket. I couldn't save Shelly, but at least I could save Candy.

CHAPTER 14

RORY

"HEY, LUIS." I spoke into the pay phone as my car idled in front of the convenience store.

"Rory! Where the fuck have you been? Hindley's been worried sick about you."

"I'm in Denver. Sorry, I forgot my phone at home, I think. Or I lost the damn thing at the airport, I'm not sure." No one having direct contact with me for this trip was probably best anyway. I had shit I needed to settle on my own, in my own way. I loved Hindley with all my heart, but not even she could fix my past mistakes. I had to settle things on my own.

I gazed out of the phone booth and glanced at the rental car.

Candy leaned on the steering wheel, her front paws placed as if she were about to drive away.

I laughed.

"What's so funny?"

Luis's question brought me back. "I had some things here in Denver I needed to settle. Hindley was right. I have to bury the ghosts of my past."

"Have you?"

"Almost," I said. "But I need some help."

"What?"

"Can you do a search for me on a Royce Hamilton?"

"Who's Royce Hamilton?"

"My dad."

"Oh, shit," Luis exclaimed.

"Yeah, my mom finally told me."

"You saw your mom?"

"Yep," I nodded my head as if he could see me.

"Holy hell, man, how did that go?"

"Like I expected." I paused. "But at least she gave me one thing." I watched Candy bounce around the front seats. "Well two." I chuckled.

"Okay, let me get on this. I'm sure I can find him. No problem."

"Great. I'll call you back in an hour. I have one more stop to make."

"Wait!" Luis's voice cracked with desperation, something I never heard from him. "It's Hindley."

"Oh, God, what's wrong with her?" My heart squeezed tight and my vision blurred.

"She's worried. She thinks you're upset with her for forcing you to confront your past. What the hell happened?"

"It's a long story."

"Well, since you haven't been answering your phone, she's worked herself up into thinking you don't want to get married any more, like you've pulled a runaway groom or something."

Oh, shit. "Look, just tell her…just tell her I'm all right, I've got closure. Tell her if she'll have me, I'll always be hers."

"Fuck, dude, you must have really screwed up," he laughed.

"You know me."

"Rory Gregor, King of the Fuck-Ups." He chuckled.

"Like I said, you know me so well. Look, I'll call you back in an hour and see what you've got."

"Is this guy from Denver? I gotta know where to start."

"My mom said he's from here. It was a one-night-stand. That's all I know. That's all I've got. I'm sorry, man."

"No problem, we'll find him."

"Tell Hindley I love her and I'll be home when I can."

Candy's paws perched on the steering wheel again and she barked at me as if to say, "Come on, dipshit, I want to go."

"And tell Hindley I have a surprise for her." I smiled, staring at the small dog.

"You better have a huge piece of jewelry to make up for this screw up."

"Hindley's not into that stuff. Tell her I'm making peace with my demons."

"Okay, man. Well, be safe. I'll work on this Royce Hamilton on my end. Talk to you soon."

"Thanks, Luis, for everything."

"No sweat, mi amigo."

I hung up the phone and walked back to my car.

Candy scratched at the window, her ears perked high with anticipation as if she were welcoming me back from a long journey. In reality I think she'd always been waiting on me.

I swung open the door. She tumbled forward and I caught her in my hands before she fell to the pavement. She'd forgone all sense of safety to be near me. I understood instant devotion like Candy's. I'd fallen for Hindley just as hard.

I had one more person to make peace with before I could be Hindley's, completely.

I squatted down in front of the small metal stake marking my sister's grave.

"Hey, baby girl." I wiped the frost clinging to the small sign, pissed the fuck off that the piece of shit marker was the only indicator Shelly had once inhabited this earth. She deserved better.

I gazed over the dilapidated cemetery that was covered with a light dusting of snow. "I'm sorry this place isn't nicer." I gazed down at her grave. "Actually, I'm sorry about a lot of things, Shelly. I should have stayed, I should have beat the shit out of Victor McKinney and taken you away."

My eyes burned with tears and my hands trembled, but not from the cold. I ran my finger over her birthdate and death date. She'd died just a few days shy of her nineteenth birthday. She'd be almost twenty-three if she were still alive.

I dropped my head into my hands and sobbed, rocking back and forth. The pressing guilt was a boulder on my chest and I couldn't catch my breath. "I'm sorry," I choked out.

"She didn't blame you." A deep voice echoed behind me.

I jumped to my feet and wiped my eyes.

A tall man with light blond hair stood stark still, his leather bomber jacket zipped tight as bare hands gripped a bouquet of daisies.

"I'm sorry," he said, stepping closer. His steel gray eyes surveyed my sister's grave. "I didn't mean to startle you or interrupt your time with your sister."

How the fuck did he know Shelly was my sister?

"Oh, sorry." He extended his hand. "I'm Owen Tucker. I was friends with your sister."

I stared at his outstretched hand.

He was too polite to be a grave robber. And his heavy coat and matching scarf indicated he wasn't a vagrant. My brows furrowed. Who was this guy? Unable to answer my own question, I took his hand in mine and accepted his welcome.

He gave me a firm grip. His glowing smile assured me he wasn't trying to intimidate me.

"Nice to meet you, Owen. I'm Rory Gregor, Shelly's brother."

"I know who you are." He smiled wider and released my hand, stepping toward the marker. His dark leather boots crunched the frozen grass.

"How do you know me?"

"Are you kidding?" He chuckled. "You're all Shelly talked about. She was so proud of you."

My gaze fell from Owen to Shelly's grave. "Really?"

"Oh, yeah," he said.

"She didn't hate me?"

"Hate you?" He mocked and shook his head. "God no. She *adored* you. You were her idol. Her hero."

"Seriously?" I couldn't believe his words. "I thought she would hate me for leaving. Everyone told her..." My throat constricted. I couldn't voice the lies my mother had told Shelly. How they'd convinced my sister I'd molested her and not Vic.

"Shelly was a survivor. She knew the truth," Owen said.

His gaze pinned me. He knew. Shelly had confessed everything about our dysfunctional home to him. I couldn't fault her. She needed a confidant, especially since I'd left her.

"How long are you in town?" Owen asked the question as if we'd been friends forever.

"I'm sorry, how did you know my sister?"

Owen bent down and placed the daisies on Shelly's grave. "They were her favorite flowers you know." He gave me a quick glance over his shoulder then turned his attention back to Shelly's grave.

"Yes, I do know." Shelly's room had been decorated in yellow with daisies painted and pasted everywhere. "How do *you* know that?" The protective brother bear was rearing his head.

"I met Shelly in fifth grade." He situated the flowers just so, fanning them out until they were positioned to his liking. "She loved order, thrived on precision." He chuckled as he stood and admired his handy work. "Just like you." He turned toward me.

I was stunned, floored he knew me so well.

"It's typical for kids who grow up in abusive homes." He explained as if he were a fucking therapist or something.

"When kids grow up with chaos, they become controlling people," he went on. "The problem is, life can't be controlled. Shelly clung to her perfection too tight and eventually lost control."

"What the hell does that mean?" I jerked back, a little offended, but mostly intrigued by this stranger's accurate depiction of my own personality.

"What, the controlled part?"

"Yeah."

"You know what it means." He tilted his head. "You lost control too. Years of booze and drugs, remember?"

The reminder cut deep, opening wounds I didn't want examined.

"Who the fuck *are* you? And why the hell are you analyzing our lives?"

"I'm sorry, I didn't mean to intrude."

"And yet, you are." I steeled myself and planted both feet firmly on the icy ground, crossing my arms across my chest.

"It's okay, man." He held up his hands. "I just meant that what you and Shelly went through in your dysfunctional home is reason enough to end up the way you did. You were able to right your wrongs, move past the pain. Shelly couldn't. Existing in this screwed up world became too much for her and she finally just," he paused, "let go."

"It's my fault," I said.

"How?"

"I left her. I left her in a shithole house with a demented mother-fucker, knowing what he'd done."

"You didn't leave her, Rory. She let you go."

"What?" I looked at him in surprise. "What are you talking about?"

"Shelly *wanted* you to succeed. She knew you couldn't if you took her along."

"But—"

"No buts, Rory. That's the way she wanted it."

"But she died. She fuckin' overdosed, man. How could she have wanted *that*? I'm the reason she died." I pounded on my chest then spun on my heels to avoid Owen's scrutiny.

"Rory," he laid his hand on my shoulder and squeezed, "none of us wanted Shelly to die. Not even Shelly. Her death wasn't your fault. Shelly made her own choices."

"What the fuck do you mean?" I whipped around and studied him from head to toe, about to throat punch him. He didn't know me and Shelly at all. And worse than that, he was intruding on my time with my sister.

"You don't think *I* don't feel guilty?" he said. "I work hard every day to fight those demons. I tried to save Shelly. We were best friends until our sophomore year. But then…" His hand fell.

"But what?" I moved closer, wanting to know more about my sister from a man who'd obviously befriended her after I left. Knowing I hadn't been there for Shelly in the end still haunted me.

"Then Shelly hooked up with the wrong crowd. I mean, she'd already been drinking. I tried to tell her, but she wanted to be liked, to be popular, hang with the cool kids. Turns out the 'cool' kids,'" he used air quotes, "were into some serious drugs and partying."

Fuck.

"The drugs, the partying, they were her escape from her home life. The momentary high numbed the pain. I'd like to think I'd been her high for all those years until the thrill of drugs influenced her." He gazed down at her grave. "But at some point, my friend-ship wasn't enough."

The pain in his voice was palpable, the sorrow in his eyes heart-breaking. I understood. We'd both lost someone we loved and cared for. And we were both overwhelmed by our profound guilt and grief.

"Once the drugs got into her system, Shelly was hooked," he continued. "I don't really think she could have stopped even if she had wanted to."

"What happened? I wanted to come back but my mother convinced Shelly it was me who—" Even acknowledging that Shelly ever thought I'd molested her gutted me. I swallowed the bile rising in my throat. My mother and Vic had poisoned my sister against me.

"It's okay, Rory. Shelly never thought you hurt her. She stayed away so *you* would stay away."

"What the fuck are you talking about?"

"Shelly was your biggest fan." He smiled at some unseen memory. "She wanted you to succeed no matter what. She understood the torment you'd endured at the hands of your stepfather."

"But she did too. I should have been there."

"Eventually she left," Owen continued.

"Where did she live?"

"With friends, here and there. I tried to stay in contact with her but she thought she was the plague and wanted to stay away from me for fear I would catch her disease. She distanced herself from you too, to protect you. Only, her efforts didn't work, did they?"

"What? What didn't work?"

"When she died, you lost focus. You fell from grace, from your high ranking in the extreme sports world." He kicked at the snow and paused. "I'm glad you made it back. Shelly would never have wanted you to go down like she did." Owen walked closer and touched my arm.

I bristled at his contact.

"Shelly was a warrior, Rory. She fought for as long as she could. When the drugs took over, she lost her battle. Even though she didn't die right away, her death was inevitable."

Sorrow etched his young face and his gaze fell to the ground.

I stood in silence.

"She was strong," he continued, "but not as strong as the drugs. They had her in a vise grip." His gaze lifted and he stared at me. "Even if you were here, Rory, there was nothing you could have done. Nothing either of us could have done. Believe me, I tried. I tried so hard."

Owen let out a heavy sigh and shook his head before releasing his hold on me. He walked back to Shelly's grave. Sinking to his knees, he stroked her marker as if the structure were Shelly herself.

"I tried, Rory. But in the end, the choice was Shelly's. Just like your decision to get clean was yours to make." He glanced at me over his shoulder. "Never, ever blame yourself for her death, Rory. Shelly never did. She never would. Just love her, the way she used to be. The way she'll always be. The little girl with hair so blonde the color looked like spun cotton, and curls so tight they bounced like the springs on a hobby horse."

Owen's head fell back and he stared up at the sky. The clouds parted and sunshine lit up his face. He closed his eyes and smiled. "She's free, Rory. She's finally free. And she would want you to be free of the guilt and shame I'm sure you still carry."

I gazed up at the sky, half expecting, fully wishing Shelly would fly down and wrap me in her delicate arms. The clouds reformed and took on the shape of wings. Maybe they were Shelly's wings. Maybe she'd flown away to a safe place to escape the hell she'd lived in here on earth.

"Sometimes dying is a better option than living," Owen whispered.

The pain in his voice decimated me.

I thought of Hindley, of all she'd been through. Those same words had been her mentality, her reality just a few months ago. She'd wanted to escape the demons that haunted her too.

"Oh, here." Owen stood and reached in his back pocket, pulling out his wallet. "I should have sent this to you a long time ago." He shoved something at me.

"What's this?" I studied the folded piece of paper then gazed up at Owen.

"Open it." He nodded.

I unfolded the worn paper. My breath caught as I gazed at the photo staring back at me.

I must have been all of thirteen, gangly and awkward. I was holding Shelly's hand, helping her balance as she rode on my skateboard. I was focused on her, but she was looking at the camera. The smile on her face stopped my heart. Her golden blonde hair waved behind her in the wind and the sun cast a light against her green eyes. She glowed from within like an angel. She was happy. And so was I.

"She had it in her purse. The police gave it to me," Owen said.

"When?" My fingers traced over her face on the photograph. The edges were worn.

"When the police found her body," Owen said. "She had my name and phone number in her wallet and they called me."

My gaze darted to Owen's.

"I never said anything to your parents," he continued. "I told the police I was her next of kin." He kicked at the ground. "I know lying to the cops was wrong, but I just couldn't stand the idea of those assholes being the one to claim her. Ya know?"

I stared at Owen, observing him. He was heartbroken, devastated. He loved Shelly. He was *in* love with Shelly.

"Thank you." My words choked out through my gravelly throat.

He shoved his hands in his pockets and stepped closer. "Will you do me a favor?"

"Sure. Anything."

"Will you send me a copy of the photo? I love to look at her, to remember Shelly when she was happy and full of life." He took out his wallet again and pulled something out then shoved the item toward me. "This card has my email address on it."

I stared down at the business card and read the name.

Owen Tucker, MS, LSSP, LSW
School Counselor

Shit, there were a lot of letters after his name. I stared at him.

Owen shoved his wallet back in his pocket, his gaze locked on the frozen ground.

"You're a school counselor?"

"Yeah." He shrugged. "I figured maybe if I couldn't save Shelly, I could help another kid, catch them before they make the wrong choices, ya know."

His words held a flippant tone, but I understand how profound his job was and why he'd selected a career so personal. My sister.

"That's amazing, Owen."

"It pays the bills." He chuckled and shrugged his shoulders.

"You know, I'm working on a program in Austin, an after school thing where kids can hang out. We're almost done with the building. My friend designed a badass skate park next door. I want to give the kids in Austin a safer alternative to the gang-infested streets."

His gaze met mine. "That's awesome, Rory. Shelly would be so proud of you."

"We're naming it 'Shelly's Hang Out.' After Shelly." I smiled with pride.

He chuckled. "I'd love to come see the place sometime."

"We'd love to have you. My fiancée, Hindley and I, I mean." I patted my pants but forgot I'd left my phone. "Do you have something to write down my number?"

Owen pulled out his own phone and tapped on the screen.

The moment reminded me of the first time I'd asked for Hindley's phone number at her sister's wedding. She'd snapped a photo of us. The picture was still one of my favorites. In fact, I'd enlarged the photo, framed it and wrapped it to give her as one of my wedding presents.

"Shoot," Owen said.

I rattled off my phone number as he typed away. I slid his card into my back pocket. "Send me a text," I said. "I don't have my phone on me, but I'll store your info too. We'll keep in touch."

"Definitely." He smiled.

"If I'd had a younger brother, I'd want him to be like you, Owen. Thanks for watching out for my baby sister. You give me hope."

"It really was my honor, Rory. Shelly was an amazing person." He bowed his head as he labored to catch his breath. "I miss her every day."

We both stared at her grave. The daisies colored the cold hard ground.

"And congrats on all your success," Owen said.

I glanced up at him.

"Shelly has always shared in your victories, Rory. She would scream so loud and jump up and down when you won a competition." He chuckled at the memories. "She still cheers for you now I'd like to think. I know when she passed from this world to the next, she did so loving you, Rory. She was proud of you. Her only regret was in herself." He glanced at Shelly's grave one last time and wiped at his eyes. "Talk to ya soon, man." He waved.

Without another word, Owen walked past me. The crunching of his heavy boots was the only sound in the stark cemetery.

I stared down at Shelly's grave. The daisies spread bright across the ground and reminded me of the smile she always wore. I knelt and ran my hand across the metal marker. I would build a better monument for her as soon as I returned home. She deserved more than this piece of shit thing.

"I'm sorry, baby girl." I closed my eyes as a cold blast of air whipped around my face. I could feel Shelly's spirit standing above me, her hand pressed on my shoulder, her love penetrating my jacket and warming me deep inside.

Candy barked inside my coat. I'd forgotten I'd brought her along.

"It's okay, girl, we're going." I laughed and patted my jacket.

I stood and wiped away the tears from my eyes, refusing to buy into the fact my sister hated me like my mother had said. Shelly was my biggest supporter. She loved me, she protected me. Owen had confirmed the truth.

Shelly Renee Gregor had been, and always would be my hero, just like I'd been hers.

CHAPTER 15

RORY

I STOOD on the porch of the old Victorian style home. My legs wobbled so much I feared I might topple over. I stared at the address on the note in my hand then compared the numbers to those nailed on the side of the door. This was the house.

I'd called Luis over two hours ago and as promised, he'd found my father. Or rather, discovered my father had died twenty-four years ago. My mother hadn't lied. My father was not Shelly's. Lineage didn't matter though. Shelly and I were one hundred percent family in my heart.

Luis's information found Royce Hamilton had served in the Air Force and died in combat. The address in my hand was his widow's, Sarah Hamilton. God, I hoped my dad hadn't been married when my mother slept with him. Only one way to find out.

My hand shook as I knocked on the plate-glass storm door. I stepped back and held my breath. What if she refused to see me, refused to even talk to me? What if she denied my existence? Oh, fuck, this could go bad, very bad.

Before I could bolt back down the steps, the front door creaked open. Behind the glass stood a tall, thin woman dressed in jeans and a loose fitting T-shirt. Her dark blonde hair was pulled back in a low ponytail and wisps of hair framed her face. Yellow latex gloves covered her hands—cleaning gloves.

Shit! I'd interrupted her.

"Oh my god." Her hazel brown eyes shot wide.

"Um…hello." My heart lodged in my throat and I couldn't swallow. "I'm—"

"My God, you look just like him." She pushed open the storm door with one hand while the other clutched her chest.

"I'm Rory Gregor." My voice broke like a pubescent teen. "Are you Sarah Hamilton?"

She stared at me, paralyzed from the neck down as her head bobbed up and down.

"I uh, I'm sorry to interrupt your cleaning, but I was wondering if I could speak to you for a minute about your late husband, Royce Hamilton." His name rolled off my tongue as if I'd said it a hundred times growing up. I didn't even know him and still a pang of familiarity hit me in the gut.

Sarah's hand fell away from her chest as her eyes perused me from head to toe. "You're his son."

Her words weren't a question but a statement, not a trace of doubt in her voice. The sliver of a smile spread across her mouth. Maybe this wouldn't be so hard after all.

"Yes, I think so," I answered quietly. "I'd like to talk to you, if you'll let me."

We stood silent and stared at one another for several seconds, absorbing the shock of my revelation.

She nodded. "Please, please, come in." She swung her arm wide and ushered me inside.

The house felt homey. A staircase sat in front of me with a room on either side. One area housed a small piano perched against the wall with formal furniture strategically placed throughout the space. The other room appeared to be a studio with canvases perched on easels and a shelf full of painting supplies on the far wall. The room was cluttered and unkept, but appropriate given the space was the birthplace to what appeared to be a creative genius.

"Oh my goodness, please excuse this mess." She shut the French doors.

"Are you a painter?"

"Yes, I paint. And sculpt." She yanked off the yellow gloves and tossed them in a chair next to the front door.

I noticed the gloves were splattered with paint. Maybe she hadn't been cleaning after all.

"Please, have a seat." She motioned toward the other room.

I stepped over the low rise of the threshold. The room smelled like fabric softener and lavender—clean and comforting. My childhood home always reeked of stale beer, smoke and Vic's body odor. I drew in a deep breath. A sense of calmness cloaked me. Sarah's place felt like home.

I lowered myself onto the small sofa.

Sarah strolled around the coffee table, her gaze never leaving mine. "God, you two could be twins." She shook her head and sighed.

"Me and my father?" I asked, still surprised she hadn't kicked me out.

"Yes, you and your father." She smiled.

"So you believe me? That Royce Hamilton is my father?"

"Even if I had doubts, they'd be washed away with one look at you, Rory." She moved to a cabinet butted against the wall. Bending down, she pulled a drawer open and withdrew several photo albums. Making her way around the furniture in the small confines of the room, she sat beside me on the sofa, albums held against her lap.

She slid the top two to the side and opened the bottom album, flipping through several pages until she found the photo she wanted. She shifted the opened album into my lap. "Royce Hamilton," she proclaimed, pointing to a picture on one of the yellowed pages.

My gaze followed her finger and I stared at the photo. My body stiffened as I studied the man in the picture. She hadn't lied. He really could have been my twin.

Royce's light brown hair was streaked with blond, like mine. His bright blue eyes matched mine and sparkled in the afternoon sun. He held the same mischievous smile I'd seen in my own photos a hundred times.

His arm was draped casually around a woman who wore a strapless blue and white striped dress with a matching wide-brimmed hat. He sported fatigue pants tucked into tan combat boots, his dark green shirt pulled taut across his chest.

"We were just back from our anniversary trip."

Sarah's words resonated with love, regret and disappointment mixed into one.

I glanced at her and noted her light brown eyes were now shimmering with tears. Shit!

"I'm sorry," I said, "I didn't mean to upset you."

"Oh, no, thinking of Royce is never upsetting. I loved your father. I still do."

She grasped a locket hanging on a chain around her neck. Letting out a shallow sigh, she stared at an invisible scene before her. Several moments passed as she stroked the locket. Soon her eyes lightened as the darkness passed, and she smiled brightly.

"We were at the Air Force base in North Carolina," Sarah began. "Your father was just about to ship off to Saudi Arabia for the Gulf War. He'd had a few days of R&R so we'd snuck off to the coast, to a bed and breakfast on Emerald Isle."

Her voice quivered and sounded strained.

A tear rolled down her cheek. She wiped at her face with the back of her hand then turned the page and pointed at other photos. "The beach was beautiful. Your father loved the ocean." She smiled.

I laughed.

"What?" Her brow furrowed.

"I live in California on the beach. I love the ocean too."

"Of course you do." She grinned.

Genuine love lit up her face.

"So my father served in the war?"

"Yes." She nodded and flipped to the next page. "Here." She pointed to another picture.

My father wore fatigues and a long sleeved shirt, a heavy vest covering his chest. A helmet sat atop his head and goggles hung loose around his neck. He stood in front of a large helicopter surrounded by several men.

"This was the air base in Al Kharj."

"Where's that?"

"In Saudi Arabia. Your father was serving in the Gulf War, Operation Desert Storm. Do you remember that war?" She turned to me.

"Uh, no." My answer was brief. She didn't need to know I'd been a juvenile delinquent and dropped out of school.

"That's okay." She gave a reassuring smile. "Kids today aren't into history, I guess."

"I wasn't really good at school." I justified my ignorance.

She nodded once and smiled.

"What did my father do? In the military I mean? Was he a helicopter pilot?"

"No, he was an air combat pararescue jumper."

I stared at her. "A what?"

"He rescued injured soldiers. He supplied trauma and medical assistance on the ground, an EMT. He also participated in combat search and rescue missions. He and his group would look for missing soldiers."

"Are you serious?" Oh my God, was my dad a real life hero?

"Yes, very serious."

"You said 'jumper.' He's standing in front of a helicopter. Did he jump out of planes and stuff to rescue people?"

"Sometimes." She shrugged. "Sometimes they rappelled if they had to do an ocean rescue, or if the injured soldier was on a mountain and the terrain was too rocky to jump."

"Holy shit," I said under my breath.

She laughed.

"Oh my God, I'm so sorry." I slapped my hand over my mouth.

"Don't be." She shook her head. "Your father and his band of Air Force buddies had the filthiest language I'd ever heard. I think you come by your colorful language honestly." She winked. "Oh, here." She flipped the page and pointed to another picture.

My father dangled on a rope below some kind of aircraft. The ocean was at least thirty feet below him with ten more to go before he reached the top of the helicopter. Another soldier dangled in front of him as my dad gripped his waist with one hand and held on to the rope with the other. My father stared up at the lens of the camera as if someone had called his name. A snorkel was attached to the side of his helmet and he wore thick goggles, but through the shield his bright blue eyes glowed. He was in his element, doing what he loved, and his pride shined through.

"This picture was from a water rescue of a downed pilot in the Red Sea."

I sat silent, in awe of my father. No words came to me. I stared at him, half expecting him to jump from the page and join us. "I can't believe it." I shook my head.

"Believe what?"

"He was incredible."

"Yes, he was."

I glanced over and noticed Sarah tracing my father's eyes, her own lost in the memory of him.

"I'm sorry, I don't mean to upset you by going through these albums."

"Oh, heavens no. I love looking at Royce." Her eyes never veered from the photo.

"You loved him?"

"Very much." She lifted her finger and dropped her hand in her lap as she turned to gaze at me. "He was my world, Rory."

I understood. Hindley was *my* world and I couldn't imagine anything happening to her.

"I'm sorry he's gone," I said. What a trite thing to say. But I had nothing else to offer.

"Thank you." She smiled.

"May I ask how he died? I'm assuming in combat."

"Yes. On a mission to rescue soldiers who'd been attacked on the ground. I don't have a lot of facts. Your father served in what they call the Special Ops unit so a lot of their information is classified. They'd already rescued several men from their downed battle tanks. They were returning for their third CSAR."

"What's a sar?" I asked.

"Oh, I'm sorry, CSAR stands for combat search and rescue."

"He saved a lot of guys?"

"Yes, he did."

We sat in silence as Sarah stared off into space. She was revering my father and I didn't want to interrupt her time with him. She stared down at the picture again before continuing. "Their helicopter was hit by ground-fired weapons from the Iraqi soldiers and went down almost immediately they said. He died on February 25, 1991."

An ominous silence echoed through the room, like I was at my father's funeral. A sense of misery and reverence pervaded every inch of the room.

"Wait, February 25th is tomorrow, Sarah."

Her hand covered her mouth and she bowed her head.

Holy fuck! "Oh, God, I'm so sorry." I slid my arm around her shoulders.

She gripped my father's picture. "Thank you, Rory. That means a lot." Sarah inhaled and closed her eyes. She held her breath for several heartbeats before exhaling. Her shoulders slumped as her eyes fluttered open.

"Did he know about me?" I blurted out. I'd waited my whole life to ask this one question.

Sarah closed the album and slid the sacred memento behind her as she turned on the sofa. She tucked one leg underneath her and studied my face as she gripped her knee. Her hazel brown eyes held mine captive for several seconds.

I held my breath. The ultimate rejection would be if Royce Hamilton had known about my existence but had never claimed me.

"No, Rory. We never knew about you." She shook her head, her eyes sad and weary. "I can promise you, if Royce had known, if *I* had known, we would have found you and brought you to live with us." Her voice wavered then broke.

Relief flooded through me like a burst dam. Did she know my history? "What are you saying, Sarah?"

"I saw your interview with Paloma Monroe."

The interview. Well, shit. Of course she knew my history. Thanks to Paloma and other relentless reporters and photographers, the entire world knew about my and Hindley's past.

"I'm so sorry, Rory." She reached out and squeezed my knee. "I had no idea you existed. Neither did Royce. But as soon as I saw your face on the screen I almost dropped my drink. You looked just like him."

"So my mother never told my father about me?"

She shook her head. "No. Your father would have told me if he knew he had a son."

"Was he married to you when I was conceived?" *God, please say no, please say no.* My father was a hero. I didn't want to taint his image.

"No, you were born in 1986. We weren't married until 1988. Your father never talked about your mom to me. I don't know if they had a relationship."

I dropped my chin and stared at my twisted fingers. Why had I imagined my father to be promiscuous? *Maybe because* you *were?*

"I'm so sorry, Rory. Royce wasn't like that. I mean, he had his wild times before we—"

I assumed she'd stopped mid-sentence because she was remembering *my* past infidelities and trysts.

"It's okay." I covered her hand with mine.

"What's important is you're here now," she said.

Her radiant smile warmed my heart.

"Why didn't you try to find me after the interview if you thought Royce was my father?"

"I wasn't one hundred percent sure you were his. I mean, you look just like him, but sometimes my mind plays tricks on me. I loved your father so much that for years I thought I saw him everywhere." Her smile faltered. "And I didn't want you to think I was a glory hound, seeking you out just because you were famous."

I shook my head, already sensing Sarah would never do something so selfish.

"I think you and I would have both been crushed if we found out you weren't his son." Her eyes brimmed with tears. "But, oh, Rory." She hiccupped a sob and shook her head. "You are *so* Royce's son. The things you've done, the heroic measures you've gone through for those you've loved, the obstacles you've overcome." She clutched my hand and squeezed. "You're *just* like your father. And he would be *so* proud of you."

My vision blurred with tears. All I'd ever wanted in life was to have a mother and father who would be proud of me.

Sarah scooted close and wrapped her arms around my shoulders. "*I'm* so proud of you, Rory. Thank you *so* much for finding me, for bringing a part of Royce back to my heart."

Candy barked.

Sarah jumped back.

I'd forgotten the dog was tucked in my jacket. "I'm sorry, I couldn't leave her in the car."

Candy crawled to the top of my jacket as I unzipped the coat.

"Oh my goodness, she's adorable." Sarah held out her hand and Candy licked her fingers. "Is she yours?"

"She is now." I smiled.

Candy clawed out of my jacket and jumped into Sarah's lap.

"Hi, cute thing." Sarah scratched under Candy's chin. The dog rubbed against Sarah's hand then dropped like a lead weight, curling up in a ball and falling asleep in Sarah's lap.

"I think she likes you." I laughed.

"I think so." Sarah stroked Candy's back.

With Candy settled, Sarah glanced up at me. "When they brought Royce home from Iraq there was nothing left of him, just a casket filled with his remains, remains I didn't want to look at. The war had taken him from me, left me with nothing but my memories."

Tears spilled down her cheeks but she made no move to wipe them away as she stroked Candy's back. Her hazel brown eyes stared into mine. "You are the *best* gift Royce ever gave me, Rory."

Her words filled the parts of my soul that craved unconditional love.

"Thank you, Sarah." I slid my arm around her and held her close while she sobbed. Together we mourned the loss of a man she loved, a man I never knew, but whose spirit and purpose lived inside of me.

CHAPTER 16

HINDLEY

I STOOD beside the luggage carousel and stared at the two-story escalator, biting my lip in nervous anticipation as I waited for Rory. He'd been competing in Colorado for a week and I'd missed him so much. I'd been busy with last minute details for the wedding and I knew he needed time to process things, so I hadn't bothered him.

I fumbled with the poster in my hands. I'd thought my creation was romantic when I'd made the sign yesterday. I'd seen Rory's fans wave posters and banners during competitions that they'd made for him. But now I felt foolish, standing in the middle of the airport holding a sign outlined in glitter asking, "Will you marry me...in 3 days?"

"Yes." A stranger's voice behind me interrupted my thoughts.

I turned. "Excuse me?"

A middle-aged man dressed in a business suit held a briefcase and smirked. "The sign."

My brow furrowed and I stared blankly at him.

He nodded toward my hand.

I looked down. Oh, my poster. *For Rory.*

"My answer is yes." He smiled like a used car salesman does

when he promises you the piece of shit turdmobile you're looking at isn't a lemon.

"Oh, uh, sorry." I chuckled.

"So, not really a sign for just anyone?"

"No." I shook my head. "This is definitely for *someone.*"

"Well," he leaned in closer, "if he says no, I'll be right over there by carousel four, waiting for the rest of my luggage."

I stared at him, my mouth agape.

He nodded at the spinning luggage rack.

I drew in a breath, about to retort when I inhaled the scent of a familiar cologne.

A deep voice growled behind me. "I'm pretty sure the man she made the sign for is going to say yes, you douche."

Rory.

"So why don't you do us all a favor and back the fuck off my girl, ass wipe."

I spun on my toes.

Rory glared at the poor businessman, the brim of his flat back hat pulled low as his eyes narrowed.

The man ducked his head and scurried away.

A high pitched yap that sounded like a dog echoed through the large atrium.

I jumped.

"That's right, asshole," Rory shouted. "Me and my dog got your number." Rory patted the nylon case hanging off his shoulder.

Was that a dog carrier?

"Rory." I hit his chest. Yes, he was being boorish, but I liked my cave man and the way he protected me.

Rory's blue eyes softened as they focused on me. "Did you have something to ask me, ma'am?" His voice rumbled deep and gravelly.

Everything south of my navel clenched in anticipation. "Ma'am?" I mocked him.

He tugged at my sign and raised his brow.

"Oh, yes. I'm looking for a man to marry." I gazed down at the words on the poster board.

"Not just *any* man, I hope." He slid his arm around my waist and drew me closer.

"Oh, no, not just *any* man." I batted my lashes and exaggerated my southern drawl. "The man I'm looking for is amazing, suave," I paused for effect, "and extremely handsome." I peeked behind him as if looking for someone else. "Have you seen him? I can't find him anywhere."

He lowered his head, the brim of his cap covering us as he kissed my neck. "Watch it, Drunk Girl or you may not get a honeymoon." His breath caressed the skin below my ear.

I swallowed a moan. We were in public which reminded me of our first kiss in the grand ballroom of one of Austin's swankiest hotels. I'd lost control with Rory that night, and the truth was, I'd never regained my senses since then, not that I wanted to.

I tilted my head to give him better access.

He kissed his way toward my ear then nipped the lobe.

"I missed you." The words rolled off my tongue in a whimper.

He chuckled, the sound vibrating against my neck.

"I mean, I missed *you*." I pulled away.

He tugged on me, thrusting his hips into mine. "I missed *you* too." His erection pressed firm against my body.

Oh, hell. I jerked out of his hold before our actions turned obscene and got us kicked out of the airport, or worse yet, thrown in jail for lewd and lascivious behavior.

"Is that a dog in your bag?" I pointed to the red case he was carrying over his shoulder as I regulated my breathing.

His eyes raked over me from head to toe, devouring me, captivating me, claiming me.

"I brought you some candy from Colorado." He chuckled.

The way he said *candy* sent shivers across my heated skin.

The dog barked. Well, yapped was a better description.

I peered through the mesh opening. Big, bulging brown eyes stared back at me. They were attached to a dog the size of a rat. Maybe the creature was a rat. "What is it?"

Rory unzipped the carrier and pulled out the smallest dog I'd ever seen. He was tan with a white diamond patch on his forehead. He trembled like, well, like a scared puppy. His ears fell back against his head. The poor guy was frightened to death.

"Oh, it's okay, little guy." I held out the back of my hand to his nose to gain his trust. He burrowed deeper into Rory's chest.

"*He* is actually a *she*." Rory nuzzled his face against the dog's.

Her ears perked up at his voice and she littered his nose with kisses. Couldn't blame the girl for being smitten.

"Oh my gosh, she's adorable. What's her name?" I reached out again. The dog let me stroke under her chin.

"Candy, this is my soon-to-be wife, and your new mommy, Hindley."

The dog barked.

Rory's face lit up with a smile. I loved Rory when he was like this, carefree and lighthearted. The trip had obviously been a good one.

"Hindley, my love, I'd like to introduce you to our daughter, Candy."

I gasped and stepped back. Did he say *daughter*? Did his introduction mean he actually *wanted* a daughter now?

"Yep," he nodded, answering my silent question. "She's ours."

"But…" He'd said *daughter* as if the thought of being a father now thrilled him. I wanted to question him, but didn't know what to ask. Or if I even should. "Where did you get her?"

"It's a long story, but suffice it to say, she needed help."

My face split into a knowing grin. "So you saved yet another damsel in distress, Mr. Gregor." I kissed his cheek then scratched under Candy's chin. "I love her already."

She leaned into my hand.

"I think she likes you," Rory said.

"I hope so. If she's my daughter we need to get along."

He chuckled.

"I'm proud of you, babe." I stared up at Rory as I rubbed the small animal.

"Why?"

"I can tell you put some ghosts to rest while you were gone. You look different, lighter, more you."

"I feel better too. Thanks for making me go."

I cocked my head. "I didn't *make* you go."

"Ohhh…kay." He laughed.

"I *suggested* you go. Big difference."

Candy jumped into my arms.

I balanced her with one hand and the sign in the other.

"So, this guy you're looking for." Rory straightened his cap and readjusted his bag as he searched the area. "Any clue what he looks like? I mean, you're smokin' hot so I'm guessing the guy can't be a total chump."

I nudged his ribs with my elbow. "Come on." I nodded toward the exit. "I've got something to show you."

"Does it involve you with less clothing than you have on now?" He swatted my butt.

I yelped. "Rory." I glared at him before surveying our surroundings.

He leaned in closer as his hand slid up to the small of my back and he escorted me through the exit. "You can pretend you don't like to be spanked in public all you want, Drunk Girl," he whispered in my ear, "but I know the truth."

His hand slipped away and he broke our embrace, leaving me hornier than I'd been in days.

We walked toward the garage and I led him to our car. "I'll drive." I bumped his hip, pushing him toward the passenger side door. He hated not being in control, especially when driving, but I had a surprise.

I popped the trunk and slid the poster in as he placed his bag on top.

He took Candy from my arms. "Yes," he whispered.

I leaned in, barely able to hear him. "What'd you say?"

"Yes." He grasped my chin and turned my face toward his. His bright blue eyes searched mine. "If you'll still have me, I would love to marry you. In three days."

I wrinkled my nose. "What do you mean, if I'll still have you?" I cocked my head and raised a brow. "Did you do something illegal in Colorado?" I chuckled.

"No, nothing illegal," he sighed. "I just know I scared you before I left, with the talk of family and all."

I couldn't deny he'd scared me. "It's okay, Rory, I—"

"I found my father." He blurted out.

"What?" I shrieked.

The dog barked. No, she yapped. The sound echoed in the garage like a gunshot.

"Well, I didn't find him, physically. I found out about him. He passed away years ago. But he was a good person, Hindley."

My mouth fell lax. "I never knew you were looking."

"I wasn't really." He shifted Candy in his arms and closed the trunk.

He'd found his father, his birth father. The discovery would have a huge impact on his own decision to be a father.

"Well of course he was a good person, Rory," I said. "So are you."

He stared at me, his eyes searching mine as if he didn't believe me.

"I want to hear *everything*." I wrapped an arm around his lean waist and rubbed Candy on her head. Our family was forming on its on—all because my brave fiancé chose to exorcise his demons instead of run from them. And he'd accomplished this incredible feat for me, for us.

"You can tell me on the way to the surprise I have for you." I shoved him toward the passenger side of the car.

"What surprise?" He slid into the seat and I walked around the car and settled into the driver's seat next to him.

"It wouldn't be a surprise if I told you, now would it?" I winked and threw the car into reverse then backed out of the space.

As I drove, Rory shared his trip with me—how he visited his mom and kidnapped Candy, how his mother disclosed the information about his birth father. I was so glad Luis had been able to help Rory locate him. And he told me about his new stepmother. She was an artist, and devoted to his father. There was so much to process.

"Can I meet her?" I asked

"Who?" Rory tilted his head.

"Sarah, your stepmom, silly."

"Oh, hell yeah, definitely. I promised her you would call. You two will get along so well. I invited her to the wedding, I hope that's okay."

We were stopped at a red light and I turned to stare at him. "Are you serious?"

"What?" He frowned.

Candy's ears perked up from her spot in his lap.

"Of course she can come, silly. She's family. She's *your* family, Rory. I would be honored to have her at our wedding. I *want* her there."

He sunk back in his seat and sighed.

"You really didn't think I would want her to come to our wedding?"

"I don't know." He closed his eyes.

The light turned green and I drove on.

"This is all just such a mind fuck," he said.

"What?"

"Me, having a dad, a *real* dad."

"Royce Hamilton," I said. "I like that name. Sounds strong. Like you." I glanced over.

He stared at the roof of the car.

"It would make a good name for a son one day, don't you think?" I asked. Okay, so maybe I was pushing him a bit. I held my breath.

Rory remained silent.

Shit. Too soon.

"Yeah, I thought the same thing. Royce Hamilton Gregor."

My heart skipped a beat and my fingers tingled as I gripped the wheel. The demons from his childhood weren't completely gone, but Rory had made progress. He'd made enough peace with his past to create a future with me.

"We're here," I announced, shoving the car into park.

"This is Shelly's Hang Out." His brows pulled together as he stared through the front windshield.

"They finished the last touchups yesterday. We'll have a final walk through tomorrow, if you're free. Then we can schedule the grand opening of Shelly's Hang Out when we get back from our honeymoon."

"What about the funding? We were still short on some of the program costs." He gazed at me in confusion, worry etched across his face.

"You have a very persuasive fiancée, Mr. Gregor." I waggled my brows and smirked.

In actuality, our friends and sponsors in the extreme sports world had come through for us when government funding had fallen short of our budgetary needs.

"No one can resist my charms." I batted my eyes.

"No, I guess they can't."

His deep, husky voice detonated a spark that set my blood on fire.

He leaned over the center console, his eyes staring at my lips.

Oh, shit. Heat pooled between my legs. "Come on," I squeaked, throwing open the door to break his hypnotic hold. "Let's go inside so I can show you around."

He grasped my wrist and tugged me back. "Thank you, Hindley."

The sincerity in his eyes, the gratitude staring back at me, warmed my insides.

"For what?" I stroked his strong jaw. The burn of his whiskers against my palm made me want to crawl over the gearshift and plant myself in his lap.

"For loving me. For teaching me to read. For giving me and Shelly this." He nodded toward the building.

"Rory, this is all you, sweetheart. I gave you the tools, but you built this place. You made your own way."

"Thanks for giving me a safe place to fail."

"You didn't fail, Rory."

"Not this time. But I will."

"We all will," I said.

He raised a brow.

"Yes," I smiled, "I know I'm not perfect either and I will fail too."

We stared at one another for a long time, both of us in awe of how far we'd come, realizing our progress couldn't have happened without each other.

Candy barked, her ear-piercing sound ringing through the cabin of my car.

We jumped.

"Someone's excited to see the inside." I laughed. "Either that or she needs to pee."

"I can't wait to see inside either." Rory slid his hand under my jaw then nestled his fingers in my hair as he pulled me close. "I can't wait to start my life, my *real* life, with you."

CHAPTER 17

HINDLEY

THE DOORBELL ECHOED inside the massive entrance of my parents' home.

"She's here! She's here!" I shouted as I ran down the hallway. I nearly slammed into the front door as I threw it open and flung myself at her. "Sarah!" I yelled.

Her eyes went wide.

I couldn't explain my exuberance. She was the first *real* connection I'd had to Rory's past. Sarah was an extension of the man I loved. More than anything I wanted to be close to her, for her to be close to us.

She clutched me tight. Just like the first time we'd seen each other on our camera phones, our connection was soul-filled and instant.

"Hindley," she sighed into me. "Oh my God, it's so good to finally hug you."

"Oh, I know, Sarah, I'm so glad you're here. I know our invitation was short notice, but...you're here. And I'm so happy."

We clung to one another. Sarah had lost the man of her dreams decades before, but his love lived on in the man who was about to be my husband. I wanted her to feel the connection, feel the life still living on despite her husband's death.

"If you two are quite finished, *I'd* like a chance to say hello to my mother," Rory said behind me.

Mother?

Sarah's arms went limp in my grasp.

I scooted back and stared at her face.

Her mouth hung agape, her eyes wide and brimmed with tears.

Rory's title had obviously caught her off guard.

"Hi, Sarah." Rory grinned. His eyes shined, alight with love radiating from deep inside. I recognized the expression. Rory reserved this type of adoration and reverence for those he held most dear. Sarah may not be blood, but there was no doubt Rory regarded her as if she were his birth mother. The thought warmed my soul.

"Thank you so much for inviting me, not only to the wedding but to the rehearsal tonight." Sarah's eyes filled with tears. "I'm just so…so honored, Rory."

"Come in, come in and I'll introduce you to everyone." I stepped aside and ushered her in.

Rory lifted her suitcase.

"Oh, I can get that," Sarah gazed from her bags to her stepson.

"No need." Rory smiled.

"God, it's uncanny," she mumbled.

"What?" I stared between the two of them.

Sarah patted Rory's cheek. "Your father would be so proud of you, Rory."

He stared at Sarah and smiled, absorbing her words. The fact she could touch him on a level none of us could amazed me. Rory believed her words. The confidence of her love flashed in his eyes.

"Come on, I want you to meet the rest of the family." I slipped my hand into Sarah's and tugged her toward the living area.

"This is such a beautiful home." Sarah surveyed the area as she trailed behind me.

"Rory and I looked at several venues, but to be honest, I've always pictured myself getting married here at my parents' house." I gazed up at the tall ceilings and wide open expanse of the home I'd grown up in. "The back yard is amazing. That's where the ceremony will be tomorrow."

Tomorrow.

Sarah rammed into the back of me.

Without realizing it, I'd stopped walking. My feet were glued to the floor as worry pounded me like a tidal wave.

"Hindley, are you all right?" Sarah asked.

"Oh my God, my wedding is tomorrow." I stared off into space. "I'm getting married. *Tomorrow.*" A tight band cinched around my chest, suffocating me.

"Hindley?"

Rory's breath brushed across my face, his scent bringing me back.

"Yes?" I squeaked out.

"What's wrong, baby?"

My eyes focused on his confused expression. "You really want to do this?" I asked.

"Do what?" He frowned.

"Get married? To me?" My voice broke.

He laughed. "More than I want to take my next breath."

I willed away the tears burning my eyes. Our wedding was supposed to be a *happy* time. Why was I suddenly doubting everything?

"Are you sure you want to still marry *me*?" Dark shadows eclipsed his blue eyes. Did he really doubt my love for him?

"Oh, Rory." I caressed his face. "There's nothing I've ever wanted more."

He leaned in, his lips just a breath away from mine.

"Save the indecent exchanges for the honeymoon, you nauseating fuck monkeys." Dana's shrill voice rang through the living area. "You've got a crap-ton of family and friends outside who want to meet your mom, Rory. You can eye-fuck your fiancé later."

Rory and I pushed away from one another and stared at Sarah.

She surveyed the two of us, her eyes filled with a knowing look of adoration and recognition. She shook her head and smiled.

"Sorry." I shrugged my shoulders.

"For what?" Sarah asked.

"For me, probably," Dana answered. "I'm Dana, the bratty cock-blocking best friend." She thrust her petite hand toward Sarah. "It's my job to make sure these two horny creeps spend the night apart and don't fuck like dogs in heat."

"Dana!" I hit her arm.

"What? If she was married to Rory's dad she's gotta be used to this kind of shit talking, right, Sarah?" Dana stared at Rory's stepmother.

"Yes, I'm afraid in the art of colorful language, the apple didn't fall far from the tree there. Rory's father had quite the sailor mouth, even though he was in the Air Force." She laughed. "It's a pleasure to meet you, Dana. I've always said a girl needs a special friend to block all the worthless cocks in her life."

Rory's eyes popped wide.

Dana hooted with laughter.

I grinned.

Sarah was officially family.

"Excuse me everyone," I butted into the conversation between Sarah and my family and friends. Watching her immerse herself into our lives was a joy. "May I steal Sarah away for just a moment?"

"Where are you going?" Rory grabbed me from behind.

"Just girl stuff." I pushed him off.

"Of course," my mother said. "But do come back, Sarah. I want to hear the end of your story about Royce and the *alligator*." She used air quotes and the group sitting around the outdoor fire pit burst into laughter.

I was sad I hadn't been there for the story telling. Instead, I'd let Rory talk me into one last make out session in my old bedroom. I'd forbidden sex for the last six weeks in hopes of making our wedding night special. You would think I'd asked for his right hand, he'd been so pissed at me.

I shook my head and touched my lips, remembering our illicit acts just moments earlier. I glanced up at him.

His gaze roamed over my body as he drank me in.

Would we ever get enough of each other?

"Tomorrow night you're mine," he whispered in my ear.

Before I could respond, he turned and strutted toward the pool area, taunting me with the sway of his hips as he joined Leif and their friends. "What's up, fuckers," he shouted, waving his hand in the air.

I shook my head.

"He's so much like his father," Sarah said beside me, staring at Rory. "In looks, in gestures…and in vocabulary."

We stared at one another and burst into laughter.

"Thanks again for inviting me, Hindley."

"No need for thanks. You're family." I smiled.

She leaned forward and hugged me. "Thank you, just the same," she whispered. "You wanted to talk to me?" She pulled away.

"Oh, yes." I led her inside my father's study then closed the door behind us and motioned for her to sit on the sofa across from his desk.

"I feel like I'm in trouble, sitting in the principal's office." Sarah laughed and fumbled with the seams of the leather cushion.

"No, not in trouble." I chuckled. "I have a favor to ask you and I didn't want Rory to hear."

"Oh, okay."

"Rory told me you're an artist, a painter and sculptor."

"Yes, that's right."

"Well, as you can imagine, buying Rory the perfect wedding gift has been impossible."

She chuckled. "I can only imagine, the man probably has everything."

"Yes, he does. And he said the only present he wants is me. But he bought me these beautiful diamond earrings." I touched my lobes and blushed. Rory had said the earrings were the only things he wanted me to wear tomorrow night. I didn't share Rory's request with Sarah.

"They're gorgeous, Hindley."

"And I know he's going to give me something tomorrow, he's already hinted to a gift. And, well, I have nothing." I bit back my emotion. "But, a thought came to me last night."

She inched forward on the sofa.

"Do you know about the learning facility Rory is working on, Shelly's Hang Out, named after his sister?"

"Yes, he told me a little about the place when he was in Colorado. Your parents were telling me more earlier tonight. I think it's an amazing thing what you two are doing for the community." She reached out and touched my knee.

The warmth of her affection hit my heart like a bolt of electricity.

I placed my hand over hers. "Rory loved his sister so much. He's been weighted down from the guilt of her death for so long. That's one of the reasons I encouraged him to visit his mother and find out more about what happened to Shelly."

Sarah nodded but remained quiet.

"Apparently while he was there, Rory met a friend of Shelly's from their old neighborhood. He moved there after Rory left his family to go pro. His name is Owen. He grew up with Shelly and assured Rory he looked out for her, but in the end, he told Rory the choice to turn to drugs was Shelly's. Nothing he or Rory could have done would have stopped Shelly's downfall." I drew in a deep breath to settle the nerves in my stomach.

"I suppose that's true," Sarah said.

"While he was there, Owen gave Rory a picture." I stood and walked around Paul's desk. I pulled open the bottom drawer and removed a manila envelope then walked back to Sarah and sat beside her, holding out the envelope.

She looked at the package then glanced at me with furrowed brows. "What's inside?"

"Take it out." I nodded.

She slid out the photo. "Oh, Hindley, it's amazing. Look at them."

"Owen gave Rory the photo of him and Shelly and said she carried the picture with her everywhere. Owen said she had the photo in her purse when the police found her body." I hiccupped a sob.

"God, I can't even imagine." Sarah stared at the picture for a few moments then gazed up at me. "Losing a child, a sister."

"I wanted to ask if you could paint the photo for me on canvas, recreate the picture. I want artwork to hang in the facility. We have nothing and the building opens to the public in a few weeks. Initially, I thought if I could enlarge that photo it would look amazing hanging in the entrance to the place. Then Rory told me you paint and I just thought…"

"Oh, Hindley, I'd be honored." She scooted closer. "I promise I'll try to do the two of them justice, but portraits aren't really my specialty."

"Just having *you* paint them will be special."

A huge smile spread wide across her face. "You have a way with words, young lady."

"I'm an attorney." I laughed.

"No wonder Rory fell so hard for you."

"Lucky for me he has a hard head."

"Like his father."

We both giggled.

"You don't have to have the portrait ready by the grand opening," I said. "I don't want to pressure you. I just thought of the idea last night."

"I'll definitely have the portrait ready by then. Would it be all right if I delivered it personally? I'd love to be there for the opening."

"Oh, Sarah!" My hand covered my mouth as new tears threatened. "Having you here would mean so much to both of us. Rory will be ecstatic. I know he wanted to ask you to the grand opening, but he didn't want to impose on your time, especially if you didn't like us."

"Not like you?" She laughed. "Rory is my husband's son, which makes him *my* son. Royce lives on in Rory. I couldn't ask for a more perfect gift. I'll do anything I can for Rory. I feel awful I didn't do more, all that time he was suffering." Her head bowed.

"Please don't feel bad, Sarah." I moved closer. "Rory doesn't blame you. No one knew who his real father was." I took her hand and squeezed. "I'm just glad we know now, so you can be a part of our lives going forward."

"I'd like that, Hindley. I really would."

"Good." I smiled. "It's settled."

"Royce would have loved you," she said softly. "He would have loved Rory so much. It breaks my heart Royce didn't know he had a son. Royce was such a good man." She wiped at her eyes. Despair gripped her voice.

"That good man lives on in his son. I think somewhere Royce is smiling down on all of us."

She nodded as a tear trailed down her cheek. "Cherish the time you and Rory have together, Hindley. Royce and I took our youth for granted when we were married. I thought I would have a lifetime to love him." She wiped at the tears with the back of her hands.

"Now you have a lifetime to love his son." I reached for the box of tissues behind me and held out several for Sarah.

She dabbed at her face. "And a lifetime to love you and your babies."

CHAPTER 18

HINDLEY

I SAT on the twin bed in my childhood room and stared at nothing. *You can do this. You can do this.*

My mother bustled around the room, straightening all the wedding garb strewn about.

Dana stared at her reflection, straightening her dress and smoothing out her hair.

I sat stock still, willing myself not to vomit.

A soft rap on the door broke my spell.

"I'm sorry to interrupt." Sarah stuck her head inside the door. "Could I steal Hindley away for just a moment?"

I glanced up at Sarah.

"Of course." My mother smiled at Sarah.

Sarah Hamilton and Caroline Hagen-Barton were fast becoming friends. *Don't mothers-in-law usually fight like wet cats?*

I stood from the bed and smoothed out my wedding dress.

"Hindley, you look beautiful." Sarah grinned as she scanned my body.

I turned and glanced at my reflection in the full-length mirror. Growing up over the years, I'd stared at my image a thousand times in this reflective glass. Most of those moments were filled with degrading thoughts. *You're not pretty enough. You're not smart enough. You're fat and no one will ever love you.*

While not fully extricated from my mind, today those voices were silent. Today I was marrying Rory Gregor, the love of my life. A man who had taught me I was beautiful, inside and out. Someone who wanted me, just for me—for the rest of his life.

My hair hung in loose curls over one bare shoulder, pulled to the side with a braided twist.

I'd never found the perfect wedding dress, so taking my mother and Dana's advice, I'd designed my own using an older dress Dana had discovered at a vintage shop downtown.

I'd removed the antique lace, utilizing the material for an overlay on my strapless bodice. The ivory mesh wrapped around my upper arms in an off-the-shoulder design, accentuating my alabaster skin. The dress fit snug along my waist then plumed out in a flowing skirt that fell gracefully to the floor. I looked elegant and regal, like Cinderella about to marry her prince charming.

I lifted the skirt and poked out my foot, smiling as I stared at my lilac colored peek-a-boo pumps. Purple was Rory's favorite color and I'd incorporated the shade into our wedding. But I'd painted my toes blue per Rory's instructions last night.

"I remember those toes from the first night I met you," he'd whispered in my ear last night as he was leaving my home, headed for Leif's. "And I want them painted blue and wrapped around my neck tomorrow night."

I shivered, remembering Rory's words. I could feel his warm breath trail across my neck, and he was nowhere in sight.

"Hindley?" Sarah whispered, standing next to me.

"Oh, sorry." I laughed, praying no one could read my sordid thoughts.

"We'll leave you two alone for a moment," my mother said as she walked toward the door.

"You look amazing, Hindley." Dana stared at me, her arctic blue eyes shimmering with tears.

"So do you." I took her hand in mine. "I love you, Dana."

"I know." She winked. "Love you too." Dana slid out the door, closing it gently, leaving Sarah and I alone.

"Thank you again for inviting me to your wedding, Hindley. I can't tell you what it means to me." Sarah's voice broke with emotion.

I turned to face her. "Oh, Sarah, I'm just so glad you came. And I'm so glad you want to be part of Rory's life."

She smiled. "It was never a question of if *I* wanted to be a part of his life. As soon as I realized who Rory was, I prayed he'd reach out to me. But I knew it had to be *him* wanting to let me in. I just never dreamed he would."

"Why?"

"When I saw you and Rory during that interview, I knew without a doubt he was Royce's son. Rory's mannerisms, his voice, everything was exactly like my husband's. But Rory was already in the limelight. I didn't want him to think I was chasing him to ride on his coattails."

Sarah drew in a deep breath and stared at the wall.

"When Rory told Paloma he never knew who his birth father was my heart broke," she said. "I had no idea what to do. The two things I knew for sure were—Rory was Royce's son, and Royce had no knowledge of Rory's existence. If he had, Royce would have turned the city upside down to find his son. To save Rory. I just thought Rory might blame me for…"

"Rory is a lot like his father, in many ways I'm sure." I reassured her. "He can be stubborn and bull-headed, he flies off the handle easily and thinks the worst of people from the get go." I paused, remembering how I'd met Rory. "But he's also a protector and a nurturer. He would never purposefully hurt those he loves and cares for, or blame them for things outside their control."

Sarah's lips pressed tight.

"And that includes you now, Sarah."

She wiped at her eyes and nodded. "Just like Royce. That's how he died you know, protecting others, trying to save them."

"Rory's told me some of his story, but not everything."

"May I?" She pointed to my bed.

"Of course."

She perched herself on the edge of my bed and set a black box trimmed with gold on her lap.

"Rory's father died in combat."

Her words were flat and her voice steady. She'd obviously trained herself over the years to keep her emotions in check.

"Yes, Rory told me. I'm so sorry, Sarah."

"Thank you." She gazed up at me and patted the spot beside her.

I smoothed my dress and sat down.

"When they brought Royce's body home, I was a mess, as were most of the loved ones who'd lost a soldier. Then they presented me with his medal at a special ceremony in Royce's honor. The award still didn't make his loss any easier." She held up the box. "Royce was the love of my life, and I knew I'd never be the same."

I slid my hand into hers.

She glanced at me. Her hazel brown eyes were wide. "Royce was awarded the Air Force Cross for his valor. The award is the second highest medal a soldier in combat can receive."

I drew in a sharp breath and clutched my heart. Rory had never told me his father had received a medal.

Sarah stroked the shiny box. "At Royce's decorating ceremony, posthumously, his commanding officer presented the medal to me with the story of Royce's bravery, how he went in to rescue a second batch of wounded soldiers. He told me Royce never once stopped to consider the consequences of what his actions may do to himself, his only concern was for the welfare of his fellow soldiers."

Sarah gazed at me, her eyes brimming with tears. "I gave this medal to Rory when he came to visit me."

"You did? Rory never told me about the medal." Why hadn't he? "Wait, if you gave it to him, why do you have it now? Didn't he take it?"

"Yes," she smiled, "he took the medal, but not for himself. He said he had special plans for it. Once he shared his plans with me, I couldn't have been more thrilled."

"What plans?" How could Rory have not told me about such a prestigious award?

"He wanted to give the medal to you."

"What?" I recoiled. "No way." I shook my head.

Sarah slid the box onto my lap along with an envelope. "This is for you, from Rory."

I stared at the box. The package blurred from my unshed tears. "Rory," I whispered as my hand ran along the envelope.

"He asked me to bring the medal in to you today and help you pin it on." She popped open the box.

Inside was a bronze cross with an eagle spread across the middle encircled by a wreath of leaves and attached to a light blue, white and red striped ribbon.

"The medal is too large for today I think." She removed a small pin clipped above the medal. "So we'll just use the ribbon on you."

She pulled the pin from the box. The brooch was small, just a few inches wide and less than an inch high, adorned with the same colored ribbon as the medal.

"I don't want to mess up your dress." She gazed over my body. "Why don't we put the pin in your bouquet instead?"

"Mess up my dress?" I laughed. "Are you kidding me, Sarah? I would be honored to fasten this on my wedding dress."

"Really?" Her eyes glistened with tears.

I jutted my chest. "Of course. Here. Pin it here." I tapped the top of my dress just above my heart.

"But that's lace, Hindley."

"Royce Hamilton died defending the men who fought in war so I could live in freedom. His death means I'm able to *choose* the man I want to marry. And I chose his son, the man of my dreams." I smiled. "I will wear Royce's medal with pride and with honor, lace be damned."

Sarah's face split wide with a grin. "I'm so happy you want to wear his pin. I feel like Royce is here with us, shining down on his son." She affixed the badge to my dress.

I gazed down at the medal as I ran my fingers over the material. "Amazing," I sighed.

"I'll leave you alone to read the note." She stood.

"Sarah." I grabbed her wrist. "Would you please sit on Rory's side, on the first row, with Kara and Jack?"

She stood silent.

"It's where Rory's mother *should* sit."

She bent down and grasped me tight. She nodded against my shoulder, unable to speak.

After she stood, I closed the lid on the box and handed the case back to her. "And will you take this too? Keep Royce's medal on your lap. That way we'll know Rory's dad is here too. He'll be close to my heart." I patted the pin on my dress.

"Oh, Hindley." The tears once held at bay slid down her cheeks.

"I didn't mean to make you cry."

"They're happy tears, dear." She stroked my face. "Happy tears." She smiled one last time. "Thank you, Hindley. I hope you and Rory are as happy as Royce and I were. I hope your love lasts an eternity."

"Just like yours and Royce's, right?"

She nodded. "He ruined me for all other men." She laughed with mock annoyance.

"I know the feeling."

"You look beautiful, Hindley. Read the note and I'll see you outside, okay?" She squeezed my hand. "I'll send your mom and Dana back in in a bit to help freshen you up."

Obviously she knew the note would make me a blubbering mess. "Thank you." I whispered.

After Sarah left, I caressed the pin over my heart. "Nice to meet you, Royce Hamilton." I gazed at the envelope in my lap. "I love your son. I'm marrying him today." I giggled. What kind of person speaks to a stranger on the day of her wedding? *Hindley Hagen does.* But Royce Hamilton wasn't a stranger to me. He lived on through his son.

With trembling hands, I turned the envelope over and tore at the seam. Pulling out the piece of paper that matched my dress, I let out a long sigh then unfolded the letter.

Etched across the paper was what I called Rory's chicken scratch. His penmanship had never been neat, but then neither was he. He wrote like he lived...fast and hard with no apologies. I steeled my grip on the paper and drew in a heavy breath to calm my racing heart.

Dear Hindley,

Well, here we are, the day we've planned for months now. If you're reading this, that's a good sign. It means you haven't run away yet. Thank God.

As I sit and write this letter to you, I can't help but smile, knowing it's only because of you I can. Your faith in me, not only to learn how to read and write, but to grow up and be a better man, gives me hope that one day I can be the type of father our children deserve.

Tears stung my eyes as I envisioned a family with Rory. At least he was considering the possibility.

You know part of the reason I was afraid of being a father was because I didn't have one of my own. But now that's changed. Even though I never met my birth father, I feel like I know him, like he's always lived inside me. He's been the voice inside my head, pushing me to be better, to do better my entire life. It's because of his voice, warning me something was wrong, that I couldn't let a beautiful drunk girl outside of a bar go home in a cab all alone. (Insert smirk here.)

I laughed out loud.

When Sarah first gave me my father's medal, I wouldn't take it. I mean, I never knew him in life so why should I have it now? Sarah had loved my father. She'd known him. I hadn't. But the more she talked about him, the more stories she shared, I realized I did know him, he lives on inside me. I think Sarah saw him inside me too. Knowing my life could give her peace made me happy.

She told me the Air Force Cross is the second highest medal a soldier is awarded, second only to the Congressional Medal of Honor. My father received the cross because the military said he showed extraordinary heroism against an enemy during wartime. Because of his brave, selfless efforts, many lives were saved, even though he lost his own.

I didn't want to take the medal at first, I didn't feel worthy. But then I remembered a brown-eyed drunk girl with bright blue toenails, a woman who was the epitome of the word brave. (Do you like my big word-of-the-day? "Epitome"- ha ha!) I remembered a woman who is a hero to many, especially to me, a lowly, lost skater boy.

Since the day I met you, Hindley, I have wanted to be a better man, for you. You are so brave. You have walked through the fires, you've faced the devil himself and have come through the flames a stronger person. Not only that, but you fight for others who can't or don't know how to fight for themselves. Look what you did for Hannah. If anyone deserves a medal for extraordinary heroism, it's you, Hindley Hagen.

The tears, which once trickled down my cheeks, now rolled down my face and dripped on the letter. I couldn't believe the kind words Rory had written for me. He thought I was a hero.

They say there are traditions in weddings, special shit a girl is supposed to do for good luck. We don't need luck because we have each other. But just in case you buy in to all that superstition bull-shit, I thought this medal might help.

Your something OLD – Because my dad received it nearly twenty years ago.

Your something NEW – Because it's new to me, Sarah just gave it to me.

Your something BORROWED – Because I'm letting you wear it today.

And finally, it can be your something BLUE – Because the blue ribbon represents bravery and valor, two things that best describe you.

Plus, blue reminds me of those delectable toes. I hope you've already painted them because I can't wait to wrap your legs around my neck later tonight. Come on, baby, you didn't think I could be serious for long, did you?

So put my father's pin close to your heart and get your sweet little ass down the aisle because I can't wait to make you my Mrs. Gregor.

I promise to protect you and our children. I promise to work hard every day to be the man you deserve. And I promise to love you, always.

Loving you has never been a choice, Hindley. Falling in love with you and winning your love in return has been the best thing to ever happen to me in my life. Saving you that night saved me.

I love you, Drunk Girl.

Your Skater Boy...Forever

Tears poured down my face and I wondered why anyone had allowed me to put on make-up at all. I folded Rory's letter into a small square and tucked the note inside my dress, just behind his father's pin, close to my heart.

Rory thought I was brave, but he'd showed *me* how to be courageous by stepping out into the world and saying, "Look at me, I can't read." Any courage I'd shown had been a reflection of his.

"Knock, knock," my mother spoke softly as she opened the door. "May we come in?"

"You better if I stand a chance of looking halfway decent at my own wedding." I circled my finger over my face. "Fix me."

My mother laughed.

Dana scooted in behind her. "Oh, shit, you look like someone doused you with a firehose, girl. Not a good look for your wedding day."

"Here, have a seat." My mom pointed to the chair sitting next to my desk. "We'll clean you up."

I moved to the seat.

She wiped at my make-up.

I grabbed her hand. "Thank you, Mom."

"For what, sweetie?" she asked as she dug through the basket of make-up with her free hand.

"For keeping me."

My mother's hand froze and her gaze fixed on mine.

When my mom found out she was pregnant with me at eighteen, her parents had wanted her to abort me. She refused, and two months after I was born, they'd kicked us out.

"Hindley," my mother whispered, "that was *never* an option for me. You're my world."

"I know." I smiled.

"You're my hero, Hindley. I've always admired you."

"Really?"

"Of course I have, baby girl." She stroked my cheek. "And now, you're starting this new life with such a wonderful man."

"He is pretty special, isn't he?" I gazed out the window over the lawn below, now decorated for the outdoor ceremony. My stomach fluttered.

"There," my mom announced as if she'd finished a masterpiece.

"You look perfect." She tapped my nose. "Now you're ready to get married."

"I'm getting married..." My lungs burned as I heaved for my next breath. "Holy shit, I'm getting married."

"Breathe." Dana knelt in front of me, her hands clasping my knees. "You're gonna be fine. Everything will be fine."

I blinked rapidly and bit my lower lip, not one hundred percent convinced of her declaration.

A soft tap on the door interrupted my thoughts.

"You ready, Hinny-Bin?" My father, Paul scooted through the door.

I stood on wobbly legs.

"Oh my God, Hindley." He stopped, his mouth gaping.

"What?" I ran my hands up and down my dress.

"You look stunning, sweetheart." He moved toward me took my wrists and held my arms out to the side. "Just stunning." He slipped his hands into mine and held them up between us. "You are so beautiful, Hindley. I'm so honored to be your father, to be walking you down the aisle."

"No more tears, Paul, I just cleaned her up." My mother swatted at my father.

We all laughed.

"You ready?" Dana peeked up at me through her long lashes. "You *so* deserve this, Hindley. I'm really happy for you."

She smiled and her Di Grazio dimples went on full display.

"Me too." I gave her a quick hug then looked at the three people I loved the most. I was nervous, but I was confident. Rory was the man of my dreams, the love of my life. "Let's do this."

They filed through the door.

I drew in a deep breath then exhaled as I placed my hand over Royce's pin and Rory's letter. "Let's go get married, Drunk Girl."

CHAPTER 19

RORY

I STOOD tall and admired Paul and Caroline's backyard. The vast green expanse had been transformed into a bride's wonderland—romantic and inviting. Hindley deserved nothing less. Our wedding would be her one and only, and I was bound and determined to give her anything her heart desired.

Most grooms suffered from weak knees and sweaty palms right before the ceremony, but not me. Marrying Hindley had never been a question. Getting married? Yes. But marrying her? No, I had no doubts or fears about sharing the rest of my life with her.

Leif nudged me as we walked toward our assigned spots at the end of the aisle. "Dude, I know this may sound totally gay, but this place looks incredible."

I studied the decor. I'd balked at the idea of hiring a wedding coordinator, but I'd been overruled by Hindley *and* her mother. Surveying the area now I had to admit the money was well spent. I beamed, knowing Hindley was about to walk out into her fairy tale wedding. And who was I to deny her. She was my Cinderella.

A pale ivory runner bordered by lavender rose petals ran up the aisle and divided the chairs into bride and groom's sides. The seats, once empty earlier, were filled with our friends and family.

Lanterns with glowing candles dangled from the trees overhead and provided the perfect amount of light as the sun slowly set behind us.

I walked toward the judge who was stationed underneath a canopy of trees. The full limbs hung as if they'd grown to house a bride and groom.

"Are you ready?" The judge waggled his brow.

"As ready as I'll ever be." The nerves I thought I'd escaped suddenly hit me like a prized fighter's punch to the gut. My legs wobbled like jelly, and my hands trembled and beaded with sweat.

Leif leaned closer. "Dude, get your shit together. You look like you're about to pass out."

"Man, I seriously think I'm going to," I whispered over my shoulder. Before I could vomit, or faint, the string quartet near the mass of trees began playing. Hindley had requested "Cannon in D" —or E or F or G or some shit like that. Holy hell, I couldn't remember now. I was about to shit in my pants.

"Breathe." Leif nudged me.

I drew in a deep breath, willing myself to calm the fuck down. *If you pass out Caroline will kill you.* Music filled the backyard and my nerves settled into the soft melody of the string quartet's performance.

"Wow," Leif said.

"What?" I glanced over my shoulder.

He nodded down the aisle.

Your wedding, dumbass, that's what. I'd forgotten where the fuck I was.

I glanced down the aisle. Dana walked toward us. Holy shit. Words escaped me. Usually I was able to sling bullshit at her with ease. But today, the woman floating toward me was a goddess. Her black, wavy hair tumbled over her shoulders and swung along the V-neck of her lavender silk dress. The shimmering material clung to her body like Saran Wrap. She held a simple bouquet of ivory roses and walked with grace and style, two things I'd never associated with the pixie vixen before today.

Her crystal blue eyes glimmered from the light of the candles overhead. As she moved nearer, I noticed they glistened with unshed tears. I'd never seen Dana Di Grazio cry. Not once.

She moved closer still, but rather than dart to the bride's side, she made a beeline for me. She braced herself on my arm as she leaned in.

I bent at the waist to accommodate her petite frame.

She placed her mouth close to my ear. "Hurt her and I'll cut your balls off and feed them to your new puppy, got it, One Nighter?"

I bit my lip to keep from laughing at her directive, and my nickname. Leaning back, I peered down at the pint-size dynamo who had kept her best friend safe for years. Now the job was mine.

"Got it, half-pint," I whispered, "but after today, I'm *Every* Nighter, got it?"

Dana pulled away and surveyed me.

Oh, fuck, was she gonna pull the ultimate cock-block and keep Hindley from marrying me?

Slowly those famous dimples lit up her face. She winked and leaned in to kiss my cheek. "Okay," she said. "I love you, Rory. Take care of her."

"I love you too, Dana. And I plan to." I kissed her lightly, and without another word, she floated across the aisle to her rightful place.

I turned my attention to the end of the aisle from where Dana had approached. My breath caught in my throat, and my heart stopped. I couldn't breathe.

My love. My life. My Drunk Girl was walking toward me.

Her hand was looped through her father's arm, his hand

clutching hers. She tilted her head and stared at me. A small smirk spread across her beautiful face—as if she had a secret she couldn't wait to tell me.

Her love for me was no secret.

She glowed from within, her love radiating out like the setting sun behind us.

Her dress was simple but elegant, leaving her shoulders bare as I'd asked. The lace wrapped around her arms and matched the color of her flawless skin. Her hair was down but draped to one side. I smiled as I thought of having unhindered access to her neck and shoulders. She wore no veil and I was grateful. I didn't want anything between us, anything to obstruct my view.

Her dress flowed behind her as Paul and she strolled down the aisle. The small bouquet of lavender roses matched the petals at her feet. Those feet weren't moving fast enough for me though. I fought the urge to race toward her and yank her to me like a caveman. She wouldn't want me to cause a scene. Not today anyway. Today was Hindley's fairytale, a formality she needed and an experience I wanted to give her.

Before I could blink twice, she and Paul stopped a few feet away from me. I could smell her perfume. Hindley's alabaster skin shimmered in the amber light from the candles hanging above us. The scene was ethereal and otherworldly. Hindley was my princess. I just prayed I could be her Prince Charming.

Her face glowed with love and adoration. The candlelight created a kaleidoscope effect in her chocolate brown eyes. She stared at me, almost through me, to my core, only now I wasn't afraid of what she would see. I hoped my eyes radiated the love she so freely gave me.

"Who gives this woman in matrimony?" the judge asked.

"Her mother and I do," Paul said.

His booming voice brought us both back to earth. Hindley and I snapped our attention to him.

Paul was delivering one of his most prized possessions to me today. I prayed I could be worthy of his trust.

He held out Hindley's arm for me.

I moved closer.

He leaned in. "I always knew it would be you, Rory with no last name."

My eyes snapped wide from the reminder of the first time I'd met Paul. Hindley had been mortified when her father thought we'd had a one-night-stand. I'd wanted to protect her from Paul's judgment. My need to shield her from harm had never faded.

Paul winked at me, then leaned over and whispered something in Hindley's ear before kissing her cheek and handing her over to me.

He was relinquishing the care of his daughter to me, and for a powerful man like Paul Barton, surrendering control was huge. For Paul's sake, and for a multitude of others, I vowed never to disappoint him.

Hindley was my life now. Truthfully, she had been since I'd rolled over and caught her staring at my body the first morning we woke up together.

"Look," she whispered as she pulled her skirt up and stuck her shoe out from under the ivory material.

I thought she was pointing at her lavender shoes, but as she moved her foot from side to side, I noticed what she was drawing my attention to. Her toes wiggled through the opening in the front. They were painted bright blue, just as I'd asked.

I chuckled. A satisfied smirk spread across my lips. My eyes rolled up to meet hers. The same smile lit up her face. Her expression screamed anticipation.

No matter what I'd thought the first time I'd seen her puking up her guts on the sidewalk outside an Austin night club a year ago, I knew life with Hindley Hagen Gregor would never be boring.

"You look stunning," I said.

She tipped her head and her eyelids fluttered. "Thank you."

She believed me. Finally. Her soft words of appreciation hit my heart.

"So do you," she said. "Are you ready?"

"Honey, I was born ready." I winked and kissed her on the cheek. I wrapped her arm around mine and stepped us closer to the judge.

"Friends and family, we are gathered here today to celebrate the union between Rory Gregor and Hindley Hagen in marriage."

The judge's eyes studied Hindley and she nodded. Then his gaze swept to mine. I could hear him ask silently, "Are you *sure* you want to do this, dipshit?"

I laughed under my breath and nodded my head.

"As we all know, marriage is a covenant, a sacrament, and should not be entered into lightly," the judge said. "Rory, Hindley, as you stand before me today, I trust you both know the seriousness this ceremony represents."

I gazed at my bride. Her eyes glistened and her lashes batted once, twice, three times in that coy way she used when she wanted something.

"Yes," we responded in unison, our gazes never leaving one another.

"Well then, let's get on with it." The judge paused and cleared his throat.

Hindley and I blinked, breaking our spell and turned to face him.

"In their short time together, I understand Rory and Hindley's love has withstood many obstacles." The judge's gaze moved from the crowd back to me and Hindley. "Through all the trials, you both have stayed true to yourselves and each other."

The words were a statement but his remark sounded like a question, so I nodded.

"As you trudge through the trials of married life, I want you to cling to those early tests of your love." The judge's words were soft but firm. "Look back and know it was your sacrificial love for one another that brought you through the hard times.

"Your lives as husband and wife will not always be easy, just as your lives up to this point haven't been. But together your marriage will be filled with blessings and joys which will enhance and add to the love and the happiness only you can bring one another. During hard times, remember the things that brought you together, the reasons you fell in love with one another."

Images of Hindley's blue toes flickered in my mind and I stifled a laugh.

Hindley elbowed me.

I gazed down.

She stared straight at the judge, but her lips were caught between her teeth.

"Would you face one another please?" the judge asked.

Hindley passed off her bouquet to Dana then took my hands.

I peered at her fingers sheltered within mine. They seemed so small, but they'd done mighty things—for both of us. Her hands had held on to our love like a life raft when I'd given her every reason to let go. She'd clung to me, held on to me, saved me. I silently vowed to never let her go.

"Hindley, please repeat after me," the judge said.

Hindley's gaze never left mine. Her flawless face held my heart captive.

Please say yes, please say yes.

I held my breath, praying she wouldn't come to her senses and bolt back up the aisle.

"I, Hindley Hagen," the judge said.

"I, Hindley Hagen."

"Take you," the judge continued, "Rory Gregor."

"Take you," her eyes flashed and she squeezed my hand, "Rory Gregor."

"To be my lawfully wedded husband."

"To be my lawfully wedded husband." Hindley smiled.

Her words washed across my wounds like a salve to my soul. She wanted me. I blew out a sigh of relief.

"To have and to hold from this day forward, for better, for worse," he continued.

Her eyes remained fixed on mine as she repeated the vows.

From the corner of my eye I noticed the judge glance between us. "For richer, for poorer, in sickness and in health," he said.

"For richer, for poorer. In sickness and in health," she recited, staring into my eyes.

The judge remained silent.

Hindley's eyes broke my gaze as she turned to face the officiant.

"As long as you both shall live." He raised a brow.

I held my breath, awaiting her final vow.

Hindley paused.

Oh, shit, this was the moment of truth. Would she agree to forever with a mook like me?

Hindley drew in a deep breath and held it for several heartbeats before releasing the final words on an exhale. "As long as we both shall live."

In those few words, Hindley gave me everything. She offered me the promise of forever.

It took all my willpower not to snatch her up right then and carry her out of here, throw her down somewhere and smatter her with kisses on every surface of her body. And then fuck her senseless.

My dick twitched. Shit. Dude, what the fuck? *Not now, boy. Later.* I smiled.

The judge turned to me and I recited the vows Hindley had,

racing through them as if doing so would get me closer to unwrapping her from that dress.

"Hindley," the judge faced her, "it is my understanding you and Rory have written vows to one another."

Vows? Shit! I'd completely forgotten. I knew I'd fuck it up, so I'd taken the time to write down everything I wanted to say. But now I would have to read them, out loud, in front of God, an officiant, our family and friends—and most important, in front of Hindley. What if I fucked up?

"You'll be fine." Hindley stroked my cheek.

I drew in a deep, cleansing breath. The only person I cared about was Hindley.

I looked down at our clasped hands. What a miracle she had said yes. And even more surprising was how she'd stayed with me through the stress of wedding planning, a new trial with her attacker, and me having to resolve the issues of my childhood. The judge was right. We'd endured more heartaches than most couples did in a lifetime. And yet we'd stood tall, stayed strong and were more committed to each other than ever.

Hindley tugged on my hands.

I pulled myself from my thoughts and stared into her mocha colored eyes. They held me captivated.

"Rory." Her voice cracked. Tears glistened in her eyes. "When I was a little girl, I dreamt of Prince Charming, riding in on his trusty steed to rescue his damsel in distress. Then *you* showed up in my bed."

The crowd burst into laughter.

Hindley's eyes shot wide and she covered her mouth. "Oh, crap." She shook her head, her face flushed scarlet. "It wasn't like that, I swear," she mumbled, staring at the judge.

The judge coughed out a laugh and cleared his throat.

I grabbed her hand and tugged. "Go on."

"Anyway," she sighed, "what I realized when I met you is,

Prince Charmings come in all shapes and sizes and not necessarily on white horses. But you know what?"

I shook my head. Where was she going with this?

"Turns out I didn't need a Prince Charming after all." She smiled.

Oh, shit. What was she saying? She didn't need me? Would she leave me now, after everything we'd been through?

"What I needed was someone to help me help myself—someone who would show me just how strong *I* could be, how strong I *had* been all these years. I didn't need salvation, I needed emancipation."

"You need what?" I mouthed.

She giggled.

My eyes narrowed and I tapped down my frustration.

"Calm down, big guy," she squeezed my hands. "What I meant was, I needed to be freed from the weights of my past. Freed from the thoughts that told me I wasn't smart enough, I wasn't pretty enough, I wasn't good enough." She paused and stepped closer. "You, Rory Gregor, are my emancipator. You freed me from myself. And because of you, I have a life free of limits. With you, I *have* a life, period."

Oh, shit, not only did she *want* me, she *needed* me. My chest swelled with pride.

"A prince means someone preeminent, royal, in any class," she said. "*You*, Rory are worthy of that title. You are *my* prince." She paused. "Charming? I'm not so sure." She shook her head and wrinkled her nose

Everyone laughed.

"But prince," she continued, nodding her head, "yes. Very much so. You are superior, you surpass all others. You are *my* prince. You came for me. And stayed with me, even when I was cruel."

Tears blurred my vision. My chest heaved and the dam broke.

With trembling hands, Hindley reached up and wiped them away.

I caught her hand and pressed my lips into her palm. "Thank you," I murmured. "You are my queen."

"I think it's princess if you're a prince." She laughed. "But yeah, I am."

I was proud of her in that moment. She believed my words of adoration and didn't brush me off. Maybe I was her prince after all.

Hindley nodded toward the judge indicating she was done.

"Rory?" He raised his brows.

I cleared my throat and released Hindley's hand, digging in my coat pocket for the note I'd written. "I didn't want to forget any words, so I wrote them down." I unfolded the paper. "I hope that's okay." I stared at Hindley.

"That's *more* than okay, that's amazing."

Her smile radiated pride. For me.

I drew in a deep breath that did nothing to calm the stampeding bulls racing across my chest. *You can do this.* Blowing out a heavy sigh, I licked my lips then focused on the words written on the paper.

"It's okay, Rory." Hindley's knuckles grazed my cheek. "Take your time. I've waited for this moment my entire life."

I leaned into her touch and nodded. Sensing I had gathered my strength, her hand slid from my face. My heartbeat slowed. I swallowed deep and willed my voice to speak. "Hindley," I started, staring over the edge of the paper at her expectant eyes.

Her hand stroked the ribbon of my father's medal.

How had I not noticed the pin attached to her dress? I peered at her face.

"Brave," she mouthed. "You are brave."

I could do this. *Just go slow and focus, man.* I cleared my throat. "Hindley," I read from the paper, "if I'm being honest I will tell you, the first time I saw you, I wasn't impressed."

She grimaced.

Shit. "Wait." I held up a hand. "You know *why* I wasn't impressed, right?" I raised a brow. I knew she didn't want to disclose how ridiculously drunk she'd been the night we'd met.

Her frown morphed into a warning scowl. "Honeymoon," she mouthed.

Nope. Keep that story for another time.

I remembered her neighbor at the time, Franny, aka "Red," wiping Hindley's drunken face with a rag. Hindley had been just as breathtakingly beautiful then as she was now. *Get back to the written shit, dumb ass, before her dad throws you out of your own wedding.*

I gazed at my note again. I would stick to the prepared words.

"The first time I saw your face I was in awe. You were void of make-up, your hair was in a ponytail, you were wearing work-out clothes. Basically, you were a hot mess." I paused and chanced a peek at her face. She wore an expectant glare. "And I'd never seen anyone more beautiful."

Her face relaxed and a reassuring smile replaced the "I'm going to kick your ass from here to China" look from earlier.

"Go on," she whispered.

"From that moment on, all I can see is your face," I said. "When I'm skating, when I'm eating, even in my sleep I see your face. It's not just your outer beauty that takes my breath away, your inner beauty drives me to be a better person, a better man, a better *me*." I tapped my chest.

"When I told you I couldn't read, you never judged me. In fact, you made it *your* mission to teach me. You gave me a journal and told me to fill it with my thoughts. Back then I only had one. Through the days and weeks and months after, I filled each page with the words racing through my head. I wrote, 'I love Hindley Hagen' on every page."

I glanced up.

Hindley's chin trembled and she bit her bottom lip.

I peered down at my note to distract myself, fearing I may break down any minute too.

"Your strength and your bravery astonish me," I continued. "Every day I can't believe out of all the men on the planet, you said yes to me, a guy who can't read and skates on a silly board for a living. When the world was against me, you believed in me, Hindley." I stared into her dark brown eyes. They glistened with tears. "You gave me the courage to believe in myself.

"A smart girl once told me we have so much faith and confidence in each other, but so little in ourselves. We're changing, Hindley. You and I, we're peas of a pod, but in a different way now. As long as I live, whatever road life takes us on, I will spend my days thanking God you're my pea and that you're sharing your very special pod with me, a humble Skater Boy." I chanced a look.

Tears rolled down her face.

"And apparently a prince too." I chuckled.

Hindley giggled.

Her laughter was my heart's song.

I silently read the last paragraph before speaking out loud. "I love you, Hindley Hagen. I'm not sure why you love me, I'm just grateful you do. And I promise you today and always that I will honor you and the trust you've bestowed upon me. Your love is the greatest medal I've ever won."

I folded the note and stuffed it back in my suit jacket. My heart beat so hard the pulse in my temple momentarily blinded me. Taking a steadying breath, I glanced up.

Tears streamed down Hindley's face. She didn't even fight to brush them away.

I'd hoped she would cry. Yeah, it was a shit thing to hope for, but I wanted my words to touch her like hers had me. I wanted my declaration to fill her with so much love, the emotion had no choice but to spill over into tears of joy. Shit, I hoped they were tears of joy.

I reached down and rubbed my thumbs along her beautiful cheeks, careful not to smudge her make-up.

She pressed my hand against her face. "Thank you," she whispered. Then, just like I had done earlier, she turned my hand and pressed her lips into my palm.

My dick twitched. Again. God, what this girl did to me.

Hindley's brows waggled and she smiled. "Later," she whispered, giving my hand one more kiss before releasing it.

We stared at each other for several breaths. I didn't want to look away for fear I would wake up and find the whole year had been a dream, I'd discover Hindley had never even existed let alone devoted her life to me.

"Well, if you're finished," the judge said.

I nodded, but my eyes never left Hindley.

"May I have the rings?" he asked.

I turned to Leif and watched as he handed Hindley's rings to the man. I peeked at Dana and watched her do the same.

"These rings are a symbol of your love and fidelity," the judge said. "They are round to fit your finger, but the symbolism goes much further than just these pieces of jewelry. There is no beginning or end to these rings. Unlike your love, which can be marked with a beginning, as Rory just mentioned." He gazed at me with a smirk. "But your love from this day forward will have no end. May these rings be a blessing and a constant reminder of the vows you have declared today. Please take your rings." He held his palm up.

Hindley and I grasped the rings. My hand shook so bad I had to concentrate to keep from dropping hers.

"Hindley, would you please place Rory's ring on the third finger of his left hand and repeat after me."

I held my hand out as she slid the platinum band onto my ring finger.

"Rory, this ring is a sign," he started.

"Rory," she said, her voice hoarse with emotion, "this ring is a sign."

"Of my love and fidelity." The judge nodded.

Hindley looked up at me, her face filled with adoration. "Of my love and fidelity." She slid the ring on my finger then pulled my hand to her lips. Her eyes remained fixed on mine as she kissed the ring.

My legs wobbled and my heart pounded against my ribs so fast I feared the fucker might explode.

"I love you," she mouthed.

"Rory," the judge nudged me, "would you please place your ring on Hindley's third finger of her left hand and repeat after me."

I gazed at the rings in my hand—one engagement, one wedding. A promise and a commitment. I drew in a steadying breath and slid both on her dainty finger. I held the rings in place and marveled at how natural she looked wearing jewelry that marked her as mine. So what if I was a chauvinistic son of a bitch. She was mine and I wanted the world to know it. Claiming her with jewelry was better than pissing all around her.

"Hindley." The judge said, staring at me expectantly.

Oh, shit, wedding, ceremony, rings.

I stared at Hindley, her smile so wide I thought her face might crack. My own expression mirrored hers. "Hindley," I said.

"This ring is a sign," the judge recited.

"This ring is a sign," I repeated.

"Of my love and fidelity."

"Of my love and fidelity." I slid the rings in place and lifted her hand to my lips, gently pressing a kiss against her knuckles. All I could think of was my lips pressing on other parts of her body.

"By the giving and receiving of these rings and the reciting of your vows to one another." The judge cleared his throat.

Focus, dude, you're almost done.

I stared at the man, willing him to hurry the fuck up.

"And by the power vested in me by the state of Texas, I now have the esteemed honor of pronouncing you husband and wife."

The judge's words rang in my head. I understood he was declaring us married, but thoughts of Hindley, naked and wrapped in my arms, kept flashing through my sick, demented mind. Christ, I couldn't picture her in such sordid positions, she was my wife now for God's sake. *Wife?* Oh, holy fuck.

"Rory," Leif nudged me from behind.

Oh, shit. Kiss her? *Yeah, kiss her, dumb ass.* I glanced at the judge.

He nodded his head toward Hindley.

Fuck yeah, kiss her!

I slid my hand around the exposed skin of her neck, my fingers digging in to the lush curls of her hair.

She shuddered under my fingertips.

I slipped my other hand around her waist and drew her toward me. Before our lips met for the first time as husband and wife, I stared into her beautiful brown eyes. I remembered every moment I'd spent with her, even the cruel ones which had broken us apart. I wasn't sure what our future held, but I knew with Hindley by my side, we'd make it through.

"I love you," I whispered. Before she could answer, my lips covered hers. I worked to tame our embrace since this was a family affair, but just like our first kiss, anytime our lips met, a spark ignited that sent Hindley and I catapulting into overdrive.

I pressed her against my growing erection as my tongue seeped between her lips. She willingly parted, twining her mouth with mine. I increased the pressure as her moans reverberated straight to my dick. Shit!

"Um, hmm," someone cleared their throat.

Fuck them.

"Rory." Leif nudged my back.

A thought rumbled through my head, warning me of impending danger. *Stop. Stop now.*

Hindley threaded her fingers in my hair and tugged me closer, anchoring my lips to hers.

All thought escaped me. I was lost to her.

"Get a room!" Someone shouted from the crowd.

I pulled away from Hindley's mouth. Her eyes were closed and her lips puffed from my assault, but she was smiling. "Already got one," I whispered against her mouth. "Already got one."

CHAPTER 20
RORY

"Oh my gosh, Rory." Hindley exclaimed, covering her mouth as we strolled through the reception area.

A canopy of lights shimmered above like twinkling stars. Someone had designed a tent like draping effect with nothing more than strands of lights. The night sky was still visible and the full moon gazed overhead.

Hindley released my hand and meandered through the round tables littering the yard. They were adorned with varying shapes and sizes of candles all flickering bright. Hindley's face caught the iridescent light. She looked like an angel as she floated through the area. Her head tipped up to the sky as she surveyed the lights and the stars.

"I just can't believe how beautiful it is." She sighed.

"Do you like it?" Geneva called from behind me.

Her voice churned my stomach. I'd worked hard to forgive her, to temper the need to throat punch her any time she was around, for Hindley and her family's sake, but I wasn't as forgiving as Hindley. The bitch had nearly cost me *everything*.

"You did this, Geneva?" Hindley's eyes stared beyond me.

"Yeah." Geneva whispered.

I would be with Hindley and her family for the rest of my life, and so would Geneva. I had to let this shit go. After all, it *was* Geneva who'd eventually come clean and confessed to drugging me. And because of her admissions Geneva had lost everything—her husband, her family, even her social status, which I'm sure hurt her the most. Hell, she damn near faced jail time. For Hindley, I would try harder to have a relationship with Geneva.

I drew in a deep breath and counted to ten, tallying the reasons I loved Hindley Hagen. There were too many to count so I opened my eyes. My stomach relaxed and my need to vomit and/or smash Geneva's face into our wedding cake was *nearly* gone.

I studied the area. The reception space really was quite spectacular, everything Hindley wanted and deserved.

"Geneva, the place looks incredible. And the ceremony too, with all the candles." Hindley met Geneva in the middle of the reception area.

"The dance floor is up on the deck." Geneva pointed to the patio a few yards away.

The family usually gathered on the terrace for outdoor eating when we came to visit. All the furniture had been removed and replaced with even more candles. Large balloon shaped lanterns crisscrossed overhead. Beaded crystals dripped from the trees and draped the patio. They caught the light of the lanterns, giving the appearance of thousands of fireflies dancing overhead. The area was breathtaking. I hated to admit it, but Geneva had done an amazing job.

I glanced at her. "It looks incredible, Geneva."

She stared at me, her mouth agape so wide I feared a bug may fly in.

Geneva and I didn't speak much. And I *never* gave her compliments.

"R-really? You like it?" She stood paralyzed.

Her face was so forlorn and desolate I actually felt sorry for her.

"Yeah." I smiled, nodding. "I do, Geneva. You did an amazing job." That was the truth. She'd given my princess her fairytale reception and I could meet Geneva halfway. "Thanks."

"Oh, Rory," she whimpered as she laid her hand on my arm. Her shoulders slumped. "I'm so glad. I w-wanted you to be…" Her chin quivered.

Shit.

"I just want you and Hindley to be happy," she said.

Her voice trembled as much as her hand on my arm. An unsure, humbled Geneva was a sight to see.

"We are." I patted Geneva's hand.

Her blue eyes rolled up to meet mine. Tears brimmed and sparkled from the lights all around us.

"We *are* happy, Geneva." I said.

"Good." She withdrew her hand and brushed away her tears.

"Oh, Geneva." Hindley sighed. "The reception, the ceremony, they've both been incredible. I don't know how to thank you."

I did.

"Thanks again, Geneva." I slid my hand around her shoulders and gave her a small hug. Surprisingly the need to hurl had disappeared.

Geneva's shoulders shook as she wrapped her arms around my waist. She buried her face into my suit jacket. "I'm so sorry, Rory," she whispered.

Geneva had offered words of apology to me a million times before, but this time the plea sounded different. Her fervent confession pierced my hardened heart. Her remorse was genuine. I'd done a lot of shit things in my life. Who was I to judge? It was time to let go and move on.

"I know you are," I whispered, squeezing her tight. "I'm sorry too."

She leaned back and stared at me, her brow wrinkled and her face glistening with tears as she shook her head.

"No, no, Rory. You have nothing—"

"Yes, I do." I held up a hand to silence her.

She nodded once. "Thank you, Rory." Geneva pressed her cheek into my chest and squeezed.

And with one small gesture, Geneva Barton and I started over. Our relationship would still take time, but it was a start.

Geneva released me. "Well, if you guys are ready," she smiled and clapped her hands, "I think your guests want to come inside. I just wanted you two to see it first."

My eyes surveyed the area one last time as it stood void of people mingling about.

"The place looks like a fairyland," Hindley said, grasping Geneva and pulling her into a tight embrace. "Thank you, Geneva."

Geneva pulled away from Hindley and dabbed at her eyes. "Okay, you guys stay here and I'll announce to everyone they can come in now." Geneva's red-rimmed eyes darted between Hindley and me. "I'm so happy for you both." Without another word, she scurried away.

I watched Geneva trail out of the area. "Well, blow my dick with a rubber hose."

"Rory," Hindley hit my chest.

I grabbed her wrist as she pulled away, yanking her toward me.

"Oh, Mrs. Gregor," I chuckled, "you've done a very bad thing, hitting your husband."

She drew in a quick breath. "Oh my god," she squealed then slapped her hand over her mouth.

"What?" My head darted around us as if a gang of mobsters threatened to attack.

"You said, *Mrs. Gregor*." Her hand slid inside my jacket. "*I'm* Mrs. Gregor now."

Her eyes rolled up to meet mine. Her delicious pink lips spread wide with a smile brighter than the stars overhead. She was a goddess among mortals.

"And *you're* my husband," she sighed as she pressed her hand over my heart.

The heat from her palm raced through my veins like an IV drug. Our hearts beat in sync and one word rang out with the rhythm. Love. God, I sounded like a sappy son of a bitch, but Hindley brought out my softer side. My *wife*. My wife.

"Yeah I am," I answered. "I'm your husband. And according to the judge you have to obey me."

"I do not." She swatted at me again.

I caught her hand and wrapped her arm around my waist, tugging her in close to me. I leaned in and whispered in her ear, "You keep hitting me and I'll tie you up and *make* you obey me."

"You think so, huh?" She giggled.

"Oh, I know so." I kissed the shell of her ear.

She trembled in my arms.

I felt powerful, but in a good way.

She stood tall and pressed her lips against my cheek then moved closer to my ear. "I'm not wearing anything under my dress," she whispered.

Fuck! My dick throbbed and pressed painfully against my zipper.

"Except a garter belt and stockings." She moved lower and licked my neck. "And tonight I'm going to make you beg me to fuck *you*, Mr. Gregor."

Yeah, that did it. My eyes rolled back in my head and I damn near collapsed just thinking of Hindley in nothing but garters, shaking her round ass for me while my hands molded to her breasts and twisted—

"Rory, Hindley, the ceremony was magical." Hindley's mother's voice rang through the area.

My chubby fled, thanks to Caroline. I blew out a sigh of relief.

"This is not over, *Mrs.* Gregor," I growled in Hindley's ear.

Hindley's hand rubbed over my fly. "Oh, I hope not, my beautiful husband," she whispered then turned to face her mother, covering my hard on with her ass.

Fuck, what this girl did to me. I adjusted myself behind Hindley's back. The little sex nymph had me in her vise grip. And I loved it. But I *would* get her back. Tonight.

I kissed her bare shoulder as her family made their way toward us. "Payback's a bitch, Mrs. Gregor," I murmured against her skin.

"I'm counting on it, Mr. Gregor." She pressed her ass into my dick. "I'm *so* counting on it."

Family and friends flocked the reception area, showering us with hugs and kisses and compliments.

"I'm so proud of you, Rory." Kara kissed my cheek and squeezed my shoulders. She'd been the only mother I'd had, until I met Sarah.

"You're not upset, are you?" I asked Kara.

"Why would I be upset with you, sweetie? You know I love Hindley, I couldn't be happier, or more proud of you."

"No," I chuckled, "I meant, are you upset because I invited Sarah?"

"Oh, heavens no, Rory. Have you ever known me to be so silly?"

I shook my head at the truth. Kara was one of the strongest women I knew, confident in ways that still boggled me. She didn't break under pressure, and she sure as hell had never been threatened, not even by a homeless, delinquent skateboarder she found in the middle of a park one day.

"Rory, I think it's wonderful you've connected with someone from your past. Sarah seems like a lovely woman."

We both turned and gazed at Sarah who was busy mingling with the crowd.

"And it seems as if she doesn't know a stranger," Kara said. "Much like someone else I know."

"Me?" I laughed, gazing down at my surrogate mother, the woman who had showered me with unconditional love.

"Yes, you, silly." She swatted my arm. "You look so handsome, Rory. Sarah says you look just like your father."

I swallowed a lump in my throat.

"He would be so proud of you, of the man you've become."

"You really think so?" My voice cracked with emotion.

"Rory," she smiled, "I *know* so. Jack and I are so happy for you. We're proud you went to Colorado and confronted your mom. In the process you found your father, and Sarah too. And you got closure with Shelly. Your sister loved you, fiercely, sweetheart, just like we all do. Apparently it's the only way a Gregor knows how to love."

I laughed and nodded, letting her words of praise and love wash over me. I *had* come a long way since Kara had found me destitute and alone at sixteen.

"And now you're opening the facility in Shelly's memory." Kara drew in a deep breath and smoothed the lapel of my jacket with her palm. "Yes, Rory, your father and your sister would be *so* proud of you. Just like I am."

She reached up to kiss my cheek. I bent over, knowing she'd never reach me on her own.

"I love you, Rory. Always have."

"Always will?"

She laughed and nodded.

"I love you too, Kara. I would never be here without your love and support, you know that, right?"

Her smile spread wide as tears glistened in her eyes. "You would have found a way, Rory. We just gave you a straighter path. The hard work was all you."

We stared at each other in mutual admiration.

"Ladies and gentlemen," a voice boomed over the speakers. "At this time I'd like to welcome the bride and groom to the dance floor."

"Oh, shit," I whispered. I'd completely forgotten about this part of the reception. My stomach twisted in fear.

"What's wrong?" Kara asked as she glanced around the area.

"It's time for the first dance," the DJ announced.

First dance. Fuck! When Hindley and I had met with the DJ a few weeks earlier to discuss the songs we wanted at the reception, he'd talked about the dreaded "first dance," but I hadn't thought much more about it. Until now.

I'd asked him to keep the song a secret from Hindley. I knew she'd expect "I Won't Give Up," by Jason Mraz. It had become our anthem. But for our first dance I'd chosen "This I Promise You." A boy band from a decade ago made it popular but my version was an acoustic mix by Anthem Lights.

I loved the lyrics. The song reminded me of our love story, one filled with battles and losses, but hope and strength too. Tonight I would take Hindley in my arms and give her the promise of forever with a single vow.

I just prayed my legs wouldn't fail me or my feet trip Hindley on the floor.

"You'll be fine, sweetheart." Kara released me. "Go find your bride."

The crowd parted, revealing my wife.

Wife. Yeah, I liked the sound of that. I even knew how to spell it. I stopped just short of her and held out my hand.

Hindley placed hers in mine. "I forgot about our song."

Love and adoration glimmered in her eyes.

"What did you pick?" she asked. "You never told me."

The piano and guitar solo of the song strummed through the speakers as I led her up the two steps to the patio-turned-dance-floor.

"Just listen to the words, baby," I whispered in her ear as I pulled her close to my body.

She sighed and leaned into me.

My footwork wasn't professional, but I managed to stay upright and not step on Hindley's toes. "Till the day my life is through," I sang into her hair, "this I promise you."

"Oh, Rory." Hindley hiccupped a sob. She moved to raise her head from my chest but I held her firm against me.

If I saw her eyes brimming with tears now, I knew mine would follow. Instead, I closed my eyes and sang along with the song as I nestled into her bare shoulder. "Our forever has now begun," I hummed. I drew in a deep breath and inhaled the scent of *my* forever. My Drunk Girl.

CHAPTER 21

RORY

THE DELICIOUS MEAL they'd served earlier sat like a rock in my stomach. I was two hours into our fucking reception and my dick throbbed like it'd been beaten with a sledge hammer. All I could think about was ripping Hindley's dress off and pounding my dick so far inside her she wouldn't walk straight for a week.

Okay, that wasn't the most loving or romantic thought, but Christ, she was my *wife* now. She was mine and I wanted her. Now.

Every time I even glanced at her, I was hard as stone. I swore twice and thought about running inside to lope my mule just to ease the pressure.

"Something bothering you?" Hindley leaned over my lap. Her hand gripped my thigh. She moved higher, precariously close to my manhood.

I drew in a sharp breath. "Hindley," I growled through gritted teeth. My eyes roamed over the mass of guests.

"What?" she whispered in my ear.

"You *know* what." I grasped her hand and slid it from my thigh. Shit! What I really wanted to do was slide her fingers around my dick. Or better yet, scoot back, wrap my hand around her neck and lead her sweet little mouth to my cock. *She's your wife dude! Not cool.*

"Sorry," she giggled and leaned back in her chair.

I raised a brow. "No, you're not." I bent over and kissed her shoulder, trailing my lips up to her ear. "But trust me, sweetheart, you're gonna be sorry."

She shivered.

I leaned back, proud of the reaction I'd prompted.

Hindley's eyes were wide in anticipation. A slow smirk lifted one side of her plump lips. She wanted to say more but my warning glare stopped her. She would pay for making my dick so hard tonight. And for making me wait two months to touch her.

I discreetly trailed my tongue up her neck and whispered in her ear. "I may not even let you come at all tonight if you keep this shit up."

Her body went ram rod stiff, like my dick. Good. Rory—one. My new bride—a bazillion.

"Everyone, if I could have your attention." Paul's words rang through the crowd.

His voice was like pouring ice cold water on my raging hard on. *Thank you, Paul.*

Hindley and I sat upright straight as if we'd been caught doing something sordid. I was reminded of the first time I met Paul at Geneva's wedding reception.

"I'm Paul Barton, Hindley's father," Paul announced into the microphone as he stood on the patio.

His face beamed. All the lights surrounding us could have flickered out and his smile still would have lit the area. I turned and stared at my bride.

Hindley's face shined with just as much adoration. She had a father. And maybe one day, if we were lucky, I'd *be* a father too. A *good* father.

"My wife Caroline and I would like to welcome you to our

home," Paul continued, "and to the wedding reception of our daughter and now son-in-law, Rory."

Son-in-law. More like son-of-a-bitch if he knew what I had planned for his naughty daughter tonight.

"Caroline and I are both so happy to welcome our new son into our family." Paul smiled at me.

Son. That had a nice ring to it.

"Although, I have to admit, the first time I met Rory, I was pretty rough on him." Paul chuckled.

Oh, shit, please don't go there.

"I told my wife that night there was something special about Rory. I'd never seen Hindley so happy."

What? I glanced at Hindley, but her blank expression told me she was just as surprised at Paul's admission.

"I'm not sure if I would have said it would lead to this." Paul swept his hand around the area. "But somewhere deep inside, I knew the first night I met him, Rory Gregor would protect Hindley and keep her safe. That's how they met. Or so I'm told."

Paul's blue eyes fell on me and held my gaze, but he held no animosity. He was truly thankful.

Hindley reached over and grabbed my hand, giving it a tight squeeze.

I glanced at her.

Her eyes brimmed with tears as she shared the same affections with me her father did.

"Before I let her go though, I'd like to have one more dance," Paul said. "A father daughter dance, if she'll have me." Paul held his hand out toward Hindley.

"Of course," she spoke softly, her voice hoarse with emotion.

I slid my chair out and helped Hindley from hers. I walked with her toward the steps, holding her hand out for Paul.

Paul walked down the stairs to grab her hand, but misstepped. His ankle buckled and the full weight of his body fell on me, causing me to stumble backward and fall flat on my ass with Paul Barton, my new father-in-law, crumpled on top of me.

He grasped his ankle and moaned in pain.

People fussed and a few shouted.

I worked my legs underneath me and pushed up with my free hand as I helped Paul stand with my other.

"Oh my God, Dad." Hindley rushed to him. "Are you all right?"

Paul clutched my shoulder, and despite his nod to Hindley, his grip told me he was in pain.

"Is it your ankle?" I leaned in and whispered.

"I think so." He gritted out.

"Oh, Paul, sweetheart." Caroline ran up beside him.

"Daddy, are you okay?" Geneva joined the throng of people surrounding us.

"Back up and let me get him into a chair." My voice rang sterner than I'd intended, but Paul was in pain and my concern was for him, not in comforting others.

Jack appeared and grabbed Paul's other arm. "Here." He walked us to a chair he'd dragged close. "Sit down and I'll take a look at it."

Jack had been a firefighter and paramedic at one time. Funny, I'd never realized how much Jack was like my birth father.

Jack lifted Paul's pants leg. "It's already swollen. Grab me a towel full of ice, would you." Jack pointed toward a waiter.

"I'm fine." Paul pushed up in his chair.

"No, you're not." Caroline said. "Now stay in that chair and let Jack look at your ankle."

"Hindley," Paul called out.

"I'm here." She knelt beside him, her eyes wide with worry.

"I'm so sorry, sweetheart, I ruined your reception."

"You didn't ruin it." She smiled and her love for him poured out with every syllable. "This has been the most spectacular day of my life."

"Until now." He laughed and nodded toward his leg.

"We may need to get you to the hospital for X-rays," Jack said, "to make sure your ankle isn't broken."

"I am *not* going to the hospital." Paul's voice rang with vehemence, his power shaking everyone to the core.

You did *not* fuck with Paul Barton, even if pain was etched all over his stern face.

"I want to dance with my daughter." He clutched my shoulder and attempted to stand but winced with the motion.

"Dad, please," Hindley begged. "We can dance later. Right now I'm worried about you."

Paul plopped back into his seat with a huff. "Fine," he sighed. "Just let me prop it up and put some ice on it. I'll be good to go in twenty minutes."

Everyone surrounding him exchanged knowing glances. If the pain etched on his face was any indicator, Paul Barton would be flat on his ass for a while.

"Can they at least play your song?" Paul glanced up at Hindley. "Maybe you and Rory can dance."

"No way," I said, waving my hands. "That song is for you and Hindley. You save it, Paul and I promise one day you'll have your dance with Hindley." I grabbed his shoulder. I wasn't sure how the fuck I would keep my promise but I would. I would give Paul his special moment with Hindley. One day.

"Thanks, son." Paul laid his hand over mine and patted it. "Thanks." He smiled through his grimace.

"Here's the ice," a waiter said. "I also brought an Ace bandage to wrap your ankle. And some ibuprofen, sir." He handed the bandage and ice to Jack then opened his palm to Paul.

"Thank you." Paul took the three orange pills and threw them into his mouth.

"Here." Caroline pushed a glass of water in his face.

"Thanks, sweetheart." He winked at her.

She smiled but concern marred her face.

"I'm really sorry, Caroline." Paul grasped Caroline's hand. "I know you and the girls worked so hard to make this day special."

"It was beyond special, my love." Caroline knelt and kissed him on the cheek. "And it was all because of you." The two shared a knowing, sexual glance. I wondered if Hindley and I looked like her parents anytime we were close to one another.

Uncomfortable much? Yes! These were my in-laws for fuck's sake. No one wants to imagine their in-laws doing the dirty deed.

Caroline reached for a chair and set it so she and Paul faced one another. She took his hand in hers. "Thank you for giving Hindley and Rory this." She waved her hand around the area.

I moved to squat next to him. "Yeah, Paul. I know I haven't said it enough, but thanks, not just for the wedding but for making me feel a part of your family. For accepting me, warts and all."

"I kind of like your warts." Hindley's voice echoed behind me as her fingers ran through my hair.

Shit, my hard on was back, stiffer than ever. How the hell was it possible to sport a raging boner while kneeling next to your father-in-law? *Not good, man, not good at all.*

"You two kids get going." Paul winked.

Oh, God, he knew what I wanted to do with his daughter. I didn't know whether to vomit or wrap my arms around the man and offer my thanks and praise. Paul was unleashing me like a pit bull from a tethered chain. A salacious smile spread across my face as I stared at my wife. She was mine.

Hindley bit her lower lip and swallowed.

Fuck.

"Everyone," Paul shouted from his chair, "Hindley and Rory are leaving now. Let's go inside the house. There are bubbles in the entry way." He glanced at me. "Could you help an old man inside, Rory?"

I willed my cock-a-saurus rex down to a more manageable size. I couldn't walk beside my father-in-law with a stiffy in my pants.

"I've got him," Leif sidled up to Paul. "You and Hindley go on ahead."

"I want to walk with him," Hindley said.

"Hindley, go on with Rory," Paul said. "I'll be there in a minute, I promise. I won't let you leave without saying good-bye."

Hindley's eyes filled with tears. "You promise?"

Paul nodded. "I promise, sweetheart."

"Come on, sweetie." Caroline grabbed Hindley's arm. "I'll help you change."

"No!" I shouted. Heads snapped and eyes stared at me. "I… uh…I just meant, I want Hindley to stay in her wedding dress because she looks so beautiful."

Lie much? You're a fucking caveman and you want to rip that dress off yourself and see what's underneath. Yeah, that was more the truth but I couldn't say that to her mother.

Hindley smirked and licked her lips.

My cock rocket pulsed and damn near shot off in my pants.

"Yeah, Mom," Hindley said, saving me, "we're leaving in what we have on."

Caroline's eyes darted from her daughter's to mine, then back to Hindley before the same smirk on Paul's face two minutes ago spread wide across her own.

Oh, fuck me, double gag. Now my mother-in-law knew our intentions. I shook my head. Not good, not good at all.

Hindley went to Paul and wrapped her arm around his waist then draped his arm over her shoulder. "Let's go, old man." She laughed.

He leaned over and kissed her temple. "I see no old man here."

"You're right." She smiled. "I only see you, my very handsome, very *young* father."

Tears glistened in Paul's eyes.

"I love you, Dad." Hindley's head fell on Paul's shoulder.

Leif, Paul and Hindley waddled toward the house.

"Here, let me." I grabbed Paul's arm from Leif's shoulder and scooted Leif out of the way as I slid my arm around Paul's waist. My hand clutched Hindley's arm at Paul's back and I squeezed her.

"Thanks, Rory." Paul said. "Seeing as you're Hindley's husband now, I guess it's okay for you to peel your banana and feed it to her tonight, right?" He smirked, reminding me of his earlier words from a year ago.

I coughed and choked on my own saliva.

"Dad!" Hindley slapped Paul's chest.

I stared at the ground. My face burned like fire and I gulped hard.

Paul's body vibrated with deep laughter.

I glanced behind him, avoiding his gaze.

Hindley leaned back and peeked around Paul's shoulders. Her brown eyes sparkled from the candlelight overhead as she stared at my ass. Her gaze caught mine and she waggled her brows and winked. Oh, she was looking forward to tonight as much as I was.

"Banana," I mouthed.

Her face flushed red.

I chuckled. Oh, she was *definitely* gonna eat my banana tonight. And more.

CHAPTER 22

HINDLEY

RORY PULLED the key card from his back pocket and twirled it in his fingers. His eyebrows waggled and his lips curled into that devilish smirk I loved.

Oh, God. My body buzzed with desire.

He waved the card in front of a metal panel next to the hotel room door. A small light glowed green and the lock clicked open.

"Is that a door bell?" I pointed to the round white button just below the key card reader.

He chuckled.

"Oh, wow. I've never been in a hotel room with a door bell," I said.

"Hotel *room*?" Rory shook his head and snorted.

"What?"

Rory depressed the lever and pushed open the heavy door.

I moved to step around him.

A long, lean arm shot out in front of me and grabbed the door-frame to block me. "What do you think you're doing?" he growled.

"Going in to my hotel room, which apparently you think is quite funny." I rolled my eyes.

"Oh, no you don't, Mrs. Gregor. Haven't you ever heard of the bride being *carried* over the threshold?"

"Oh my gosh, I totally forgot." I giggled.

Rory stuffed the key in his coat pocket and bent down. Sliding his arms around my waist and lower legs, he whisked me up into his arms.

"Ahh," I yelped, throwing my hands around his neck.

"Shall we, Mrs. Gregor?"

Rory's blue eyes pierced mine. They were darker tonight and half hooded with passion. Oh, holy hell. A knot of anticipation throbbed in my belly. I held the door open with my foot. "Yes, we shall, Mr. Gregor."

"Your wish is my command, *Mrs. Gregor.*"

His words vibrated through my body like an earthquake. I feared I might spontaneously combust and disintegrate into the atmosphere.

"My wish is your command, huh?" I cocked a brow. Oh, this could be fun.

"Most definitely." He grinned.

Oh, God, his smile. My heart beat wild against my ribs. My knees tingled and my head spun like I'd taken ten shots of tequila. Thank God he was carrying me.

"What do you think?" He slid me down his chest and held on to my hips while I caught my balance.

I smoothed my dress then raised my gaze to study the room. I gasped. "Holy hell, Rory."

"Not so much a *room* is it?" He chuckled.

"This is like a mini-mansion on the forty-seventh floor of downtown Austin."

"They call it a *suite*, Hindley."

I stepped inside. "They should call it the Holy Shit suite."

"I'll put that on our guest comment card when we leave." Rory chuckled and slipped off his suit coat then strolled toward the eight-person dining table. He slung his jacket over the back of a chair as if he lived here.

I gazed over the open expanse of the suite. Floor to ceiling windows covered the facing wall. The lights of downtown Austin glittered beneath us, creating a sultry backdrop. The illuminated city bathed our suite in ambient lighting.

A gray leather semi-circle couch sat in the middle of the living room adorned with coral colored throw pillows of varying shapes and sizes. Two matching coral chairs framed in steel sat across from the couch. They looked more suitable for aesthetics than function. The deep cherry wood stain of the hardwood floors stood in stark contrast to the cream-colored walls.

To the left of the huge foyer was a modern kitchen with granite countertops and state-of-the art appliances. The room was larger than the kitchen in my duplex, but that wasn't saying much.

The suite was an ultra-modern retro sex cave. The space oozed sensuality. The room was breathtaking.

"Over there is a guest bedroom." Rory pointed down the hall-way. A long, cream-colored runner lined the corridor. The walls were darker than the living area and littered with various artwork.

"You haven't seen the best part." Rory slid his large hand into mine and tugged me to the left of the living area.

As we walked through the space, I noticed a gas fireplace blazing against the opposite wall. The flames bathed the suite with an air of opulence and indulgence.

"Rory, this place is amazing." I studied every nook and cranny. "It had to cost a fortune though."

He gazed over his shoulder, his eyes roving over my body. "I spare no expense for my princess."

My panties would have exploded with the deep tenor of his voice, but I wasn't wearing any. Going commando beneath my wedding dress had been Dana's idea, but right now I was wishing I had the extra layer of protection.

Rory led me into the master bedroom.

I stopped to admire the space. Floor to ceiling windows like those in the living area adorned one side of the spacious room. A massive bed butted up to the wall facing us. Bright yellow pillows littered the top of a plush white comforter. The bedding billowed like a cloud and beckoned me. A charcoal gray throw rug lay underneath a black leather bench at the end of the bed.

"You see that?" Rory nodded toward the massive piece of furniture at the foot of the bed. His eyes cut to mine.

I swallowed and nodded.

"I'm going to bend you over that stool, spank your ass for being such a tease today then fuck you thoroughly before the night is over, my love."

I choked on my tongue. "W-what?"

He tugged on my hand, pulling me further into the room. "You think taunting me at my own wedding is funny?" He stopped just inside another threshold.

"What do you mean, taunting?" I asked. My legs wobbled but my body hummed with excitement. I was nervous about his threat but thrilled at the same time. Rory had spanked me before, so his threat wasn't a surprise. The surprise had been in the fact I *liked* his punishments.

Rory pressed against me, his hands glued to his sides. "I mean," he paused, drawing in a deep breath, "you walked down the aisle looking like an angel, that dress clinging to your sexy body, a body I haven't been *allowed* to touch in weeks." His eyes narrowed.

My breathing escalated as I clutched my dress. The wrath of Rory was building.

"Then, you told me you were totally nude underneath. Tsk, tsk, tsk." He shook his head and waved one lone finger in my face.

Oh, shit.

"Then, you put your hand on my thigh and threatened to rub my hard cock right in front of our friends and family."

"I didn't—"

He thrust his hips into me, stealing my words. His erection pressed firmly against the juncture between my thighs. "You're a cock tease, Hindley Gregor." He smiled, his expression devouring me like the Big Bad Wolf.

"Say it again," I whispered. I stroked my palm up the smooth material of his shirt.

His eyes followed the path of my hand as he swallowed. "Say what again?" His voice broke with desire.

"My name. My *new* name." I fluttered my lashes as I gazed at him.

His hand slid around my waist and tugged us flush against one another.

"Hindley Gregor," he growled in my ear.

I sighed and my head fell against his chest. "I love it."

"I love you."

His muffled words brushed over my skin as he kissed my head. He trembled and I knew he was staving off his dominant side, but truthfully, I wasn't so sure I wanted him to.

"Show me the rest of the suite so I can show you something else sweet." I stepped back and waved my hand along my body.

"That will cost you, my beautiful wife."

"I like the sound of that, my gorgeous husband." I smiled up at him.

He skated his fingertips across my bare shoulder.

I shuddered and my eyes fluttered closed.

He traced the back of my neck then wound his fingers into my hair. "I like the sound of that too." He leaned in.

His scent enveloped me, an erotic mix of male desire and brute strength. My head spun and I wobbled.

"And I love these."

My lids lifted.

His eyes focused on my lips as he dipped closer.

"No." I held up my hand. "Let's see the rest of the suite first."

"Fuck the suite." His lips crashed down on mine, his mouth soft yet demanding. Taking charge was Rory's style, and as usual I submitted to his command.

In truth, I loved surrendering to him. I loved relinquishing my power to such a strong man, even if only for a little while.

"Rory," I mumbled against his lips.

"Hmmm?" His mouth vibrated against mine.

I pushed on his chest and ducked under his strong arm, side-stepping his grasp. "Oh my god," I gasped as I stumbled into the adjoining room. I stood dumbfounded in one of the most decadent, provocative, insanely opulent bathrooms I'd ever seen.

"Worth every penny, huh?" Rory stood beside me and rubbed his chin against my bare shoulder.

I couldn't talk, I couldn't move, the space was breathtaking.

The exterior walls were solid glass from floor to ceiling and butted together in the corner, giving you a 180 degree view of the city. A modern style porcelain tub sat in the middle of the room bordered by nothing. The angle of the fixture allowed you to see downtown Austin no matter which way you positioned yourself.

A long double-sink counter with ultra-modern faucets covered the left wall. Across the room a separate vanity table butted up to the windows.

"Look over there." Rory nudged my head.

I followed his gaze and my jaw dropped. Holy shit. In the corner of the room was a free-standing shower with glass walls. Jets and knobs protruded from the far side of the stall.

"Those are called body sprays," Rory purred in my ear. "You control the pressure."

I'm pretty sure I moaned out loud.

Rory chuckled. "Check out the view from inside."

That's when I noticed the real intrinsic beauty of the shower stall. One side was the actual exterior glass wall of the building. You could see the city while you showered.

"What the…"

"I plan to fuck you in that shower, Mrs. Gregor, in front of the whole goddamn city."

"U-uh…" Oh. My. God. My body heated, every nerve cell detonating like synchronized fireworks on the Fourth of July.

Rory loved dirty talk, but this was…so much better. God, the thought of my hands pressed against the glass wall while Rory took me from behind, our eyes gazing out at the lights below. I pressed my thighs together and moaned.

"That's right, baby." He kissed my neck. "Our first night as husband and wife is gonna be so good." He stepped back and slid his hand into mine. "Now come on," he tugged, "you owe me a dance."

"A dance?" I squeaked as he led me out of the bathroom. "What do you mean?"

He stopped in the middle of the large bedroom and turned me to face him. "What I mean is…" He trailed his pointer finger along my jaw line. "You teased me all night long at my own wedding. That's not nice, Hindley." He shook his head and scowled, trailing his finger to my chin and down my neck.

Lower. Please God, move lower.

He paused at my collar bone. His blue eyes met mine and he licked his full lips. "You've made me wait to have sex with you for almost two months so you could reclaim your purity." He rolled his eyes. "Do you know what blue balls look like, Hindley?"

I rolled my lips between my teeth to stifle a laugh.

His eyes flashed dark.

My core throbbed.

"I know you want me just as much as I want you," he whispered, leaning in. "But you'll have to work to get me."

"What?" I stumbled back. "What do you mean?"

"I said, if you want this," he waved his hand along his tall, well-built body, "then I want that." He nodded toward a chair.

"I don't understand."

He stalked behind the purple velvet chair and lifted it with ease, placing it inches away from me in the middle of the room. His hands ran over the smooth material.

Suddenly, I wanted to *be* the stupid chair, I was so envious of his touch.

I swallowed. His torture was my penance. I'd known better than to poke the tiger at our wedding by disclosing I was nude underneath my gown. Rory had been so desperate. And watching his desire for me burn out of control had given me a sense of domination I rarely experienced.

"I want you to dance for me." Rory's voice growled low as his instructions vibrated through the air. He patted the chair. "I'll sit right here and you're going to shake your hot little ass around me until I say stop."

"A *lap dance*? You want a lap dance on your wedding night?"

He nodded. "Umm hmm, and you're going to give it to me as payment for making me rock hard at my own wedding."

I giggled. "Don't guys usually get a lap dance *before* their wedding night?"

He ignored me and walked toward the desk in the corner then fumbled with something on top. The room filled with the sounds of SoMo, one of my favorite singers.

I smiled and shook my head. I'd told Rory many times that SoMo's songs were perfect for erotic dancing. The familiar chords of "Fire" wafted through the room.

Rory skirted around me, his body moving with ease through the bedroom. He stopped in front of the purple chair and slowly sank into the plush cushions. His eyes glazed over with lust as he stared me up and down. He was an animal, waiting to devour me.

My aching flesh burned for his touch.

His long legs stretched out in front of him and crossed at the ankles. His hands lay in his lap and he twiddled his thumbs as if he hadn't a care in the world.

"Well, Mrs. Gregor?" One brow rose. "I'm waiting."

I cocked my head. Okay, two could play this game.

SoMo's song enveloped us like a sex blanket. I would win our game. And the grand prize would be my husband.

I strolled toward him then turned and lifted the skirt of my dress. With the material brushing near the crest of my ass, I backed up until I was straddling his legs then glanced over my bare shoulder. "Could you unzip me? Please." I purred, my voice low and husky. Hell, I was turning *myself* on.

His eyes flashed wide and his Adam's apple bobbed.

Yes! Score one point for me.

I sank down almost to his lap, careful not to touch any part of him.

His fingers brushed my back.

Oh, shit. A tingle of desire sparked between my legs and my body flexed taut.

He slid my zipper down, his thumb trailing a path along my back, lighting me on fire.

The game was officially tied.

Pull it together, girl. Concentrate, focus. Win.

The zipper stopped just above the crook of my ass. I stood and turned to face him, my legs readjusting to straddle his. I leaned forward and braced my hands on the arms of the chair. The front of my dress sagged low and teased him with a glimpse of my chest.

Rory's eyes slid down to my almost bared breasts.

I rubbed my cheek against his and whispered in his ear. "No touching the dancer, Mr. Gregor."

He chuckled.

The vibrations of his laugh shot a chill down my spine that curled my toes. I sucked in a deep breath and worked to compose myself. Instead, I inhaled his delicious scent. Shit! Rory wasn't the only one suffering from my vow of celibacy.

I backed up then turned, my back facing him again, and slowly let my dress slip down, revealing my ivory-laced garter, sans undergarments. I glanced over my shoulder.

Rory's hands white knuckled the arms of the chair and he stiffened, his feet tucked underneath him.

The cocky man from earlier was gone. I'd left him a trembling, horny mess. *Two points for Mrs. Gregor.* I stifled a giggle.

Balancing on my high heels, I gyrated my hips to the rhythm of the music and slinked to the ground. When my ass hit the heels of my shoes, I released the dress and watched the material pool at my feet

My fingers worked through my hair and released the pins holding it in place. The curly locks tumbled down my back as I shook my head. Rolling my hips to the sensual notes of the song, I rose.

Rory's ragged breathing echoed through the room. *Three points go to, Mrs. Gregor.*

My fingers trailed up my body and across my chest, caressing my neck as they moved higher. I dug my fingers into my thick hair and swept the curls high, exposing my back as I swayed my bare ass to the beat of the erotic music.

Rory growled.

I glanced over my shoulder.

His chest heaved as he gulped air. His body was taut and poised to attack. I feared he may pounce on me at any minute.

I released my hair and palmed my breasts, gazing at the shimmering crystals between my legs. Apprehension flooded my mind. Would he like my surprise? Would he laugh? Dana had assured me the jewels would drive Rory insane.

I stepped out of my wedding dress and turned to face him, my hips twisting with SoMo's sensual song. "Devil on a mission," I mouthed the words.

"Fuuuck," Rory moaned.

His single word echoed in the dark room then faded.

I stepped closer to him.

His eyes focused on the sparkling patch between my legs. "What the hell is that?"

The flat tone of his voice scared me. "You don't like it?" I palmed my breasts and curled my shoulders in.

"Oh," he rumbled, "I like it." His plump lips tipped up into a smile as he reached out to touch the crystals.

Thank God, he liked it. I sighed in relief. I covered my breasts with one arm and waggled a finger in his face as I side-stepped his grasp. "No, no, remember the rules, Mr. Gregor."

"Fuck the rules!" He lurched from the chair.

I stumbled back, almost tripping over my wedding dress.

Rory's hands slid around my waist and caught me.

Score one point for Mr. Gregor.

His rough hands slid under my bare ass, and lifted me.

I wrapped my legs around his waist.

The song transitioned to SoMo's, "Show Off."

"God, could there be a more perfect song for the way I feel about you?" Rory squeezed my thighs.

"So are we gonna bump and grind?" I drove my hips into his, mimicking the lyrics.

He strode toward the massive bed. "Eventually." He dropped me on the edge.

"Eventually? What does that mean?"

He ignored my question and knelt, spreading my legs wide as he trailed his fingers along my inner thighs.

I shuddered as goose bumps spread across my skin.

"So, can I touch the dancer now?" He raised a brow and ran his tongue over his lower lip then bit it with his teeth.

I gulped.

Ten points go to Mr. Gregor.

I surrendered. "Yes," I whispered.

Rory's fingers slipped behind my calves as he skimmed his fingers up my silk stockings. His eyes rolled up to meet mine. "Beg me," he whispered.

"W-what?"

"Beg me."

"Why?" I cocked my head.

"Because you're a tease. And now it's *my* turn to tease *you*."

Oh, shit. I was in trouble, big time. I'd been playing with fire when I teased Rory at the wedding, but I couldn't help it. He'd looked so desperate. Now I wished I hadn't poked the panther. He would make me pay. I would love his punishment—if I survived it.

His hands worked higher until his thumbs skimmed over the bare skin of my thighs just above my stockings. "I love this." He lifted the straps of my garter belt and slid his hands higher.

Oh, holy hell, his hands felt good.

"But I *really* like this." His fingers skimmed over the crystals spread between my legs.

His light touch tickled me. I squirmed and giggled.

"What is it?" His lids lifted and his blue gaze locked on mine.

My heart stopped. God, he was beautiful—strong jaw, full lips, thick lashes. I was the luckiest girl alive.

"It's called vajazzling." My face washed red and I questioned Dana's advice. My gaze darted to the window.

"What's wrong?" He stroked the crystals.

I sucked in a breath. "I just wasn't sure you'd like the jewels."

He chuckled.

I turned to stare.

His salacious grin confirmed his thoughts. Vajazzle was va-good.

His body shifted and settled between my legs then his hands slid under my hips. "I like your vajazzled va-jay-jay. A lot." His breath washed over my bare skin below the crystals.

"Oh, God," I groaned.

"Are they edible?"

"What? No!" I bolted up. "They're Swarovski crystals."

"And?" His tongue slid out between his lips.

"It's for aesthetics, Rory. If you eat one, you might choke."

"Oh, trust me, my beautiful wife, it's not these crystals I want to eat."

Fuck. My body fell back onto the feathery comforter and my hands clutched the silky material.

"But first," he said.

Cool air brushed over my skin. I pushed up on my elbows.

Rory sat back on his heels and unbuttoned the cuffs at his wrists as if he had all the time in the world. His lips curved in a devilish smirk.

He'd left me a quivering mess with my hoo-hah spread eagle in front of him.

"But what?" I licked my dry lips.

"Well…"

His eyes twinkled with mischief.

Oh, God, here came my punishment. My skin burned with desire and anticipation. I worked my hips closer to the edge of the bed.

"Someone wants what I have?" Rory chuckled. He stared at my vajazzled mid-section like a starved man.

"You want what I have too." I wiggled my hips. My sultry, raspy voice surprised me. I cocked an eyebrow and stared at him. *Uh, I thought we agreed, poking the bear was dangerous.* I was horny as hell and didn't care. I needed the bear to attack.

His tongue slid across his plump lips as a slow smile curved the corners of his delectable mouth.

I arched my back and thrust my breasts higher. The crystals covering the edges of my nipples shimmered in the ambient light from the window.

"You're right about that, Mrs. Gregor." Rory nodded and his hands moved to the top of his shirt. He undid each button, slowly, seductively.

My heart hammered with expectation.

The song in the room switched to SoMo's "Back to the Start." The words rang true for me. I wanted Rory, heart and soul. I needed him with a desperation that scared me and I feared I may spontaneously combust without his touch.

Rory peeled open his shirt, exposing his chiseled chest then slid the silky material off his shoulders and down his muscular arms, tossing it to the floor. His hips gyrated to the beat of the song. God, with those moves he could be a stripper for Thunder from Down Under.

I roamed my hungry eyes over his sculpted body and stared at his strong arms. They would keep me safe for the rest of my life. Tears burned my eyes and threatened to pool. I slammed them closed. What the fuck? Do. Not. Cry.

"Hindley?"

My eyes fluttered open.

Rory leaned over me. "What's wrong, baby?"

My hands ran over the contours of his arms and up his neck until I cupped his face. "I just don't know how I got so lucky." I meant every word.

He cocked a brow and twisted his lips. "Are you trying to get out of your punishment?"

I laughed and shook my head. "No."

"You like being punished?"

"I like *your* punishments." I smiled.

"And I love disciplining my Drunk Girl when she's been oh, so bad." He pecked my lips and stood, unfastening his belt.

I moaned, craving the sting of his strap.

"No, not that kind of punishment tonight."

I pouted.

He chuckled and lowered his zipper then slipped his suit pants down his toned thighs.

I pushed up to my elbows and waited with anticipation to see what lay underneath.

He stepped out of the pants and stood with his feet planted apart, hands fisted on his hips like he was Superman.

I covered my mouth and burst into laughter.

"A man doesn't really like to be laughed at on his wedding night when he's standing half-naked in front of his bride." Rory smirked.

I nodded toward his underwear. "Then a man shouldn't shop in the girls' department and buy thong Hello Kitty panties meant for women." I shook with laughter at his choice of underwear.

"What?" He shifted his feet and stared down at his crotch. "These are *guys'* underwear, and they're not thongs, they're boxer *briefs*. But the largest size they had was medium, and as you can see," he thrust his hips toward me, "I'm much bigger than medium."

Hello Kitty's face contorted with his movement.

"Her nose is growing." I pointed and giggled.

His brow pinched and his arms crossed across his chest.

"Ooops. Sorry," I whispered, slapping my hand over my mouth again.

"Mrs. Gregor, what am I going to do with you?" He clicked his tongue and shook his head as he stepped closer.

I gulped.

"You don't like my Hello Kitty?" He slipped his hands behind his head, flexing his arms and chest. His hips rolled with the music.

"I love your Hello Kitty. I just want your Hello Kitty in *my* hello kitty." I grinned.

Rory waggled his brows and thrust his hips back and forth.

"Do you buy Hello Kitty stuff in bulk?" I smirked.

His brow furrowed. "What do you mean?"

I held up my hand. My charm bracelet dangled on my wrist. Rory had given me the piece of jewelry the night he'd proposed, and since then, he'd filled the bracelet with more charms. I tugged on the trinket he'd given me last night at the rehearsal dinner. "Where did you get this one?"

Instead of the normal pink accessories, Hello Kitty wore a blue dress with a blue flower in her hair. Her hands gripped a blue lock.

"What?" He frowned and rubbed his chin.

"What's up with all the blue?"

He snorted. "You locked up my balls for two months with your vow of celibacy." He glanced down at his crotch. "They're pretty blue right now."

I bit my cheek to stifle a laugh.

He shrugged. "They have a Hello Kitty store in the mall." His lips curled up and he waggled his brow. "And there's always the internet."

I shook my head and giggled. Life with Rory Gregor would never be boring.

He sank down to his knees and spread my legs. "You know, the more you sass me, the more I'll punish you."

My grin fell. Oh, shit. My legs trembled in his hands.

"That's better." He smirked. "Now it's time for me to reintroduce myself to my wife's hello kitty. It's been a while." His head sank lower.

I rolled my eyes. "God, Rory, it's only been—" The words were sucked from my mouth when his tongue swiped across my sensitive skin. Oh, good Lord, the man was lethal with his tongue. "Ahhh," I moaned. My back arched as his tongue played me like a musical genius.

"Mmmm." His voice vibrated against my body as his mouth worked me to a fevered frenzy.

"Oh, Rory," I panted, my hips grinding into his face. My release wouldn't take long. I hadn't had Rory's body against mine for weeks.

What the hell had I been thinking, swearing off sex for two months?

"Oh, shit!" My breathy moans echoed through the room. I squeezed my eyes tight and gripped the comforter. I was so close. My impending orgasm burned through my veins.

Cool air suddenly wafted between my legs and the fire was gone. What the hell? My chest heaved as I struggled for air and my hips spasmed of their own accord.

Then it hit me. *Punishment.*

"It's not nice to tease, is it Mrs. Gregor?"

I opened one eyelid, barely able to breathe let alone move my body.

Rory sat back on his heels, his arms crossed over his bare chest, one brow cocked high. The evidence of my desire covered his mouth.

I wanted him. I wanted the orgasm he held captive. But more than anything, I wanted to win this game. I wanted to regain control, even if only for a brief moment.

Drawing a deep breath, I steeled my resolve and pushed down my need to grab his face and shove it back between my vajazzled va-jay-jay.

I pushed up on my elbows and shook my head, shimmying my shoulders. My hair tumbled over my jeweled nipples as I shimmied my shoulders to the beat of the music, my breasts swaying in the air. "No it's not nice to tease, Mr. Gregor," I whispered, puckering my lips.

His eyes flitted from my mouth to each breast. His nostrils flared and the muscles in his neck flexed.

Yes! He was losing control.

He jerked up onto his knees. His Adam's apple bobbed and his jaw clenched.

One point, Mrs. Gregor.

"Yeah, you're absolutely right," I pouted and stuck out my bottom lip as I tilted my head. I drew in a deep breath, jutting my breasts higher for his perusal. "I guess I shouldn't expect anything tonight since I've been so bad." I rolled over to my hands and knees, smirking to myself as I crawled up the bed. I pushed my ass high in the air, presenting him with all my lady parts as I pulled back the thick comforter.

He growled like a rabid dog about to attack.

His bark was worse than his bite, but it still scared me. I didn't dare steal a glance back.

Suddenly, his body crashed on top of mine.

"Ahh!" I yelped.

His chest hair rubbed against the skin of my back. His hard on caressed my ass.

I was in heaven.

Rory drew my hands over my head and interlaced our fingers.

I gazed up at our hands, mesmerized by our wedding bands now lying side by side.

SoMo's song switched to "We Can Make Love." God, SoMo's album was the perfect wedding night mix.

I glanced over my shoulder.

Rory swept tender kisses across my skin.

"Truce?" I asked.

"What?" He pulled away.

"No more punishments for teasing?"

"Oh, I don't think so, Mrs. Gregor." His smug expression warned of pleasure *and* pain.

I squeezed my knees. My vajazzled Swarovski crystals melted

with the heat of his voice. "What about for now, Mr. Gregor? Can we have a truce just for a little bit?"

He pushed onto his knees and flipped me over, pressing his thighs against my hips. His hands slid over my shoulders and into my hair, gripping it as his thumbs brushed against my cheeks.

The love in his eyes took my breath away.

"So what will it be, my gorgeous husband?" I asked.

He frowned and tilted his head, his brows knitting together. "What will *what* be?"

He was clueless, and adorable. I wanted to make a Baby Rory with him right now, but we needed time together as husband and wife, just the two of us, before creating a family together.

I nodded toward the sound system. "SoMo. We can make love," I paused for effect, singing the lyrics. "Or we can just *fuck*." I popped out the word with a clack of my tongue, repeating SoMo's words.

Rory shook his head. "Oh, Hindley." His voice vibrated with my name, his deep blue eyes boring through me.

I clenched my legs tight to stave off the orgasm he'd left me hanging on earlier.

"I love you, Hindley Gregor." He leaned down and fastened his lips to mine.

His tender kiss possessed me, body and soul. He didn't press for more. His caress was meant to speak words of love and adoration.

He pulled back. "I don't know why you said yes to me," his eyes darted between mine, "but I'll always be eternally grateful that you did." His gaze pierced mine. "I'll live my life trying to be the man you deserve, Hindley Gregor."

Holy hell, my brassy, ballsy, foul-mouthed extreme sports athlete jock just spoke the most romantic words ever uttered. *I* was the lucky one. "You already are the man I deserve, Rory Gregor. The man I want, for the rest of my life," I whispered.

He smiled. "We have a lifetime to *fuck*, sweetheart." He ground his hips into mine.

Okay, there was my crass, foul-mouthed husband.

Rory slid off the bed.

I moaned in disappointment.

His thumbs sunk into the waistband of his Hello Kitty underwear.

I bit my lip to stave off a giggle.

The underwear tumbled to the floor. All thoughts of laughter evaporated as I stared at the beautiful man standing naked before me, so brave and secure in his own skin. I hoped to be like him one day.

Rory crawled on top of me and spread my legs wide with his knee. "Tonight I want to *make love* to you, Hindley, make love to my wife, for the first time." His brows rose. "Okay?"

Like he had to ask. "Okay," I whimpered.

"Beg me."

I didn't hesitate. "Please, Rory. Please make love to me. I want you."

His lips spread wide in a victorious smile.

Game, set, match goes to Mr. Gregor. He'd won our wedding night battle, but I was the real victor.

He pressed against me, the length of him slowly filling me. His hips moved with the rhythm of the music.

"Thank you," I sighed as I wrapped my legs and arms around his body, drawing him in deeper.

"For what, baby?" He rose on his forearms and gazed down at me.

I rubbed at the frown line between his brows. "For being as fucked up as me, and for loving me anyway."

He chuckled and pulsated inside me, his face washing with lust and desire. "I love you *because* you're fucked up," he smiled. "Peas, remember?"

"Peas," I smirked.

His hand slipped under my hips, lifting me until his body rocked against the spot that had me seeing stars. With a few more strokes of his hips, my world flashed and shattered.

Rory's arms held me tight as I rode out the waves of pleasure and fell back to earth. He thrust harder, his pace almost frantic as his body trembled and spilled inside me, marking me as part of him. My Skater Boy. Forever.

CHAPTER 23

HINDLEY

An arm snaked around my waist as I surveyed the crowded room. I gazed down at Kara who stood next to me and I slid an arm around her shoulder.

She drew in a deep breath and sighed. "I'm so proud of him." Her voice choked as her gaze locked on Rory.

Rory circulated the room, shaking hands and greeting guests who'd arrived for the grand opening of Shelly's Hang Out.

Kara's eyes danced with motherly affection.

I stared at my husband. *Husband.* "I'm proud of him too." I hugged her tight.

"I'm proud of you too, Hindley." Kara squeezed my waist and stared at me.

"Why?" My eyes narrowed. "This was Rory's idea, his brain child. I mean, I helped with the legal stuff, but the concept and inception was all him."

"Hindley," she chuckled, "do you really think Rory would have done *any* of this without you?"

I considered Kara's question. Would he? "I don't know, maybe. Hopefully."

"I've known Rory for ten years. I tried to help him learn to read so many times, but something just didn't click. And then you came into his life and suddenly…"

"It clicked?" I asked.

She nodded.

"But it was Rory who did all the hard work."

"It was *your* faith in him, your encouragement and belief he *could* do it that gave him the confidence to try again."

Warmth spread through my body from her compliment. "I always knew he would do great things." I studied Rory.

As if hearing my words, his head popped up from the crowd and his eyes found mine. His full lips curled into a devilish smile, lighting my insides on fire. Even standing in a crowded room filled with friends, family, colleagues and guests, my stomach still fluttered with anticipation from his sultry gaze.

"Hindley?" Kara shook me.

"Oh, sorry, what?" How long had she been talking to me? Anytime Rory stared at me with his seductive gaze I lost all train of thought. I tore my attention away from Rory and focused on Kara.

"How was the Maldives?" She smirked.

Oh, the honeymoon, she's asking about the honeymoon.

"Did you know he was renting an *entire* island for our honeymoon?" I tilted my head and stared at Kara.

She laughed and nodded.

"Who *does* that?" I squeaked. "I mean I loved every minute on our private island in the middle of the Indian Ocean, but renting an entire island for a week? That seems over the top, even for Rory Gregor."

With the new trial and our wedding so close together, the media had rekindled our story from last year. The press had wanted the inside scoop. We'd given exclusive rights to television host, Paloma Monroe, since she'd been so kind to Rory in her interview months ago when news of Rory's illiteracy and our relationship broke.

We'd shared our wedding photos with her and did a brief interview together, mainly to showcase Shelly's Hang Out in hopes of securing more sponsors and donors. But other than Paloma, we'd been closed off to the public about everything. Having our own private island to escape to for our honeymoon had been a Godsend.

"When have you ever known Rory to do anything halfway?" Kara tilted her head and smirked.

I laughed. "Yeah, I guess you're right."

"I've heard the Maldive Islands are gorgeous."

"Well, I don't know about *all* the islands, but ours was breathtaking. We had a huge house on the shore and a cabana about a hundred yards out in the ocean."

"Oh, wow!" Kara whistled. "No expense spared for his new bride."

"Our trip was definitely over the top." I shook my head as images of our sexcapades in the Maldives raced through my mind. Rory had made sure all our play toys arrived at the house. It was a wonder I could walk straight, the man and I had done so much kinky shit. But I'd loved our honeymoon. And I loved him.

"Everyone, may I have your attention."

Kara and I followed the sound of the female voice. Dora Rodriguez was the facility's executive director, a long-time educator who also had extensive experience with non-profit organizations. She'd seemed like a natural fit for the position when the board had interviewed her.

Rory and I both had underestimated the amount of work involved in getting Shelly's Hang Out up and running. Thank God for Dora's vast experience and knowledge.

I gazed out over the crowd of neighborhood kids, their parents, city leaders and other extreme sports professionals packed into the facility and I realized all the hard work had been worth the effort.

"Please, everyone, have a seat." Dora waved her hands in the air.

The kids in front sat on the floor while the adults sat quietly in the rows of chairs we'd set up earlier.

"I can't believe it's actually happening." Leif bumped my shoulder. "Hi, Mom." He leaned across me and pecked Kara on the cheek.

"Hi, baby boy." She smiled. "The skate park looks amazing, sweetie."

"It really does, Leif," I whispered.

"Thanks." He ducked his head with a humble shyness I never saw. "The pros just took a test drive on it and everything seems good to go. I guess we'll find out in a second."

"It will be great," Kara said.

"Totally rad." I laughed

Leif shook his head and chuckled. "That sounds weird coming from you."

"Yeah, it really does." I'd immersed myself in the world of extreme sports after meeting Rory, but some things I would never master.

"I want to thank you all for coming out today to our grand opening of Shelly's Hang Out." Dora's voice boomed through the large room.

The facility housed four classrooms. Each could be opened to create one large room. Today we'd removed the partitions to facilitate the overflowing crowd.

Rory stood behind Dora, his face beaming with pride.

I stared down at the rings on my left hand, twirling them around. *Husband.*

"My name is Dora Rodriguez and I am the executive director of Shelly's Hang Out. As many of you know, our mission is to provide a safe environment for kids to 'hang out,'" she used air quotes, "during times they may otherwise be on the streets. We offer in-house tutoring as well as counseling. And I'm sure as most of you guys here in the front already know, we also have a state-of-the-art skate park designed by our founder's best friend, Mr. Leif Jennings, owner of Fly by Night Skate Parks." Dora motioned toward the back of the room at us.

The massive crowd turned and stared at Leif. The kids cheered and screamed, flailing their arms in the air.

He ducked his head.

I nudged him.

"Hey, be proud, cuchura," someone next to Leif said.

Luis's distinctive South American accent surprised me. Where had he come from?

I looked across Leif at the beautiful Latino man standing next to him. Luis Marquez was Rory's attorney and sports agent, and my friend and colleague at the law firm where I used to work.

Luis gave Leif a quick wink.

Luis had recently broken up with his long-time boyfriend but never disclosed why. He stared at Leif like he wanted to eat him alive. I didn't have the heart to tell Luis he was barking up the wrong tree by putting his saucy Latino moves on Rory's best friend. Leif was straighter than an interstate highway.

Leif's face lifted to meet Luis's gaze. A dazzling smile spread wide across his face.

What the hell?

Leif gazed out over the crowd and waved.

"You can try out the park after our dedication." Dora's words jolted me from my thoughts. "For those of you who don't have skateboards or equipment, we have several companies here today giving away some great products."

The kids erupted into deafening screams and chants as they jumped up and down.

"Okay, okay." Dora flapped her hands. "Settle down, guys." Her eyes narrowed as she stared at the children littering the front rows.

The educator in Dora sprang to life with the stern flash of

warning she gave the children. Without further admonishment, the kids quieted down and slid to the floor.

I laughed to myself. Dora would do amazing things with these kids.

"Wow, this crowd is fucking insane. Are they giving away free booze and porn in here?" A tiny giggle erupted.

I didn't even have to look.

"Dana!" Kara, Leif and I echoed, glaring at her.

"Ooops." She shrunk back against the wall and covered her mouth. "My bad," she mumbled.

I stared at my best friend. "If you're going to volunteer here, you have to tame that mouth."

"Good luck with that." Leif laughed.

"Fuck you," Dana mouthed to Leif. She gave him a hand gesture I didn't recognize but could only assume meant something offensive.

"You'd like to." He chuckled.

She raised a brow.

His laughing ceased.

What the hell? I'd always wanted my best friend and Rory's best friend to get together. Had they hooked up already?

"Shush, you two." Kara reprimanded then nodded toward the front.

"I'd like to introduce the man who many would say needs no introduction as his charm precedes him." Dora glanced over her shoulder at Rory. "But I'll try. He is the chairman of our board and the founder of Shelly's Hang Out. Through his hard work and dedication to the children of this community, we celebrate his dream today. A dream that is now a reality.

"When Rory first came to me and explained his vision of providing a space where kids could escape the mean streets they lived on, I was thrilled to be a part of it. He told me, 'Dora, people say it all starts with a dream, but it doesn't. Because of my home life, I didn't even know *how* to dream. I didn't know dreams were possible. I lived in a perpetual nightmare.'"

Tears burned my eyes.

Kara pulled me close.

Leif slid his hand into mine and squeezed. "You gave him a chance to dream, Hindley." Leif whispered in my ear.

Tears slid down my cheeks, but I didn't wipe them away.

"Rory found a way out of his nightmare through skate boarding," Dora continued. "And now he wants to give back, give hope, encourage the youth, give them a safe place to dream." Dora reached behind her.

Rory stepped forward and took her hand in his.

"Ladies and gentlemen, the man who needs no introduction. Mr. Rory Gregor."

The room exploded with cheers and shouts of praise. The kids and adults jumped to their feet and clapped as whistles and chanting echoed through the room.

Rory's eyes caught mine.

I smiled.

He scrubbed his jaw and raked a hand through his hair as he swallowed hard.

I could tell he was trying to tap down his emotions so he could speak.

He finally lifted his hands and leaned into the microphone. "Thank you." He waved at the crowd. "Please, have a seat."

I drew in a steadying breath. I was nervous for him. As of last night he still hadn't pieced together a speech. Public speaking wasn't his thing. Yes, he was a show-off in his sport, but not in conversation.

Rory pulled a piece of paper from his back pocket.

My hands trembled.

Kare leaned in. "He'll be fine." Her quiet, confident tone soothed me.

"Thank you all for coming today." Rory's deep voice echoed through the quiet room. "It means a lot to me to see so many people supporting our facility." Rory gazed out over the large crowd. His blue eyes shined with joy.

I was proud of him. He'd come so far from his abusive past. His beauty and strength, both inside and out, amazed me and stole my breath.

"Most of you know my story. My sister, Shelly and I grew up in an abusive home. I escaped. She didn't." He bit his lip and fumbled with the paper. He drew in a ragged breath and exhaled. "Then a very special family found me." He smiled. "They saw a dream in me I hadn't allowed myself to imagine." Rory searched the crowd. His gaze locked onto Kara.

I squeezed Kara.

She nodded, and blew Rory a kiss.

"I wouldn't be here today if it weren't for the love and support of three very important people—Kara and Jack Jennings and their amazing son, my best friend, Leif." Rory held out a hand, motioning toward us.

The crowd erupted with applause.

Rory set down his paper and joined the ovation.

"Thank you." He spoke close to the mic. "I love you, all of you, very much."

Kara wiped the tears streaming down her face. "I love you," she mouthed to Rory.

Dana pressed several tissues into her hand.

I gazed at Leif. He rubbed his cheek against his shoulder then lifted his head and nodded once at Rory, the equivalent of saying "I love you too" in man code.

"Where's Jack?" I asked.

"He's in the front with the kids," Kara answered.

Rory glanced at the audience on the floor in front of him. His smile spread wide when he found Jack.

Jack gave him a thumbs-up.

Rory laughed then stared at his paper. "Dora was right, I didn't even know how to dream when I was young. Not until I met the Jennings did I even know dreaming was possible. By the time I went back for my sister, it was too late, and I will always mourn my decision to wait."

Silence pervaded the room.

Rory rubbed the back of his neck and cleared his throat. "I hope this facility provides all of you the gift I couldn't give Shelly. The gift the Jennings gave me. The gift of dreaming."

Rory studied the children sitting in front of him, many of whom were probably enduring the same type of abuse he had as a child.

"My sister Shelly was beautiful and smart and crazy about daisies." Rory chuckled. "That's what I called her, Crazy Daisy." He shook his head as if lost in memories of his sister. "You'll notice daisies are woven into a lot of our interior design." He nodded around the room.

The pattern was faint, but if you looked closely, you could see the daisies illuminating the walls.

Rory continued. "I want to thank my sister-in-law, Geneva Barton for helping me incorporate my sister's favorite flower in a way that didn't seem too girly."

The crowd laughed.

"Holy shit, did he just *publicly* thank Geneva?" Dana whispered.

I couldn't reprimand her. The same thought ran through my mind. I'd forgiven Geneva, even though she'd almost destroyed Rory and me, but I'd had to forgive her in order to heal myself. Our family needed to mend, and harboring hate in my heart for Geneva wouldn't have helped. Not to mention, Geneva had changed, she had become a person who actually cared about others, and not just for what they could give her.

Rory had been much slower to forgive Geneva. He held out offering his pardon, assuming her actions were temporary. He'd said she would resort to her old bitch-like ways given enough time. Hopefully, time had proven him wrong.

Rory's gaze found my parents in the front row.

Geneva sat beside them, hands folded in her lap. Normally she was boisterous and outspoken, demanding attention. Today she was quiet and unassuming.

Rory gave her a small smile and a single nod.

Geneva dipped her head and wiped at her face.

Rory gazed out over the crowd. "I won't take a lot of time because I know you guys are anxious to try out the skate park and 'hang out' with other pro skateboarders." Rory used air quotes, noting the name of his facility.

Rory glanced at his pro skateboard friends, Buzz Dahlke, Manny Morales and Smitty Smith, men he competed against. In the extreme sports world, they were friends first, competitors second. The men waved to the crowd.

The kids cheered and screamed like they were at a rock concert. These men were their idols, their heroes.

Rory turned his attention to the paper in front of him as he studied the note. His shoulders heaved with another deep breath. He held it and closed his eyes.

Here it came, the hard part of his speech. My stomach flipped and I willed him the power to go on.

Rory blew out a heavy breath and opened his eyes as he stared out over the group. "Leo Tolstoy wrote, 'Everyone thinks of changing the world, but no one thinks of changing himself.'"

Tolstoy? Had Rory been reading *War and Peace*? I giggled, remembering our first morning together.

Rory had woken up in my bed and caught me studying his tattoo. *Skater Boy*. His deep voice had rumbled through my room with words of admonishment.

I'd been embarrassed but excited too, turned on by his deep, sexy voice. I would have given anything to hear him read *War and*

Peace that morning just to hear his deep vibrato. Little did I know back then he couldn't read. Maybe now I would get my wish.

"Shush," Dana scolded.

I shot her an inconspicuous middle finger.

She chuckled.

We turned our attention back to Rory.

"I never wanted to change the world," he said. "I didn't even want to change myself. I was convinced I wasn't worth much, so I didn't deserve much. Until one beautiful woman quite literally stumbled into my life."

Rory's gaze caught mine and we shared an exchange of memories. My heart burst with joy and love.

"She taught me how to read. She taught me how to love. She taught me so many things." Rory's eyes never left mine. "She helped me change. She gave me the opportunity to grow and be a better person. She never judged me. She helped me see I *did* deserve the chance to dream, to dream big."

Rory studied the crowd. "And in doing so, she helped me envision this for all of you." He spread his arms wide.

My heart swelled and burst with pride for my husband. My *husband*. My Skater Boy.

"My hope," Rory continued, "is that you will see in yourselves what my wife saw in me so many months ago—a broken person worthy of love. Through this facility I want to give you all the gift of dreaming, because I couldn't give it to my sister, Shelly." His voice cracked and he swallowed hard.

My eyes filled with tears. His words were heart felt and genuine, his emotions wrought with guilt and remorse.

Rory's gaze found mine, his blue eyes covered in a sheen of unshed tears. "I love you, Hindley." He didn't smile. He didn't wink. He didn't do any of the Rory-like quirks he always did when he showered me with terms of endearment.

His gaze paralyzed me, pierced my heart like a flaming arrow, lighting my soul on fire. I'd never felt more admired and revered in all my life.

I sensed Shelly's presence in the room.

"I love you," I mouthed back. "Thank you."

His façade cracked and his lips curled into a salacious smile.

My belly flipped and my legs wobbled. *Not here.* Dammit!

Rory's gaze left mine and he scanned the audience. "There are two very important things in the front of the facility. One is called the 'Sick Wall,' although my wife hates the term. You guys know when extreme guys say something is *sick* we mean the trick is amazing, freaking awesome, right?"

The kids cheered.

I shook my head. I was opposed to the term, but apparently I was outnumbered.

"There is a purple wall in the front called the 'Sick Wall,'" Rory said. "We will showcase all the amazing things you do on that wall, whether your work is inside or outside the classroom or within the walls of this facility. We want to teach you guys to be proud of your accomplishments, and to teach you humility, about how to be proud for others too. You'll work with the counselors and volunteers and we'll showcase your hard work."

The kids high-fived and fist-bumped one another as smiles erupted across their young faces. It was as if Rory had already fulfilled a promise to help them dream.

"The second thing you'll notice is a large painting above the front desk. The portrait was commissioned by my beautiful wife as a wedding present to me." He gazed past the crowd to me. "Thank you, baby."

I smiled and nodded once.

"It was painted by my stepmother, Sarah." Rory scanned the room until he found Sarah in the middle of the crowd. He held out his hand.

Sarah blew him a kiss and she waved to the audience.

"Like some of you," Rory gazed down at the kids, "I didn't know my birth father growing up. Recently, I was fortunate enough to find out who he was, but he'd already passed away in the war."

One small red-headed boy in the front raised his hand. Without waiting to be called on he spoke. "I loth-tid my daddy, too, Mithuh Rory."

His lisp was pronounced but it didn't keep him from speaking out.

A collective "ahhh" of sorrow and sympathy rippled through the room, even from the kids.

My heart broke.

Rory's eyes darkened and his face filled with empathy. "I'm really sorry, buddy." He glanced over at Sarah again. "Thankfully, I found my father's wife, my stepmother, Sarah, and I've been able to connect with some of my father's memories.

"Thanks to my sister's friend, Owen Tucker," Rory pointed to the young man sitting next to Sarah, "I now have an old photograph of my sister and me. Sarah painted the image on a huge canvas. Some of you may have already seen it up at the front. The picture shows me *trying* to teach Shelly to skate." He laughed. "Unfortunately Shelly, like my wife, wasn't very coordinated."

The room broke out in laughter.

I joined in. He wasn't lying. I was such a spaz when it came to sports.

"I love that photo for a multitude of reasons," Rory spoke quietly. "Mainly because I know Shelly kept it with her even after I left her at home and went pro. Shelly knew how much I loved her even though I left her." His voice broke and he paused. "My hope is that in the life after this one, Shelly looks over me and protects me and those I love, even though I couldn't do the same for her. I think she will watch over this facility too. She will protect all of us."

Several members of the audience dabbed at their eyes.

"The last thing you'll find when you enter Shelly's Hang Out is a plaque with our mission statement." Rory held up the plaque. "For those of you who haven't had a chance to read it, I'd like to share it now." Rory pointed down at an older boy in the crowd. "Would you come up here and read it for me?"

The boy glanced around as if Rory was asking someone else. When no one else answered, he stood. His shabby clothes and well-worn shoes spoke of a hard life on the streets. His smile shined brighter than his blue eyes as he shook his shaggy blond hair from his face. I imagined Rory looked like this boy as a child.

The boy snaked his way through the mass of kids, careful not to step on anyone.

Rory pulled up a stool.

He climbed on top and leaned over the podium.

"What's your name?" Rory asked.

He leaned in to the microphone. "Ryan."

Rory whispered something to the boy.

He nodded.

"Ryan is going to read the mission statement on our plaque."

Ryan stared at Rory for several heartbeats, anxiety etched on his face.

"Yeah?" Rory asked.

Ryan stared down at the plaque.

The room fell silent.

Shit, could he read?

Ryan's quiet voice skimmed through the room as he read the plaque out loud. "We dedicate this facility to Shelly Gregor, a daisy in a field of darkness."

Ryan glanced up at Rory as if asking permission to continue.

Rory smiled and nodded.

Ryan's voice grew louder, more confident. "For those who enter this place, may you always reach for the impossible, dream the unthinkable, and never be afraid to fail."

A deafening silence filled the room.

I pushed off the wall and stood tall, clapping loudly.

Rory and Ryan stared at me.

The audience followed and the room exploded with the sounds of joy and jubilation.

Rory turned to face Ryan and smiled as he clapped along with the crowd.

Ryan's face reddened and he cut his eyes to the floor but a small smile lurked underneath his shaggy hair.

Rory was right. These kids needed to know what it was like to accept praise. Rory and I were still learning ourselves.

The room quieted and Rory stepped up to the microphone. "On behalf of the board, the employees and the volunteers of Shelly's Hang Out." He glanced down at Ryan and put his arm around the boy's shoulders. "Ryan and I would like to thank you all for coming out today and celebrating with us. Please stay and try out the skate park and tour the facility." Rory reached down for the skateboard leaning on the wall behind him. "Who's ready to skate?" He lifted the board in the air.

The kids jumped to their feet, their screams of excitement vibrating off every wall.

My breath caught and tears threatened to break over my lashes when I saw the bottom of Rory's board. The deck was lacquered black and covered with daisies. In the center, someone had artfully painted the photo of Rory and Shelly. Probably Sarah.

Rory leaned back and glanced at the ceiling. His lips moved in silence. I knew he was talking to Shelly.

I pushed through the crowd, nearly knocking people over to make my way toward Rory. I was within a few feet when he lowered the board and stared at me.

"You're next you know."

I stopped as if an invisible wall had been erected between us.

"Next for what?" I tilted my head, feigning ignorance. I knew what he meant. He'd wanted me to skate for months but I'd refused, saying I didn't want to walk down the aisle in a cast.

He glared at me, one brow cocked high.

"I don't have a skateboard." I smiled and shrugged my shoulders. "Besides, today is for the kids, and for you. Trust me, you do *not* want me sprawled out in the middle of the skate park on my butt." I giggled.

"I don't know." He slid in next to me and wrapped his free arm around my waist. "I'd kind of like to see you spread out on the floor, ass up," he whispered in my ear.

I should have been appalled. I should have swatted him for his indecent comment, especially here in front of all these guests. Instead, all I could do was envision the erotic scene myself. My insides burned and I pressed my legs together.

"Mmm, hum," Rory murmured then kissed just below my earlobe. "It's gonna happen, Mrs. Gregor."

"Stop." I pushed at him. "You're insatiable. We just spent seven days with my ass…" I cleared my throat and surveyed the room. The guests were slowly clearing.

"That's right." His lips curled in a devilish grin. "And now I have the rest of my life to—"

"Mithuh Rory! Come on, leth 'kate!" The red-headed boy from earlier butted up next to Rory and tugged on his shirt. The kid barely hit Rory's waist.

"Later, Mrs. Gregor." Rory winked as he took the boy's hand in his and raced out of the door.

"He'll be an amazing father." Sarah said.

"Sooner than he knows," I sighed.

"What?"

"Shhh." My eyes darted around the room.

"Are you…" She stared down at my stomach then back up to me.

"I'm not one hundred percent sure, but yeah, I think so."

"But you just got back from your honeymoon."

She must have forgotten we'd waited for two weeks after the wedding trying to finalize things for the grand opening today before leaving on our honeymoon. "We got married three weeks ago, Sarah."

"Oh my gosh," she covered her mouth, her eyes wide. "Does anyone else know?"

I shook my head. "You're it." I shrugged my shoulders.

"Rory doesn't even know?"

"Oh, God, no. He would flip. He has the X Games in a few weeks. I don't want to freak him out. Plus, I'm not one hundred percent sure. I'm too scared to take a test. I have an appointment with the doctor next week." I choked a sob. "He's going to kill me. I wasn't supposed to get pregnant this soon." Finally, the tears I'd worked to keep at bay flowed freely and my shoulders rocked with sobs.

"No, he won't, sweetie." Sarah rubbed my back. "He'll be surprised I'm sure, but he'll be happy."

"I don't know," I whimpered through muffled sobs. "What if he leaves me? I don't even know how this happened, I have an IUD, and…" My crying grew louder. "I may even lose the baby."

"You'll be fine, Hindley. I'm sure the baby will be fine. Rory will come around." She stroked my hair. "And if not, I'll kick his ass."

I giggled.

"What the fuck happened to you?" Dana's sassy voice roared behind me.

"She's just overcome by the grand opening," Sarah said.

I drew in a deep breath and wiped at my eyes.

"Is it because you're pregnant?" Dana leaned close and whispered.

"What?"

Heads turned in our direction.

"How do you know?" I whispered as I stared at my best friend. Of course she knew.

She shook her head. "I've known you for twenty years. You're moody, you're irritable…"

My chin quivered as fresh tears threatened.

"And you have a glow about you, Hindley. It's kind of sickening actually." Dana laughed.

I wrapped my arms around my best friend and cried into her shoulder.

"Don't worry, One Nighter will understand."

I pushed away. "Wait, he told me you changed it to All Nighter."

Dana and Sarah burst into a fit of hysterics.

"What?" I stared at them.

"We decided to call him *Every* Nighter," Dana giggled, "not *All* Nighter. That is *totally* your nickname, not mine. And I do *not* want to hear the stories. All your wild-ass nights of non-stop sex is probably how his little sperm soldiers busted through that IUD of yours. I told you, taking a vow of celibacy for two months before your wedding was wrong." She wiped her eyes. "There was so much PSI behind the man's sperm, those suckers split that flimsy plastic shit to smithereens on the first try and found your egg like a heat-seeking missile."

My head fell back with roaring laughter. I could always count on Dana to make me feel better.

"He'll be fine, Hindley," Dana said. "And I can't wait to spoil my little niece or nephew." She rubbed at my stomach.

"Thanks, you guys."

"For what?" Sarah asked.

"I've been worried sick for days, not telling a soul. Finally letting someone know feels good. Please don't say anything yet. Please." My eyes darted between them.

"Of course." Sarah rubbed my arm.

"Mum's the word." Dana mimed her lips being zipped closed. "You're going to be an amazing mom, Hindley, don't worry."

"How do you know?"

"Because you have so much love in your heart, it spilled out onto a man who was able to dream this." She waved around the room. "You helped Rory become the man he was destined to be. And you'll do that for your baby too."

I smiled at my best friend.

"Mithith. Gregor!" Someone shouted from the doorway.

My heart skipped a beat at my new title.

"Mrs. Gregor," Dana repeated. "Don't know if I can get used to your new name." She laughed.

I glanced up and saw the same red-headed kid from earlier. "Mithuh Rory wanth you."

"Truer words have never been spoken." Dana jabbed my ribs.

"Even after I tell him I'm pregnant?"

"Supposedly pregnancy hormones make you super horny." Dana waggled her brows. "Pretty sure he'll be okay with the amped up sex drive." She laughed. "And besides, he's your *every* nighter now, Hindley. He's not going anywhere."

I laughed and walked toward the red-headed boy. I squatted down in front of him. "What's your name?"

"Tyyy-ler." He drew out his name in an exaggerated drawl.

"Well, come on, Tyler, let's go see what Mr. Rory wants." I held out my hand and he tentatively took it in his.

We walked toward the indoor skate park adjacent to the facility. The noise was deafening, but the smiles on the kids' faces were priceless. I glanced to my right.

Rory knelt next to a little boy near the railing and tied his shoes.

My generous husband had given the boy new shoes. My heart beat heavy as tears threatened to fall. Hormones had me clutching my stomach. Rory would be an amazing father. I just hoped he would believe in himself too.

"Hey there, buddy." Rory stood and waved.

"Hey, Mithuh Rory. I bring her to you." Tyler nodded toward me.

"You *brought* her to me, little man." Rory said.

Tyler nodded and squared his shoulders. "I *brought* her." He smiled wide.

"Right." Rory winked and ruffled the boy's hair. His hand dropped away from Tyler and his gaze traveled the length of me.

His predatory gaze surveyed me as if I was his next meal. My belly clenched and my body throbbed with need. God, how could he set me on fire every time? Right here? In a crowded skate park? With kids!

"Hello, *Mrs. Gregor*." Rory smirked.

"You wanted to show me something?" I cocked a brow.

"Ah, yes." He held out a hand to the boy on the ground.

The boy was fumbling with the laces of his other shoe.

"Over, then under." Rory squatted back down and mimicked the action.

The boy followed Rory's direction and within seconds, had the laces secure.

"Awesome!" Rory held up a flat palm.

The boy's eyes lit up and he slapped Rory's hand.

How many times had I taken something as simple as the ability to tie my shoes for granted? Realizing these kids lacked basic necessities *and* skills suddenly hit me like a bag of bricks.

"Kevin, this is my wife, Hindley."

The boy bumbled to his feet, seemingly awkward in his own skin. He was heavy set and his shoulders slumped in as if hiding himself. His black hair was thick but cropped short. His caramel-colored skin reminded me of Luis.

Looking at him was like gazing at myself fifteen years ago. The boy staring back at me seemed just as timid and shy, and hopeless as I had been.

"It's nice to meet you, ma'am."

His high voice didn't surprise me, but his serious expression did. He may not know how to tie his shoe, but he had manners. I instantly liked him.

"It's nice to meet you too, Kevin. So, what did Tyler bring me out here for?" I cocked my head and smiled at Rory.

"Kevin here just mastered the kick flip." Rory grinned. He slung his arm around Kevin's shoulder and hugged him.

Rory had admitted even though the kick flip was an easy trick in skateboarding, the maneuver had been one of the hardest for him to master. He was like that. The simple things could often times trip him up the most. But Rory was persistent and failure wasn't an option for him. He would instill those qualities in these kids.

"Kevin, that's amazing!" I held up my own palm, awaiting his high-five.

His eyes went wide as if he'd never touched a girl. He recovered quickly and slapped my hand.

"Show her." Rory nodded toward the park littered with kids and adults.

"Now?" he asked.

"Yeah, now," Tyler shouted.

I'd forgotten about the copper-haired sprite next to me.

Kevin's eyes darted from Rory's to Tyler's before settling on mine.

"I'd really like to see it." I nodded.

"Okay," he mumbled.

"Don't forget your helmet." Rory reached behind him and held out the protective gear.

Kevin secured the helmet and snapped the buckle under his chin.

"Go on." Rory motioned to the course again.

Kevin walked around the railing and dropped his board. With great care he positioned his feet and bit his lip.

Rory cupped his mouth and shouted above the noise, "No lip biting. If you fall, you'll cut a hole clean through it." Rory pulled on his bottom lip as if to share his experience.

"Go, Kevin," Tyler shouted.

"You got this," Rory yelled.

Kevin pushed off with his left foot and went sailing across the pavement. Before I could even blink, Kevin jumped in the air, his skateboard rotating beneath him. He landed squarely on his board and his hands went into the air in victory.

"Yes!" Rory cried out. He pumped his fists in the air. "Way to go, dude!"

"Whoo hoo!" Tyler screamed, jumping beside me.

I clapped my hands so hard and so loud they burned.

Kevin stopped the board and stomped the back, sending the board into the air.

He caught it with one hand as if he'd been skating for a lifetime then turned to face us. His eyes glowed with triumphant jubilation and his smile lit up the massive skate park.

I realized for Kevin, pulling off a new skateboarding trick was a momentous occasion. Skating in front of a professional athlete was probably a dream come true.

Rory had given Kevin the one thing he'd never had himself as a child. Hope.

I slid up next to Rory and snaked my arms around his trim waist.

He dropped his hand to my shoulder.

I laid my head on Rory's chest and breathed in his scent. He was my elixir, my cure for the nightmares that had haunted me. And now, he would be that for these kids too. I stared up at him.

His blue eyes peered down at me.

"You're amazing," I sighed.

He smiled, but I could sense the apprehension.

"It's true, Rory. Look what all you've done." I swung my hand around the skate park. Kids and adults littered the area.

He surveyed the space. "This was all Leif." He shrugged.

I grabbed his chin and pulled it toward me. "Hey." I narrowed my gaze. "This is *all* you, Rory Gregor. Don't *ever* forget that." I gave his chin a small shove to drive home my point.

"You're a tough lady, you know that, Mrs. Gregor." He grabbed my wrist.

"I have to be." I smiled up at him. "I'm married to an extreme sports athlete. They're pretty tough guys."

"Who's also pretty good looking too, I hear?" He waggled his brows.

I jabbed his rock hard stomach. "And extremely modest."

He tugged my hand up to his lips and kissed the knuckles then pressed my palm to his heart. His chest rose and fell with a deep breath. "I think she'd be proud, don't you?"

I didn't have to ask who the "she" was. "Shelly would be *so* proud of you, Rory."

His eyes stayed riveted to the crowd as he drank in his surroundings. Rory wasn't typically reflective. He was more of a spur-of-the-moment kind of guy. But the facility had taken a lot of planning, coordination…and dreaming.

"Yeah," he nodded his head and smiled, "I think so too." He leaned in close and placed a small kiss on my temple. "I was thinking."

"Ut oh." I chuckled.

"Shush." He slapped my hand still glued to his chest.

"Sorry." I nuzzled into him. "What were you thinking, Mr. Gregor?"

"When we have a daughter I'd like to name her Abigail."

My heart stopped and my head spun. Shit, I feared I might pass out. Did he already know I was pregnant?

"W-what do you mean?" I pulled away.

"Don't freak out." He kissed the top of my head and held me firm. "I'm not talking any time soon."

But he *was* talking about kids. My palms pooled with sweat and my mouth went dry. "So," my voice quivered, "how long are you thinking?"

"I don't know, a year or two at least. I want you to travel with me to my competitions."

Oh, holy shit. He would flip when I told him. We didn't have two seconds, let alone two years to wait. Our family was starting now...or nine months from now. Should I tell him, just pull the bandage off and get it done? No, today was his day to bask in the glory of all his hard work, to celebrate his accomplishments. Shelly's Hang Out had been his baby, his brain child. Finding out he had another kind of child could wait.

"Is that okay?" he asked.

"Is what okay?" My mind washed blank.

"That we name our little girl Abigail."

"Oh,...um..." What could I say? "Why?"

"It was my father's mother's name. My birth father."

Could my love for Rory Gregor grow any more? Apparently, yes. I wrapped my arms around my husband and squeezed him tight. "I love it," I spoke into his chest.

"And I love you." He kissed my head.

I tilted my head and rested my chin on his chest. "You're going to be an amazing father, Rory."

He laughed off my suggestion. Now wasn't the time to convince him.

"I love you so much." I smiled. "I have no idea why you picked me, but I'm glad you did."

"You're my Drunk Girl." He laughed.

"And you're my Skater Boy."

"Forever?"

I nodded. "Yeah, you're stuck with me."

He leaned in close to my ear, his breath wafting against my neck. "Tonight I'm gonna be stuck *in* you."

"Rory!" I pulled away as if offended and swatted at his chest.

His roaring laughter echoed through the arena.

"You're a mess." I scooped his hand into mine and tugged him toward the exit. "Come on, you need to mingle."

"But I'm right, right?" He waggled his brow.

Who was I kidding? I wanted him stuck *in* me just as much as he did. "Yeah, you're right." I giggled.

"There's the sound that feeds my dreams."

"What sound?"

"Your laughter."

I tugged him toward me and wrapped my hand around his neck, yanking him down for a deep kiss. I had to keep our embrace family-rated, but I wanted Rory to feel the way he made me feel. Alive. Loved. Cherished.

I broke our kiss.

He moaned.

"You're quite poetic, Mr. Gregor." I winked.

"You're my muse, Mrs. Gregor."

I shook my head. "At least you didn't say moose." I grabbed his hand and strolled toward the door.

"Your ass is as big as a moose." He swatted my butt.

"Rory!" I dropped his hand, scanning the area. All the participants were busy skating and laughing, oblivious to our antics.

"What?" He chuckled. "I love your moose ass." He gave it another slap.

"Stop." My eyes narrowed and I pointed a finger at him.

"Or what?" He leaned in closer, kissing the tip.

Oh, shit.

"Or you won't be stuck *in* this tonight." I waved my hand around my mid-section.

"Yeah, right." He shook his head and laughed as he walked away from me.

I watched as Rory filtered through the crowd, signing autographs, taking pictures. Before he left the skating area, he turned to glance back at me.

"Tonight," he mouthed.

I glared at him in mock offense.

He waggled his brow.

I was a sure thing and he knew it. I had been his since our first kiss at Geneva's wedding.

Rory held a power over me and I didn't fear submitting to him. He protected me, took care of me.

My hand skimmed over my belly as I studied my stomach. I had no idea if I was expecting a girl or a boy, but something told me Rory's penance for being such a player in his bad boy days would be worrying over a gaggle of daughters the rest of his life. I laughed.

"Don't worry, Abbi," I whispered, "Daddy's gonna protect you too."

CHAPTER 24

RORY

FIVE YEARS LATER

I CLICKED the lock on Hindley's old duplex and stared over my shoulder at my wife.

We had built our permanent house on Lake Austin, close to Dana and Peter, but still kept Hindley's duplex for our sexcapades, as Dana called it. Hindley's old house was a place for us to escape to, especially on anniversaries. Some men took their wives to Cancun or France. I took mine to her duplex. And she loved it.

I pushed open the door.

Hindley moved to enter.

I held on to the doorframe and blocked her.

"Oh my gosh, Rory, not this again. We've been married five years now. You don't have to—"

She shrieked as I bent and secured my arms around her thighs and tossed her over my shoulder. I swatted her ass for good measure, and because I could.

"Rory!"

When I didn't answer, she slapped my butt with a glorious smack. Oh, yeah.

I walked over the threshold and kicked the door closed as I ran my hand up and down the back of her smooth, shapely thigh. "You're my wife and this is our anniversary. I will do with you as I please."

"Well, I don't think men are supposed to throw their wives over their shoulders and cart them around like cavemen."

I flipped her over and leaned her against the sofa.

She stumbled and steadied herself, smoothing her skirt.

"Are you calling me a caveman?" I tilted my head and cocked a brow as our eyes glared at one another in mock disgust. God, she had the most beautiful eyes.

"Well, with that little stunt," she waved toward the front door, "you are most definitely a caveman, Mr. Gregor."

"I like surprising you." I smiled.

"Speaking of surprises." She wrinkled her nose. "What have you got planned for tonight?" She bounced on the balls of her feet.

I loved the anticipation sparkling in her eyes—the look of pure lust and desire, for me, anytime we came to the duplex. My gaze traveled over her body like a hungry animal. So many options, I chuckled to myself.

I walked to the kitchen and pulled out one of the bottles of fruit-flavored sparkling water Matt Davis had shipped to our house for sampling. Matt was the new CEO of Sonora Water. Six years later and they were still one of my top sponsors.

I chuckled silently at how jealous I'd been of Matt when I'd first signed with his company. He'd wanted into Hindley's panties from the beginning, but my beautiful bride put the nix on his attempts and cock blocked the poor bastard. I couldn't blame the man. Hindley was gorgeous. Thankfully, he'd taken the rejection in stride and years later the three of us were still good friends.

Sonora had recently ventured into the fru-fru drink shit, packaging water as if it were champagne. Matt said they wanted to attract the high society fuckers. I couldn't care less, but I figured our anniversary was as good a time as any to try the shit out.

I grabbed a glass from the shelf and walked back into the living room.

Hindley was propped against the couch, examining her blue toenails. Her long blonde hair fell forward and skimmed the tops of her breasts, framing her face like a picture window showcasing a sunset. She'd worn a loose-fitting skirt that hit her mid-thigh and a snug fitting tank top like I'd asked. I just hoped she'd complied with the rest of my instructions.

"Ooo, what's that?" She reached for the bottle.

I held it against my chest. "Oh, no, Mrs. Gregor. Not yet."

Her lips puckered and she slumped against the couch.

"Don't pout or I'll suck those lips until they bleed."

Her eyes popped wide. "Promise," she whispered, stepping closer.

I sidestepped. "Behave or you won't get your present." My narrowed eyes warned her.

She touched the diamond pendent hanging around her neck. "I thought the necklace was my present."

"That's the *good* present." I tucked the bottle of sparkling water under my arm and reached for her hand. "I'm talking about the *bad* present."

"Oh." Her eyes popped wide. "Yes, the *bad* present. I want that one too." She licked her lips.

My dick twitched. Fuck. "You do now, do you? Have you been bad, Mrs. Gregor?" I tugged her down the hall toward the bedroom.

"Very." She giggled.

"Did you do what I asked?"

"Wait, where are we going?" She stopped and her hand slipped from mine. "Why aren't we going into the rex room?" She nodded toward the spare bedroom.

I glanced over my shoulder.

Hindley stared at the door to our recreational-sex room, or "rex room" as we called it. Some people called their spaces a playroom, but I never liked the term. That language always conjured up images of small children, and that was *not* sexy.

Over the five years we'd been married, we'd filled our rex room with an assortment of fun, sexual furniture and toys. My wife was all about the kinky, and my heart, and my dick, tightened with desire.

"Ahhh, are you disappointed, baby?" I slid up next to her and slipped an arm around her waist, nuzzling my face in the crook of her neck.

"Kind of." Her shoulders slumped against me.

"Well, maybe later. But for now, I have something else in store for you." I pulled away and nodded toward the primary bedroom. "Come on."

I had big plans for Hindley later which *did* include the rex room, but we had reservations in a few hours and for now, our quick rendezvous would have to do.

I sat the bottle of water and glass on the nightstand then walked into the en suite bathroom and grabbed two towels. When I returned, Hindley was standing at the foot of the bed.

"What's that?" She pointed to a heart-shaped pillow laying on top of the white down comforter.

I tossed the towels on the bed next to her. "That's your something *bad*." I smiled.

Her eyes cut to mine.

My salacious grin gave me away.

"Okay." She reached for the pillow. She squeezed tight then flipped it around in her hands, surveying it as if it were filled with something illegal. "It's leather."

"So it will clean easier." I stepped around the footboard and took the pillow.

Hindley gazed at me with those innocent doe eyes I knew from experience were anything *but* innocent.

"Clean it?" Her nose crinkled and her brows knit together. She studied the pillow longer, running her hand over the soft red leather. "It's a wedge pillow too," she said.

"I know." I paused and waited for her to comprehend. "A *wedge*," I repeated.

Her eyes widened. She sucked in a breath. "Oh," she sighed.

I often slid wedge pillows under Hindley's hips to angle her body for better positions during sex. To me, wedges were the best invention next to the skateboard. The heart "pillow" wasn't as large, but it would do the trick.

"It has an added bonus." I waggled my brows.

"Okay." She stared at the pillow, her voice giddy with anticipation.

"God, I love you, baby." I kissed the top of her head.

"I love you too." She smiled. "Now show me the bonus."

She bounced like an excited toddler, waiting for Christmas morning.

I pulled the rounded tops of the heart-shaped pillow apart, revealing the vibrator housed inside the cushion.

"Is that a—" She reached out to touch the tip.

"Yep." I licked my lips. "A little modification to the heart wedge, thanks to our friend and sex shop owner, Regan." I chuckled. "She wants us to try it out and if we like it, she's gonna market it."

"So," Hindley tilted her head and slapped a fist to her hips, "I'm a guinea pig?"

"Oh, Mrs. Gregor." I slid in closer. "I would *never* call my wife a pig." I dug in my pocket and clicked the remote control. The vibrator sprang to life.

"Oh my God." Hindley slid her hand between the cushions and

pressed on the tip. "Holy hell." Her eyes nearly popped out of her head. "Are we going to try it out?"

I grimaced in offense, as if she'd asked me if I liked skateboarding.

She hit my chest. "Okay, so that's a yes."

I clicked the vibrator off and tossed the pillow onto the middle of the bed.

Her eyes followed the pillow's descent and her face fell. "I thought we were using it." She turned and pouted.

Her plump lips were so delicious I wanted to bite them. "Did you follow my instructions?" I asked.

"Uh…about the underwear you mean?"

"Yes."

She nodded.

Hindley hated to go without underwear but I'd instructed her to dress without them earlier. Ever since our wedding night when she'd been completely nude underneath her dress, her commando style had become something of a tradition on our anniversary.

"Good girl." I licked my lips.

Her eyes widened.

"Now, sit down on the bed." I kept my voice low and monotone. Dominant Rory just entered the room.

Hindley shivered. "Yes, sir." She bowed her head and lowered her body onto the bed.

I stalked toward her and stared down at her bare feet. Blue toes. Like the first night I'd met her.

A small smirk curled her lips.

I slid my finger under her chin and raised her head. "Was there something you found funny, Mrs. Gregor?"

She shook her head, but bit her lips to stifle a laugh.

"I'm sorry, I couldn't hear you." I narrowed my eyes.

Her body tensed. Her neck pulsed. All signs of amusement washed away.

"No." She paused, her eyes locking on mine. "No, *sir*."

I leaned in and pressed my lips to hers, pulling away before our connection could explode into something unmanageable.

She moaned.

My dick twitched from the vibrations of her groan. I drew in a deep breath to steady my desires. I didn't want to pop a load before I even started. "Would you like some sparkling water, Mrs. Gregor?"

She shrugged. "Um, sure."

I walked around the bed and grabbed the single glass along with the chilled bottle of water. I kicked off my shoes and strolled back to stand in front of her. "Put a towel under you," I demanded.

She opened her mouth to question me.

My sharp glare closed her lips.

She glanced down at the purple towels next to her and spread them under her rear end. The precaution was for my protection. If I screwed up her white comforter she'd be pissed.

"Would you like some sparkling water to toast our anniversary, Mrs. Gregor?"

"Yes, please." She reached for the glass.

I pulled it away. "Oh, no." I shook my head. "This is for me."

"Why can't I have some?" She cocked her head. The innocent expression on her face mirrored the ones my two daughters gifted me with almost daily.

I chuckled with a low grumble. "Oh, you'll have water, just not in a glass." I cocked my head and stared at her chocolate brown eyes.

"Okay, but…" She studied the bottle of water. Her eyes burst wide. "Oh, okay, I get it."

I tucked the glass under my arm and twisted off the cap and tossed it behind me. The bottle hissed with the release of carbonation. God, my dick needed release too.

I poured the bubbling water into the glass and drew in a long sip. The drink tasted sweet, like peaches, and burned, travelling down my throat. I smiled, thinking of how much better the water would taste on Hindley's body.

"Lean your head back and open your mouth." My tone was deep and authoritative.

Her eyes fluttered closed and she tilted her head back, opening her mouth wide.

The slender column of her neck begged for my tongue but I staved off my need. I pulled a satin scarf from my back pocket and slid it along her cheek.

"Rory?" she called. "Are you blindfolding me?" Her voice held apprehension mixed with a shrill of excitement.

"No."

She sighed.

"You are," I amended. "Tie it around your eyes."

"Why?"

"Tonight I want you to just *feel* me," I whispered.

She shivered. "But I like to look at you." She giggled.

"Tie it, Hindley." I swatted at her thigh.

She winced but smiled and complied.

I leaned over her body and drew in a deep breath. She smelled like sugar and spice and *nothing* nice. She was my naughty Drunk Girl. "Are you thirsty?" I asked against her lips after she'd secured the blindfold.

"Uh huh," she moaned.

I tilted the glass over her mouth and poured the bubbly liquid inside.

She choked at first but then swallowed deep.

I pictured her throat swallowing my dick. Fuck. *Focus. Focus. Hindley. Focus.* I breathed in deep to control my voice. "Is it good?" I whispered in her ear.

"Mmmm," she nodded.

"Do you want more?"

Her head dipped. "Yes, please. Sir." She smiled.

I ran my fingers over her lips. "Open."

She nipped at my fingers and reached up to bite them.

I pulled away. "Tsk, tsk, tsk, Mrs. Gregor. You know better than to try and take control. That will cost you."

She whimpered, half in fear half in desire.

Her sultry voice lit my body on fire. "Open." I barked. "No biting."

Her mouth shot open wide.

I tilted the bottle and stared at her lips. The water fell on her chin and trailed down her neck, completely missing its mark, just as I'd intended.

"Rory!" She screamed, jumping back. "That shit's cold."

I chuckled. "You moved."

"No I didn't." Her lips pressed together.

"Do you want more?"

"In my mouth," she said.

"Oh, I've got something for your mouth." I chuckled.

She shrugged one shoulder. "Promise?" Her lips curved into a smile.

Shit, she was in control. Again. Not good. I bent over and licked her neck, lapping at the liquid.

Her sharp gasp ensured her silence.

Better.

The water had reached the edge of her tank top. Not good enough. "Lean back on your elbows."

Anticipating things to come, she fell back.

I held the bottle inches above her body. "Do you want more water?"

"Yes."

"Do you promise to be a good girl?"

She smirked.

I remained silent. Fuck, this girl could take the reins of a power play faster than John Wayne in a western movie.

Her smile faded with my silence. "Yes, I promise." Her husky voice grumbled low in her throat.

I leaned over and kissed her nose. "Good girl," I whispered.

Goose bumps erupted across her skin.

Yes, much better. "Open your mouth again."

She complied with no resistance.

I poured the water on her neck and trailed it down her chest, soaking her tank top.

She jerked away. "Rory!"

I pushed her hip and held her against the bed. Fuck, she looked like a college coed in a wet T-shit contest. My mouth silenced hers as I bit a puckered nipple through her soaked material.

"Oh," she moaned, snaking one hand into my hair, drawing me closer. "This water is amazing." She chuckled.

"Change your mind?" I laughed against her skin and bit down harder.

"Ahh," she gasped.

I drew my mouth from her nipple and stood as straight as my hardened dick. I stared down at my beautiful wife.

Her chest heaved and her mouth fell lax.

God, she was gorgeous, heavenly. Long blonde hair tumbled down her shoulders and her legs spread wide. The hem of her skirt danced close to the land I was going for. I thanked God every day she'd said yes to marrying me. Hindley gave my life meaning.

"Rory," she called, her hand reaching for me.

"I'm here, baby." I stepped closer, interweaving our fingers. I drew her hand to my mouth and kissed the palm then released her and stepped back. "Put your hand behind you again."

She lowered her body and didn't argue.

I squatted in front of her and wrapped my hands around her

ankles then slid them up her soft, shapely calves. I trailed my hands behind her knees.

She shuddered.

I pushed her legs further apart as I suckled and kissed her inner thigh, working my way up.

"Oh, God," she panted, her chest heaving as her legs pressed against my hands.

"Do you want more?" I rumbled against her skin.

"God, yes."

I pulled back and stood. "Too bad."

"What?" she shrieked, lifting onto her elbows.

"You were a bad girl, Hindley, sassing me and trying to control my scene."

"But I thought—"

I pressed my fingers to her lips and leaned over her again. I thrust my body in between her legs.

She gasped as my hard on rubbed between her thighs.

"Don't think, baby, just feel. Remember?" I slipped my hands around her neck and pecked her lips. My fingers skimmed over the exposed skin of her chest, but there wasn't enough for me to see. I curled my fingers into the top. "Do you like this shirt?"

"What?"

I ripped the tank top in two and spread it wide, exposing her pert breasts and hardened nipples. God, she had the best tits I'd ever seen.

"Rory!"

"Hindley," I admonished. "Don't make a sound." My demand was low and stern.

She rolled her lips in between her teeth to keep her words contained.

I chuckled. She was such a little shit. And I loved her. I grabbed the bottle sitting on the floor and held it over her body. I tilted the bottle until the bubbling water pummeled her bare abdomen and slid toward her belly button.

Her body bucked at the cool temperature. Her breathing was labored and the muscles in her neck strained. She was working hard to remain silent.

I licked the center of her chest. The water trailed along with my tongue as I moved up to her throat. She was soaked, coated in the sticky mess but she remained still. "Good girl," I murmured against her skin as I sucked and licked away the water. "Do you want some water?"

"In my mouth?" She cocked her head.

"That's a sassy little mouth you have there, Mrs. Gregor." And God, did I love her mouth, especially when it was wrapped around my dick. "I may have to fill it with something to keep you quiet."

She smiled.

My dick pulsed. Fuck. Enough of this play shit. I couldn't take the build-up.

I grabbed Hindley's waist and flipped her over. Her legs stretched beyond the edge of the bed and her toes skimmed the floor. Her short skirt scrunched around her waist, leaving her bare ass on display.

"Rory!"

I swatted her butt. "Hands above your head," I ordered. "Interlace your fingers."

"Oh, shit," she mumbled, but she complied.

I reached over her and grabbed the wedge pillow. "Lift up your hips."

She pushed up onto her tiptoes and perched her ass in the air.

Fuck, her body... I gulped down a moan. I wouldn't make it two seconds with my wife. *Do not lose control...again.* I slid the wedge pillow under her hips and aligned the vibrator between her legs.

Her ass pushed higher.

I slid my fingers along her warm skin as I nudged the tip of the vibrator between her legs.

She clutched at the comforter with her interlaced fingers and moaned into the bed.

God, I hadn't even turned the vibrator on. She was so ready for me. I reached in my pocket and clicked the control.

"Ahh. Oh God, Rory," she sobbed. Her back arched and she ground into the heart-shaped pillow.

Shit. I was gonna blow a wad right here in my pants just watching her squirm in ecstasy.

Her body convulsed and twitched as she panted a plea. "Oh, Rory, please."

My fingers fumbled with the button and zipper on my fly. I felt like horny teen watching a porno, I couldn't get my dick out fast enough.

"Rory!" she moaned. "God, I, I need…" she gasped for air.

I yanked my pants and underwear down in one fluid motion and nudged my steel-hard dick between her legs.

Hindley's head turned and she stared at me over her shoulder.

The blindfold lay beside her, pulled away by her ministrations on the bed. She was the most seductive, sexy, wanton goddess I had ever seen.

"Please," she begged.

I bit the inside of my cheek and thought of anything other than her plump lips and round ass as I worked to stave off my impending release.

"This is gonna be fast, baby." I said as I slid closer.

"I want it. I want you. Fast and hard." She ground her pelvis into the pillow then back against my dick.

Oh, fucking hell. I slid inside with ease.

Her body inhaled me like the last breath of a dying man. She drew tight against me.

The vibrations of the pillow reverberated through Hindley and shot straight to my dick.

I drove in hard, my body slapping against her ass with an intoxicating whack.

"Oh! Oh, God!" Hindley shouted.

She was close. She tightened and drew my dick in further.

I pumped in and out, driving her hips into the pillow. Fuck! I'd never worked up an orgasm so fast in my life. But that's what Hindley did to me, even after five years of marriage.

"Rory." She panted.

"Come on, baby. I'm close too." I heaved. "Let go."

She pressed against the pillow and screamed. Her rigid body pulsated around my cock. "Oh, Rory! Oh my…oh, God!" Her voice echoed through the room.

My body thrust against her twice, driving in so hard I thought I might split her in two. I wrapped my arm around her waist and groaned into her back, lifting her higher and yanking her toward me, impaling her. My release hit hard and lightning fast, scorching every nerve ending in my body. The world faded to black and my legs trembled.

Hindley spasmed around my dick.

I gritted my teeth as I pushed further inside her and rode out my release. My orgasm rolled on for what felt like days until finally I collapsed in a heap on top of Hindley, pressing her into the mattress as we both gulped for air.

"Oh my God, Rory." She panted, her back slid against my chest with every inhalation. "That was so…intense."

"Sorry."

"Why?" She twisted but my heavy body kept her locked in place.

"I wanted to draw it out for you." I kissed her neck.

"Foreplay is overrated." She giggled.

My dick pulsed inside her.

She squeezed my cock.

I pushed my hips into her ass. "You keep that up and we'll never get to your next surprise." I kissed her shoulder and pushed off her body, pulling out.

"Ahh." She pouted and rolled over.

Her gorgeous body splayed out, sated and glowing with post orgasmic bliss. I reached for my pants and yanked them over my already hardening dick. If I stood and stared at her naked body, I'd wrap myself up in her again. With Hindley, once was never enough. But I had other plans tonight.

She pushed onto her elbows. Her eyes roamed over my body as she splayed her legs wider.

"Don't do that, Hindley." I growled.

"Do what?" She cocked her head and bit her lip as she twirled a piece of hair around her finger.

"You know what."

"Is it a crime to want my husband?"

I smiled with pride. She still wanted me after all these years.

"I'll always want you, Rory." She answered as if hearing my thoughts. She stretched out her hand.

The bracelet I'd given her when I'd asked her to marry me dangled from her wrist. I admired all the charms I'd given her since then. She'd been stark naked that night too. "You're just as beautiful today as the night I gave you that bracelet." I took her hand in mine and sank down on my knees.

"After two kids, there's a little more of me to love." She laughed and ran her hand across her belly.

I stopped the self-conscious movement of her hand and stared into her sparkling eyes. "I love your body, Hindley. You're even *more* beautiful after two kids." I squeezed her hand and kissed her abdomen. "And I'll always want more of you."

Her supple lips parted and curled up into a wanton smile. She slid her hand from mine and brushed it through my hair, massaging my scalp. Her fingers stopped and her eyes narrowed as she surveyed the room. "What's that noise?" She cocked her head and lifted her ear high.

I scanned the room. My eyes focused on the floor where the buzzing sound echoed. I laughed and picked up the pillow.

"Oh my gosh." She chuckled.

"I forgot to turn off the pillow." I reached in my pocket and flicked the remote control. The pillow stopped vibrating. "Guess we should tell Regan to put this thing on the market."

Hindley giggled. "Mass market."

"I love that sound." My fingers caressed her cheek.

"I know," she sighed. She bent down and placed a soft kiss on my lips. "Happy anniversary, Mr. Gregor."

"Happy anniversary, Drunk Girl. I'm really glad you puked on my shoes the first night I met you."

"Ewww," she shook her head and swatted at me.

"I love you, Hindley."

Her eyes sparkled with unshed tears. "I love you too, Skater Boy."

"Always?" My brows rose with anticipation.

"Always," she grinned, "and forever."

CHAPTER 25

RORY

"Are you seriously making me wear a blindfold *again*?" Hindley fidgeted in the passenger seat and reached for the material.

"Yes." I swatted her hand. "Quit messing with it or you won't get your surprise."

She dropped her hand and slumped back in the seat with a pout.

God, she reminded me of our daughters, Abbi and Renee, when they didn't get their way. Like mother like daughters. I laughed to myself.

My phone pinged with a text message.

"Who is it?" Hindley's head turned. "Are the girls all right? Is it my mom? Renee felt warm when we dropped her off earlier."

I smiled at the motherly concern in her voice.

"They're fine, baby. I called your mom and checked on them before we left."

"Then who was it?"

We idled at a red light. I glanced down at the screen.

We're ready!

Shit. My fingers tingled as I rapped them against the steering wheel. My heart slammed against my chest, each beat deafening me. Why the fuck was I nervous?

I typed then hit the reply button on my phone.

5 minutes away.

"Rory?" Hindley's voice captured my attention. "Who is it?" she asked.

"Oh, uh, it's just Jack. He wanted to make sure I got my practice schedule he emailed me this morning."

She faced me. "Liar." She folded her arms across her chest and stared as if she could see straight through her blindfold.

"Why are you calling me a liar?" *Maybe because you are.*

"I can hear you thrumming your fingers on the steering wheel and you're doing that click-click thing with your tongue like you do when you're nervous."

Did I really do that? I bit down on my tongue as my fingers gripped the wheel. "Are you serious?"

"Yeah. You do it anytime you're anxious. Like before all your competitions. And, oh my God, you drove me and the nurses at the hospital *crazy* with your nervous tics when Abbi and Renee were born." She chuckled.

"I'm glad you find my anxiety funny."

"Oh, quit pouting." She swatted at me but missed.

I gazed up at my reflection in the rearview mirror. My expression was more a scowl than a pout.

"Light's green," she said.

I peered through the windshield. Shit, she was right. I glanced at Hindley. Yep, blindfold was still in place. I eased off the brake. What the fuck? "How did you know?"

"I'm a mom." She smiled, tapping the base of her skull. "I have eyes in the back of my head."

"But you're blindfolded. And facing forward."

"Doesn't matter." She shook her head. "I suggest you watch yourself, Mr. Gregor. I see *everything.*"

Well, not everything. I chuckled to myself.

"So who was on the phone?" she asked.

"My girlfriend."

"Better not be," she huffed and swung at my shoulder.

I grabbed her hand mid-swing and tugged it to my lips, planting a soft kiss on her knuckles. "You know you're my girl. My Drunk Girl."

"Yeah, but sometimes your fans can get…"

"Ah, is my baby jealous?"

She sat silent.

"Now who's pouting?"

Her body stiffened and she sat stock still.

"Now you know how I feel," I grumbled.

"What does that mean?"

"Hindley, come on. There's a reason I want you in the same seat when I compete."

"I thought it was to ground yourself and ease your anxiety so you feel safe, knowing where the girls and I are."

"Well, there's that."

"And?" She drew her hand from mine and faced me as if she could see everything.

Maybe she did have eyes in the back of her head.

"When you're in your seat, your ass isn't parading around the skate park for all the guys to gawk at."

"Ha! That's funny." She flicked her hand. "Whatever."

After nearly six years together, Hindley still couldn't fathom the power she held over the male population. The attention she drew from men fucked with my head, but I'd learned to tamper my jealousy. Her faithful love for me was eternal and unconditional. Devotion swelled in my heart. But still, guys were guys. They gawked when she brushed by them and I didn't like the tempered jealousy their glares created in the pit of my stomach.

"Ah, come here." She slid her hand up my leg and reached for my hand.

My dick sprung to life like I hadn't just fucked her senseless an hour ago.

Thankfully, she found my hand before she discovered the evidence of my arousal.

"You know you're my Skater Boy." She kissed my knuckles and planted my hand on her thigh.

My fingers skimmed the silk.

She wore a dress she'd designed a few weeks earlier. The silk *bodice*, as she called the dress, was lavender with a sheer overlay. I felt kind of feminine knowing all these fashion terms, but making clothes was my wife's career, and I wanted to be a part of it as much as she was mine.

I glanced at her for a second as the traffic slowed. "You look beautiful tonight. I love your dress."

She slid a hand down the soft material. "I love it too. I think it's my favorite design."

"Maybe you should think about designing clothes," I teased.

"Ha ha, funny boy." She laughed.

After our second daughter Renee was born almost three years ago, Hindley was upset to find no "after-baby" clothes as she called it—for those months after the baby was born when you couldn't fit into your pre-baby clothes but didn't want to wear maternity clothes. And with her small idea and need for appropriate clothing, Hindley Gregor Designs was born, so to speak.

Hindley had struggled with the name of her company, not wanting to flaunt herself. Regan was a marketing genius and assured Hindley her name was well-known and would open doors in the competitive fashion industry.

Hindley realized her after-baby designs were just one of many clothing lines she could develop. Regan and I convinced her to put her name on the tags in the clothing, and with that, Hindley's company was born.

Hindley said, besides marrying me and having our daughters,

opening her boutique in downtown Austin had been one of the best days of her life.

I was proud of my wife for many more reasons than just her company. Her strength, her courage, her bravery to fight the demons of her past and conquer them is what made me love her the most.

I pulled into a parking spot and turned off the engine. "Ready?"

She bounced in the seat and nodded.

"Stay put, I'll come around and get you."

"Okay." Excitement radiated from her body like heat.

My stomach twisted with nervous energy. It felt like I was about to start a run at the X Games. Shit. What if she didn't like my surprise? *Too late now, man.*

I guided her out of the car and opened the door to the building, ushering her inside. The lobby was quiet but the lights blazed bright.

"Where are we?" She touched the blindfold.

I positioned her in front of the painting and undid the scarf.

As the material fell away, she blinked and squinted from the overhead light. Slowly she focused on her surroundings.

"We're at Shelly's Hang Out?" Her eyes darted around the lobby.

"Yes."

"You brought me to the center? For our anniversary?"

Disappointment rolled off every word.

I bit my lip and stifled a laugh. "I wanted to thank you again for my painting." I motioned toward the canvas hanging behind the reception area. The portrait perfectly captured the spirit of my sister.

Hindley commissioned my stepmother to paint the portrait and presented the artwork to me as a wedding present. I'd cried like a baby when I opened it.

"Rory, I gave you that painting five years ago. You've thanked me enough already."

Her words were clipped and she rolled her eyes. Oh, yea, she was definitely perturbed.

"I know you did." I bit my cheek to hide my smirk. My wife was so feisty tonight. "But it all started here."

"What did?" She glanced around the lobby.

I slid my hand into hers and wove our fingers together. "I never dreamed I could learn to read. Never dreamed I could create a space that would help kids learn to read too." I turned to face her. "But then one dark night this drunk girl fell down on the pavement in front of me and spewed her guts all over me."

Hindley covered her face in embarrassment.

I removed her hands. "It was one of the best days of my life and I didn't even know it. You, with your yoga pants, ponytail and blue toes," I chuckled. "You gave me hope, Hindley. And I never had that before."

Tears welled in her eyes.

Shit. I didn't want her to cry. Not now. "Come on." I tugged on her hand and dragged her toward the classrooms.

"Where are we going?"

I glanced over my shoulder. She was breathtaking. Her long blonde hair swung across the spaghetti straps of her dress and caressed her light skin. Her bright brown eyes sparkled with anticipation.

"You'll see." I stopped at the doors to the classrooms. "Are you ready?"

She squeezed my hand and nodded.

"Close your eyes."

For once she didn't argue and followed my instructions.

I knocked three times on the door before twisting the knob and pushing it open. The partitions had been pushed back and the large room was bathed in darkness. I pulled Hindley inside and positioned her in front of me.

"Happy anniversary, baby," I whispered in her ear just as the lights flickered on.

CHAPTER 26

HINDLEY

"Happy anniversary, baby," Rory whispered in my ear.

My eyes darted around the dark room but I couldn't see a thing. What the hell?

Bright lights blinded me.

"Surprise!"

The booming voices echoed through the massive room.

"Mommy!"

Someone squealed, slamming into my legs. *Abbi?* I reached for Rory to steady myself. She wrapped her hands around my thighs. I stroked the blonde ringlets of my precious baby girl.

"Mah-mah!" another voice rang out.

My dad carried Renee. She clapped her chubby hands then reached out to me.

I clutched her as she fell into my arms.

"You es here, Mah-mah." Renee smiled.

"Yes, your momma is here, sweetheart." I smoothed the light brown hair from her face, a face so similar to her father's. Her light brown eyes danced with delight.

"Es a par-tee for you, Mah-mah."

Her hand swept out over the crowd like she was the hostess of a game show.

Tears welled in my eyes and blurred my vision as I surveyed the room.

The walls of the individual classrooms had been pulled back to make one large space. The room had been transformed into a fairy-tale. The space reminded me of our wedding. Round tables covered with white cloths littered the room. Votive candles with decorative floral arrangements set in the center of each table. Overhead lights and fabric were strung from the rafters and crystals of varying shapes and sizes dangled overhead. A large dance floor stood in the middle of the room. At the front, a full band sat atop a stage erected for the occasion.

"Daddy gave you a party, Momma." Abbi clung to my legs.

I gazed down. Her bright blue eyes matched her father's and she stared up at me. She smiled, her small dimples tugging at her cheeks.

"We had to be very quiet," Abbi whispered. "Daddy said we couldn't say anything." She shook her head and her ringlets tossed around her face.

I turned toward Rory. He smiled, that dazzling, brilliant grin that always set my heart thumping. "You did this?" I whispered through choked tears.

"Well, I had a lot of help." He motioned toward the crowd.

My gaze followed his hand.

Dana and my mom waved. My dad stood beside them and blew me a kiss.

"I help Aunt Day-nah too, Mah-mah." Renee hit my chest, her eyes wide and bright with pride.

"You did an amazing job, angel." I kissed her temple.

"Do you like it?" Abbi asked.

I surveyed the room. Everyone I loved most in the world was present—Dana and Peter and their kids along with his family, Leif and his parents, Sarah and her new husband, along with the girls from my shop—and so many others.

"Wait," I jerked my gaze back to Rory. "Where's Geneva and Berk and JP?"

Rory pointed toward the stage.

Geneva stood next to the microphone at the front of the room and waved.

Suddenly, I realized Berk's brother Rhen and his band were behind her.

Berk stood next to the stage, JP propped on his hip. They both waved and smiled.

"Hi, baby!" I waved to JP. "Oh, God, Rory." I wiped my eyes.

My dad pressed a tissue in my hand. "We never got our father daughter dance, Hinny Bin." My dad smiled. "The klutz here fell and ruined everything." He gestured at himself.

I laughed.

"So Rory gave me a second chance, another reception for you. Happy anniversary, sweetheart."

I dabbed at the tears streaming down my face and turned toward Rory. "I can't believe you did this." I passed off Renee to my dad and stepped toward my husband. I slid my hands around his shoulders and drew him close. "I can't believe you did this for *me*."

His hands encircled my waist. "Why? You don't think I'm romantic?" He laughed.

"Your idea of romantic is..." My eyes darted around the room. "Let's just say it's a little naughtier than this."

He winked.

My knees wobbled. "Thank you," I whispered as I reached up on my toes to kiss him.

His lips engulfed mine

My hands snaked into his hair.

His arms clutched me to his strong body.

I felt dizzy and light-headed.

"Oh, God! Here they go!" Dana shouted. "Kids, cover your eyes."

The crowd broke into laughter.

Somehow I found the strength to pull away from my husband's embrace.

Rory's forehead fell against mine. "Later."

His plump lips curved up into a salacious smile.

"What about the kids?" I nodded behind me.

"Your parents have them both for a week."

"A week!"

"We're going back to the Maldives."

"Rory Gregor, you did *not* rent another island."

He cocked his head and shrugged his shoulders.

"You're just…amazing," I sighed.

"Ladies and gentlemen, if I could have your attention." Geneva's voice boomed through the speakers. "It's time for the father-daughter dance." She waved toward the dance floor.

"Yay!" Renee clapped her hands.

Rory grabbed her from my father.

"Paw-Paw dance." Renee bounced in Rory's arms.

My father had a routine with his grandkids. He would blast loud disco music from the speakers in their playroom at his house, and he and the grandkids would have "disco night" as he called it. My mom and dad and the kids would jump around to the music as if it were a mosh pit at a punk rock nightclub. The girls and J.P. loved "dancing" with their grandpa.

"Not *that* kind of dancing, Little Bit." My dad tweaked Renee's nose.

She grabbed at his hand.

"Too late." He chuckled, holding his thumb between his fingers. "I got it!"

"You no get my nose, Paw-Paw," Renee pouted.

"I'll give it back right after I dance with your mom, okay?"

"Oh-tay." Her tiny lips curved up and she slung her shoulders back.

I laughed at her animated features. She was so much like Rory it scared me. I stroked his cheek. "Thank you, for letting me dance with my dad," I whispered, leaning into Rory's body.

He grabbed my hand and kissed the palm. "Go dance with your dad." He winked. "I may take the girls for a swing myself."

God, I loved my husband. Even more than I did the day I married him. Watching him become the father I always knew he would be to our children was the most intoxicating aphrodisiac ever.

"Dah-Dah, dance wiss me?" Renee clapped her hands and sprung into his arms.

"Maybe." He kissed her cheek. "Right now this is for Momma and for Paw-Paw, okay?"

She nodded her head. "Oh-tay."

The band strummed their instruments.

My dad held out his hand.

I slipped mine into his and he led us toward the dance floor and twirled me into his arms.

I giggled like a twelve year old.

Geneva's sultry voice rang out.

I recognized the song. "Because You Loved Me." Tears burned my eyes.

"I have more tissues." Dad patted his jacket.

"Thank you, Dad."

"For what?"

He spun us around with ease and grace. No wonder my mom fell for him so hard.

"For loving me when my actions toward you weren't very loving."

"Hindley," he shook his head, "you've always loved me. I know that. You were just hurt and you had a lot of walls. I think Rory helped you knock them down."

I glanced over his shoulder.

Rory held both girls in his arms and swung them from side to side.

I shook my head and looked at Dad. "I can't believe he thought he wouldn't be a good father."

"All guys do that," Dad said.

"Even you?"

Dad always seemed so confident. No way he ever feared being a dad.

"Especially when I met you and your mom. God, I was so afraid I wouldn't do right by you, Hindley."

My head fell onto his shoulder.

"I'm everything I am because you loved me, Dad." I repeated the lyrics.

His chest heaved with staggered breathing.

I raised my head and watched as tears streamed down his face.

"I feel like I failed you so many times, Hindley."

"Never." I wiped away his tears. "Never, Dad."

He pulled me close.

"Well, there was that one time when you told Rory to keep his banana in his pocket, or something like that."

We laughed as he twirled me on the dance floor like I was Cinderella.

"I love you, Hindley. I hope you know that."

"I do." I nodded. "I didn't always show it, but in my heart I always knew you loved me." I stared into his blue eyes. "You know *I* picked this song to dance with you at my wedding."

"This song? 'Because You Loved Me?'" he asked.

"Yeah. The words were perfect."

We stared at one another for several heartbeats.

Geneva's voice belted out the song.

Our gaze traveled to the stage.

She sang the song with conviction, her voice stronger than Celine Dion.

"Wow," my dad and I said in unison.

Geneva blew us a kiss then rested her hand on her distended belly. Her daughter was due in a few weeks. The thought thrilled me. I was going to be an aunt again, to a sweet baby girl. Soon I would have another niece to love besides Dana's little girl.

"She's an amazing singer," I said.

My father stared at her. "She sounds just like her mother." His voice broke.

"Thank you."

He turned back to face me. "For what?"

"For loving my mom again after your wife passed away."

"Loving your mother wasn't a choice, Hindley." He chuckled.

"She has that effect on men." I giggled. "But with you, Dad, she didn't have a choice either. She was a goner the minute she saw your photo in that real estate magazine."

We both stared at my mother.

Caroline Hagen-Barton was nothing if not dignified, but standing at the edge of the dance floor, my mom was a blubbering mess. One hand covered her mouth to hold in the sobs as her other arm wrapped around her slender waist.

I turned back to him. "I think the writer of this song knew our story, Dad. The words are perfect."

He wrinkled his graying brow.

"You were my strength, you were my voice, you stood by me," I said.

"Oh, Hindley," he shook his head, "you were already strong. I envied your strength and your tenacity. And you're still the bravest person I know. I'm just sorry I didn't protect you."

His blue eyes darkened and glassed over with tears.

"No." I gripped his shoulder. "You were my greatest protector, Dad. I could never have done *anything* without your strength and your support. My world *is* a better place because of you." I repeated the lyrics again as tears streamed down my face. "You saw the best in me and you forced me to see it in myself."

He hugged me tight, his head burrowing into my shoulder. "Oh, Hindley." He shook his head. "I feel the same way about you."

"I know." I squeezed him tight.

He pulled away and wiped at his eyes as he reached in his pocket and handed me a tissue.

I wiped my own eyes and stared at the man who was born to be my father. I was the luckiest girl in the world. "Oh my gosh." I stared at the edge of the dance floor.

"What?" He craned his neck, gazing over his shoulder.

I watched in shock as Dana's oldest son Lucas led her onto the dance floor. He was almost fourteen and already a head taller than her.

"Wow," He said. "The boy knows how to dance."

"I just can't believe Dana Di Grazio is a mother. To *three* kids."

"Well, you have two, sweetheart." He laughed.

"Can you keep a secret?"

He nodded.

"It's gonna be three for me too."

"What!" My dad shouted.

Everyone stared at us.

"Shhhh, I haven't told anyone yet."

"Not even Rory?"

"Nope. It's his anniversary present."

He clutched me close. "Oh, Hindley, I'm so happy for you."

"Me too."

The song drew to a close.

"May I cut in?"

A deep voice rang behind me.

"I'll trade ya," my dad said as he released me and took my girls into his arms.

"Paw-Paw dance." Renee clapped and bounced in his arms.

"Not that kind of dancing, Little Bit." My dad laughed.

Renee pouted.

"In a little bit, okay?" He smiled.

"Oh-tay." She nodded and laid her head on my dad's shoulder.

Abbi sighed and wrapped her arm around her grandfather's neck, resting her head against his other shoulder.

"You girls are getting so big." My dad stared down at them. "How will I fit a third?"

I glared at him.

My dad's eyes went wide.

"Hindley." Rory growled as he drew me into his arms.

"Sorry," he mouthed behind Rory's back.

"What is Paul talking about?" Rory asked.

"Oh, I uh meant, Geneva's daughter. Yeah," Paul said.

My dad was a horrible liar.

"How am I gonna fit three girls on my lap." His deep voice cracked with nervous laughter.

"Hindley." Rory repeated, tilting his head.

I looked at the stage and watched Geneva descend the stairs.

The band took over and played "I Won't Give Up".

"Oh my gosh, listen." I nodded. "They're playing our song, remember, Rory."

He grasped my chin and turned it toward him. His blue eyes narrowed.

Shit! I wanted to wait until later to tell him.

Rory and I had talked about having a third child, but neither one of us was sold on the idea. Our schedules were so hectic.

I placed his hand on my stomach. "Happy anniversary?" I squeaked out.

"Are you…?"

My eyes widened.

"Pregnant?" he whispered.

I nodded.

"Holy shit!" he shouted.

"Shit! Shit!" Renee yelled from my father's arms.

The crowd roared with laughter.

"Dammit, Rory," I swatted his shoulder.

"Ooo, Mommy *and* Daddy said bad words." Abbi scowled at us.

"Cuss bucket." Dana giggled as she and Lucas butted up next to us. "Congrats, Every Nighter." Dana stared down at Rory's mid-section. "Looks like your little guys shot through another barrier. Boom! Those are some powerful little suckers you're packin."

"Shut up, Dana." I glared. I hated to admit it but apparently Rory did have some powerful swimmers.

She laughed hysterically and Lucas led her away.

"Congrats, you two f-monkeys," she shouted over her shoulder.

At least she was filtering her words tonight.

"Love you!" Her giggles echoed through the room.

Rory danced us away from the crowd filtering onto the dance floor. "Hindley, are you pregnant?"

He stared at me, his eyes darting between mine. His lips pressed into a firm line.

All humor vanished. My stomach roiled and the movement had nothing to do with the baby inside of me. My eyes filled with tears. Damn pregnancy hormones. I nodded and the tears spilled over my lashes. "I'm sorry," I whispered, blubbering.

"Oh, baby, no, I'm sorry." He drew me close, stroking my back. "I didn't mean to make you cry. Shhh." He wiped my cheeks with his thumbs.

"You're not mad?" I choked through sobs.

He leaned back and gazed down at me. His face beamed with pride. "Why are you sorry, Drunk Girl?"

"We didn't plan this. We're both so busy. I—"

"Our children are always surprising us." He thrust his hips against mine. "Dana's right. My boys are potent."

I giggled.

"There it is. The most amazing sound in the world, next to the laughter of our little girls'." He grinned. "I have no fucking clue how I'm going to handle *three* girls. I mean, boyfriends, weddings…oh, God."

"Who said it will be a girl?"

His head snapped to mine, his eyes wide.

"What are you saying, Hindley? Don't fuck with me. You know I love my girls, but a boy would be…"

"Would be perfect?"

"I'm holding perfection in my arms, sweetheart." He leaned down and kissed my nose. "I have more than I deserve."

"So you don't deserve to share your title?"

"What title?" His eyes wrinkled around the edges and a deep V formed between his brows.

"Skater Boy. *My* Skater Boy."

He gawked, his mouth hanging open.

"Should we call him Skater Boy Two?" I tilted my head. "Or maybe Baby Skater Boy? Or what about Skater Boy, Jr.?" I teased.

"Hindley' are you shitting me? Are we having a boy? Tell me the truth." His jaw clenched as he squeezed my waist.

Thanks to early genetic testing, I'd been able to find out the gender even though I was only eleven weeks pregnant.

"Yes," I said, "we're having a boy. You're having a son, Rory Gregor."

His face paled as his hands slipped from my body then clawed at his hair.

"Rory, what's wrong?"

"I don't know how to be a dad to a boy. What the fuck am I gonna do now?" His fingers strummed against his head with the beat of the song and his tongue clicked on the roof of his mouth. His eyes darted around the room.

I giggled.

"This isn't funny, dammit."

"I know." I couldn't stop laughing. I wrapped my arms around his waist. "I'm pretty sure being a dad to a boy is as hard and as rewarding as being one to a girl. You'll be fine, Skater Boy."

His hands fell and he gripped my shoulders. "Are you sure?"

"Yeah, I'm sure. The girls need a protector anyway."

"Oh, I'll crucify any motherfucker who tries to mess with my girls."

We gazed across the dance floor. My mom was holding Abbi and my dad held Renee.

"We're so lucky, Rory."

"I know, baby, we are." His forehead fell against mine and he stared into my eyes.

"Peas?" I laughed.

"Peas." He smiled. "Should we tell everyone else?"

"Not yet. Tonight I just want to dance with my husband, love on my family and party with my friends." I leaned back and gazed around the room. "Thank you for giving me this, giving me and my dad our father-daughter dance."

"I know it means a lot to you both."

Rhen's band ended *our* song and he spoke into the mic. "Okay, folks, enough of the sappy stuff." His deep voice rumbled through the speakers. "This next song is for all of you dancers. Let's really get this party started."

Renee squealed as my dad swung her around. Everyone shouted and jumped to the beat of Rhen's new song.

I surveyed the room. All the people I loved the most in the world surrounded me.

Dana spun in circles as she clutched Levi's hands. Peter swayed with Lilly and Lucas, all three laughing hysterically.

Berk held a giggling J.P. on his shoulders as he and Geneva shimmied and shook.

My parents held the girls between them and waltzed around the floor, the girls squealing with delight.

"I love you, Drunk Girl." Rory kissed my forehead.

I gazed up at my husband as I placed a hand on my stomach. I couldn't believe I was having another baby with the man who meant everything to me.

"Really, Skater Boy?" I cocked a brow.

"Really. I promise, Hindley." His lips caressed mine. "I'll always love you and our children."

My head fell against his chest and I breathed in his heavenly scent. "Always, and forever," I sighed.

Rory held me tight and kissed my head. "Forever, Drunk Girl. I promise."

~

Thank you for reading
Extreme Promise

~

Be sure to read the companion novelette
Extreme Gift
Trapped in Paris
X-Treme Love Series, Novelette

Only two weeks away from delivering her first child, Hindley Hagen goes against her doctor's orders (and her overbearing husband's) and travels five hours away to the small Texas town of Paris. She and her best friend, Dana Di Grazio, want to experience one last girls' only weekend. But this year Paris, Texas is experiencing epic floods and Hindley is trapped.

Against his better judgment, Rory Gregor has traveled to Paris,

France to participate in a charity pro-am, even though his wife is days away from giving birth. His sponsors assure him he'll make it home in time to welcome their new baby girl. But one day before his expected return, Paris is hit with an unexpected blizzard and the threat of record-breaking snowfall halts all travel.

Will Hindley and Rory be able to reach one another in time to welcome their new daughter together? Or will Hindley give birth to their first child alone in the confines of a small Texas hospital where the doctor-on-call has gone MIA?

Join the cast of the **X-Treme Love Series** in this funny, touching, heartwarming novelette that proves true love can weather any storm.

Available now!

WANT TO RECEIVE A FREE EBOOK?

Join my email list and I'll send you *Extreme Beginning*, the X-Treme Love Prequel for free. It's the story of Caroline Hagen and Paul Barton. Just visit the website below and join today.

I also give away free things all the time, including ebooks and signed paperbacks (my own and from best-selling authors) and more.

You'll also receive exclusive sneak peeks and teasers of upcoming books in my series.

Visit my website and join my email list now to receive your free ebook today!

www.kaymanis.com

IF YOU ENJOYED THIS BOOK

Please:

    1. Write a review. It's so important to my work.

    2. Tell your family and friends about my books.

    3. Visit my website and sign up for my newsletter. You can also send me an email. I love to hear from my readers.

    www.kaymanis.com

    4. Follow me on social media.

Facebook: www.facebook.com/kaymanisauthor2

Twitter: www.twitter.com/kaymanis

Instagram: www.instagram.com/kaymanis

EXTREME GIFT

Be sure to read the companion novelette
Extreme Gift
Trapped in Paris
X-Treme Love Series, Novelette

Only two weeks away from delivering her first child, Hindley Hagen goes against her doctor's orders (and her overbearing husband's) and travels five hours away to the small Texas town of Paris. She and her best friend, Dana Di Grazio, want to experience one last girls' only weekend. But this year Paris, Texas is experiencing epic floods and Hindley is trapped.

Against his better judgment, Rory Gregor has traveled to Paris, France to participate in a charity pro-am, even though his wife is days away from giving birth. His sponsors assure him he'll make it home in time to welcome their new baby girl. But one day before his expected return, Paris is hit with an unexpected blizzard and the threat of record-breaking snowfall halts all travel.

Will Hindley and Rory be able to reach one another in time to welcome their new daughter together? Or will Hindley give birth to their first child alone in the confines of a small Texas hospital where the doctor-on-call has gone MIA?

Join the cast of the **X-Treme Love Series** in this funny, touching, heartwarming novelette that proves true love can weather any storm.

Available now!

JOIN MY PRIVATE FACEBOOK GROUP
THE MANIS MOB SQUAD

We support and enable those diagnosed with **MOB Disease (Mania of Books) -** a rare and debilitating disease that causes sufferers to become unable and/or unwilling to stop reading and obsessing over all things book related.

Are you a book-aholic? Do you have a One-Click addiction? Then come join our support group. We're all about fun in here, no judgment.

ALSO AVAILABLE BY KAY MANIS

X-Treme Love Series

Extreme Risk (Hindley and Rory)

Extreme Devotion (Hindley and Rory)

Extreme Sacrifice (Dana and Peter)

Extreme Trust (Dana and Peter)

Extreme Attraction (Geneva and Berk)

Extreme Courage (Geneva and Berk)

Extreme Promise (Hindley and Rory)

Extreme Gift: The New Arrival (Hindley and Rory)

Extreme Beginning: The Prequel (Caroline and Paul)

Baxter Bay

You Could Be Mine (Aiden and Olivia)

Sumner Brothers Series

Born to Be My Baby (Ben and Maggie)

Never Say Goodbye (Emmett and Elle)

Thank You for Loving Me (Max and Devlin)

With These Two Hands (Aaron and Kayleigh)

I'll Be There for You (Jake and Lina)

If That's What It Takes (Grant and Sophie)

Now and Forever (Max and Devlin)

Season of Love Short Story Series

Second Chance Heart

Dance with Me

Fall for Me

ABOUT THE AUTHOR

Kay Manis is a funny chick who's sprinkled with a little crazy on top. Okay, let's be honest. . . there's ALOTTA crazy up there.

She writes books filled with passion, promise and purpose (with laughter and a few tears, but always an Happily Ever After).

She is a native Texan and lives with her family in Florida. When not reading or writing, you'll find Kay eating out with friends or napping with her favorite pillow (stolen from an Inn in Vermont - true story).

Please feel free to contact her at: **www.kaymanis.com**

f facebook.com/kaymanisauthor2

X x.com/kaymanis

O instagram.com/kaymanis